Down in the Dumps

H. Mel Malton

RENDEZVOUS
PRESS

Cover art: Alan Barnard
Book design: Craig McConnell

Le Conseil des Arts du Canada | The Canada Council
DU CANADA | FOR THE ARTS
DEPUIS 1957 | SINCE 1957

Rendezvous Press gratefully acknowledges the support of the Canada Council for the Arts for our publishing program.

Napoleon Publishing/RendezVous Press
Imprints of TransMedia Enterprises Inc.
Toronto, Ontario, Canada

Printed in Canada

05 04 03 02 01 00 99 98   5 4 3 2 1

Canadian Cataloguing in Publication Data

Malton, H. Mel , date
   Down in the dumps

ISBN 0-929141-62-8

I. Title.

PS8576.A5362D68 1998   C813'.54   C98-931871-0
PR9199.3.M34D68 1998

To Simon and Irma, who gave me space (in different ways) to write this, and to my parents Anne and Peter, who are truly magical. Thanks to Karen Hood-Caddy for a million things and to Sylvia for everything that went after.

One

Howie's got a backhoe, Howie dug a hole.
It's big enough for Daisy
and he didn't tell a soul.
—Shepherd's Pie

When one of George's goats dies, he just crams the corpse in a feed sack and takes it to the dump. It's no problem as long as it's a weekday when Spit Morton is working. Spit wouldn't care if you dumped nuclear waste in the "wood only" pit as long as you were quiet about it.

Freddy, the other guy who works at the dump on weekends, is the one you have to watch out for. He comes up to your truck as soon as you drive in.

"What'cha got?" he'll say. I guess you could lie if you wanted to, but Freddy has an instinct, like an OPP officer running a spot check. He would smell your lie and he is perfectly capable of wrenching the bags open with those big red hands of his and pawing through your shame. I would never lie to Freddy. Neither would George, which is why we saved the dead goat for Monday morning.

George is older than he looks, tall and spare with hair the colour of a larch in late autumn—a sort of yellowy-orange, which he wears long. He is my landlord, a Finn with charming manners and the strength of an ox. He farms a couple of hundred acres of northern Ontario soil, rocks mostly. Every spring a fresh crop of boulders heaved up by the frost pokes through the melting snow, ready to take the edge off the disc harrow. We collect them and haul them off to the edge of the hay field, where we will one day build a wall with them.

I am the hired hand. Three years ago, I came up here to Cedar Falls from Toronto to rent George's old homestead cabin for the summer. I had put the word out that I needed a place to work, a quiet, out of the way hovel somewhere, and I heard about George's place through my aunt Susan, who runs the feed store in Laingford.

She called me the day before the lease ran out on my awful little basement apartment on Broadview Avenue.

"Got a place for you," was the first thing she said.

"Susan? That you?"

"No, it's Jim Henson." I'm a puppet-maker by trade, and the joke wasn't funny. Henson created the muppets and was sort of a god to me. When he died, the world got a little bit darker.

"Har, har. Kermit is watching you, Susan. What kind of place?"

"A shack in the woods. Right up your alley. No plumbing. Rent's cheap. Expect you on Friday." She hung up. She'd always hated the phone and carried on a running battle with Ma Bell, refusing to pay the phone bill until the last possible moment, then writing out the cheque and leaving a few cents off the payable account, just to piss them off. Getting a phone call from her was something of a miracle. I borrowed a truck the same day and headed north.

Dweezil had died of asthma, George said. He was a breeding buck who had suffered through six winters of wheezing and coughing, dying slowly from a ridiculous, tragic allergy to hay.

As a child I had buried my fair share of gerbils, budgies and kittens, but although I was fond of Dweezil, I wasn't about to build a cardboard headstone for him. Besides, he was way too big to put in a shoebox.

When we found Dweezil, stiff and silent in his pen, on Sunday evening, we simply shook our heads and bagged him, ready for the next morning when Spit Morton would be manning the dump. After the chores were done, we each went our separate ways, agreeing to meet at dawn to do the deed.

George's old cabin, the original homestead building on his farm, is the perfect place for someone like me. I'm broke most of the time, and I'm a slob. Because of what I do for a living, I can't afford much rent and I need lots of space. I do sell the puppets I make, occasionally. My specialty is marionettes, but I have been known to accept commissions for foam-constructed, muppety-things.

I had just completed a set of Audrey-the-Plant puppets for a Toronto production of *Little Shop of Horrors* when Susan called about the cabin, but I was up north for a week before the contact-cement headache went away.

The contrast between the Broadview basement apartment, crammed with foam rubber, Kraft dinner boxes and beer bottles, versus George's airy cabin, my new home, was breathtaking.

The cabin was primitive, but there was a woodstove, an outhouse, a well and privacy. Everything that mattered. I wasn't just escaping the city to work in solitude, actually. I was also on the run from an unwise affair with a narcissistic actor who had been pressuring me to move in with him. I didn't leave a forwarding address, and he would never have followed me up here anyway because there is no television, no phone, and only one small mirror in the bedroom.

George didn't like me at first. I have a feeling I was mildly obnoxious for the first few months—I wanted to do everything myself and I wasn't very gracious about accepting help. Later, though, we found a balance. I started helping out with the goats and I let him teach me how to chop wood properly after I almost cut my foot off. Now we're buddies, and I get to live on his land for free.

When we got to the dump on Monday morning we had poor old Dweezil wrapped up in his feed sack and buried discreetly under a stack of rotting timber in the back of George's pickup.

Spit Morton was sitting asleep at the wheel of his hearse, in which he lives.

Nobody knows where Spit goes on weekends when Freddy's working. Maybe he drives out onto a back road somewhere and parks, waiting for Monday. I have rarely seen him get out of the hearse, which is a two-tone pastel monster, like a bad pantsuit. It's dented and rusted, but it still has the original sheer curtains masking the back windows.

Rumour has it that Spit's Dad, Laingford's undertaker, had groomed both his sons to take over the business when he died. At the funeral, Spit and his brother rolled dice to see who was going to be boss. Spit lost, so he decked his brother out cold on top of the casket and stole the hearse. Hunter Morton never tried to get it back.

I guess if you're going to live in a vehicle, a hearse is a pretty good choice. There's probably even a bed back there somewhere, although nobody I know has ever had the pleasure of finding out.

Spit chews tobacco, which slows down his conversation a bit. He doesn't say much, until you get him going.

My first chat with him was in the early days when I thought he was like Freddy, requiring me to ask permission and perhaps pay him off before carting anything away. I had my eye on a dented but serviceable zinc tub in the "metal only" pile, right next to a stack of crushed bicycles and an old fridge. I was willing to pay a price for it.

"Hello there!" I said. He spat and looked at me from the cab of the hearse.

"Do you have any problem with me taking that old tub over there?"

He spat again and his eyes followed my pointing finger. The hearse was parked ten metres or so away from the metal pile. Without a word, he started up the engine, which purred with so little noise it was uncanny. I suppose that hearse manufacturers make that a specialty—you don't want revving engines when you're in mourning. He got into gear and whispered it over to the tub. I ran to catch up.

"What do you think?" I said, panting.

"Got a hole in it," Spit said. His voice was thick and rough, like a mud creek running over gravel.

"I know. I figured I could patch it, though. It's not a very big hole."

"Nope."

"Well?"

A stream of brown goo landed to the left of my foot. "Well what?" he said.

I replied slowly, distinctly. "Well, do you mind if I take it?"

"Why should I mind? It's a dump, ain't it?"

"Yes, but I thought you might...umm. Do you think it's worth anything?"

He smiled broadly, showing the stumps of three sepia teeth.

"Might be, if I was Freddy."

"I thought maybe five bucks."

"On Saturday she would be worth five bucks, maybe," Spit said and spat. Pause. "You want to wait till then, you can pay Freddy five bucks, I guess."

"But...?"

"But lady, I don't sell other people's garbage. Ain't mine to sell, though Freddy might believe 'tis."

"Oh. I thought—well, I guess you don't mind, then."

"Nope. Take her away. Take it all. People throw too damn much out these days anyway."

"You've got that right," I said.

"Why just last week a fellow come in here with a couch— nothing wrong with it I could see. Freddy said he could sell it for ten bucks, easy. Just about shit when I give it to a youngster was getting married. What did you do that for? Freddy says. Went for me. Had to pull my gun on him. You seen my gun?" He reached into the back of the hearse and brought out a big old blunderbuss of a shotgun, which he showed off like it was a new baby. I gulped and stepped back.

"It's all right. I ain't aiming to shoot you. Use it to scare away the bears, mostly. And for protection. Got a lotta valuable things in this here automobile. Don't want nobody sneaking up on me at night, eh?" He grinned again and spat before putting the hearse carefully into reverse and backing silently all the way up to where he had been parked before, near the dump hut. The hut was Freddy's domain, and I wondered suddenly if Freddy also kept a gun on hand "for the bears".

I took the tub, not willing to wait until the weekend, when it would cost me five bucks.

George drove slowly past the hearse which cradled the sleeping Spit. We didn't want to wake him up. Spit probably wouldn't care about Dweezil, but it is illegal to dump livestock (or deadstock, I suppose) at the landfill, and we wanted as few people to know as possible. Spit's head was down on his arms, resting on the wheel.

"That can't be very comfortable," George muttered, as we headed for the "wood only" pit.

We put Dweezil in as gently as we could, out of respect perhaps, but also because a hoof sticking out would have given the game away. We threw the rotten lumber in on top of him, but George was a stickler for protocol, and the bag did look kind of obvious. I climbed in to move an old screen door on top as well. That's when I found the body.

It was a man, about forty years old, definitely dead, with no feed sack to make him pretty. There was a tattered, meaty cavity where his torso had been, and the flies had found him. I gagged and called for George, scrambling up the steep sides of the pit as if the corpse might reach out and grab me.

I gabbled out the information, and George peered over the edge of the pit to have a look as I raced for Spit Morton and the hut phone.

Spit was unconscious—alive and breathing, but off somewhere in a place I could not pull him from. I tipped his head back and sniffed for signs of alcohol, which was a mistake, because Spit's odour is ripe at the best of times. Then I noticed the lump on the back of his head, pushing up out of his matted hair like a turnip in a bed of moss. I probed it gingerly with my supporting hand. It was spongy.

Now, I am not a first-aid-y person, and he didn't seem to be in any danger—that is to say, his breathing was regular and he wasn't bleeding, externally anyway. I put his head gently back where I had found it and went to the hut to call 911.

Then I lit a cigarette and walked back to George. I suppose we were both in shock, because the first thing we did was to haul Dweezil up out of the pit and put him back in the truck. This, after all, was a police matter.

TWO

Grant me a taste of your experience, stranger,
Give me a sip of your blood.
—Shepherd's Pie

Police officers make me nervous. I could be driving perfectly legally, all the insurance and my license up to date, keeping to the speed limit—a responsible citizen in every respect, but the minute I see a police cruiser, my face flames red and my throat gets tight. I start to drive erratically, out of sheer nervousness.

It's all that dumb power that gets me; men and women in uniforms with bored, bovine faces, carrying guns. I don't see brave "Servers and Protectors", I just see people in stiff blue hats who have every right to interrogate you if they feel like it. I'm the same with customs officers, and I am invariably searched at airports.

By the time the police finally arrived to deal with Spit Morton and the body in the "wood only" pit, I had worked myself up into a lather of fear. I was all for dragging Dweezil off into the bush somewhere and leaving him, but George would have none of it.

"They will be searching the area," he said. "I'm the only goat breeder around here. They would know."

"Get real, George," I said. "As if the police, in the middle

9

of a murder investigation, would give a damn about a dead goat." Still, George wasn't taking any chances.

I believed that George and I, as the first to find the body, would immediately become prime suspects. I'm no fool. I've read my Eric Wright and Sue Grafton. The police would ask us all sorts of awkward questions, they would go to my cabin and search it and they would find my modest stash of homegrown weed (kept for medicinal purposes only, you understand) and I would go to jail.

The police officers who arrived first were from Laingford, and they were both men. The thinner of the two, who introduced himself as Detective Becker, looked to be in his mid-thirties and obviously worked out with weights. He was wearing a short-sleeved uniform shirt, and the muscles on his arms were ropy and interesting. The other, from what I could see of him, weighed about three hundred pounds. He stayed in the car, talking on the radio.

I wondered if Detective Becker was any relation to the mogul Becker who owned the famous chain of convenience stores, and I asked him—you know, to break the tension, but he gave me a cold smile and said he wasn't.

I gave him my name. Pauline Deacon. Polly, to my friends.

"Can I have your address, please, ma'am?"

"My, uh, mailing address?"

"No, your place of residence."

This was a problem. My beloved cabin—George's homestead—was not strictly legal. What I mean is, although I had been living there for a number of years, it wasn't zoned as residential. There was no record, anywhere, that someone was living in George's cabin. His tax returns certainly didn't include that information, and although most of the locals with whom I was acquainted were aware of where I lived, they were very good about keeping it to themselves. I hadn't filled out a tax return in years. I didn't have a credit card or a phone. Actually, I didn't exist. I liked it that way.

So, the question made me uncomfortable. I glanced at George, who came to my rescue, smelling trouble.

"She lives with me," he said, his voice full of hidden meaning. Interesting, I thought. Why not? I took his arm possessively.

Becker's upper lip twisted for a moment, and then he switched his attention to George.

"You live together, then, on the Dunbar sideroad." He checked his notes. "Lot forty-two, concession six?"

"Correct," George said.

"You married?"

"I don't think that's any of your business, detective," I said. I could feel a hideous blush creeping up my body.

Not that the concept was wholly far-fetched. I mean, George was well into his seventies, but hard-bodied and more flexible than I was at six. He was probably quite capable of getting it up if called upon to do so. Our relationship was entirely platonic and the thought of being intimate with him had never crossed my mind, but Becker didn't know that. We were, after all, covering our butts.

"We are not married," I said, after a nasty little pause which Becker filled by scribbling in his little black book. I can just imagine what he wrote: "May/December relationship between suspects. Check this."

"Domestic partnership," George said, which was true in a way. Becker wrote that down as well.

"Now, Mr. Hoito and Ms. Deacon, can you tell me in your own words just how you came to find the deceased?"

"Well, we were getting rid of, er. . ."

". . . some scrap lumber and Polly thought that she—"

"I thought I saw a piece that we could have kept. You know? Re-use? Recycle? So I jumped down to haul it back."

"And she moved that old door."

"It looked like maybe we could save it too, eh? And the decea— I mean the body—was there underneath it."

"Slow down, please," Becker said. "I don't do shorthand." He smiled, and I started to like him. Nice eyes. Crinkles at the corners.

The fat guy still hadn't moved from the driver's seat of the cruiser, but I could see an ambulance arriving to deal with Spit Morton. Fatty noticed it too and gunned the cruiser over to meet it.

We had met the cops at the dump hut, after we had replaced Dweezil in the back of the truck and covered him up. The truck was still parked by the pit where the body was.

The cops had checked out Spit, and, like me, they had decided that he was in no danger and left him there to wait for the first-aid people. I'll bet Spit would have received more attention if he had been dressed in a three-piece suit and found unconscious in a BMW.

Anyway, that left us alone with Becker. He had caught up with his notes and was looking at me expectantly.

"Uh, sorry. Did you ask me something?" I said.

"Did you touch the body in any way?"

"Are you kidding? The guy was not in any immediate need of CPR, you know. Just look at him." Becker peered obediently over the edge of the pit. I looked over too, to keep him company, which was a mistake. The corpse's appearance had not improved. The most horrible part was that his eyes were open. Once you see dead eyes, you never forget them.

"Right. So you didn't move him."

"He might have shifted a bit when I moved the door that was covering him," I said. "I took one look and scrammed."

"Don't blame you. You recognize him?"

Now this is the weird thing. Up until then, I hadn't. It had just been a body. A horror-filmy, yucky, dead human body, and that was all my outraged mind would accept, but when Becker asked me that question, I did recognize him. I knew who it was.

"John Travers," I said.

George gasped. "Really?" he said and went back to take another look over the edge.

"Travers. Local?"

"He's—was—an auto mechanic living about two kilometres down the dump road. He has a wife and baby daughter— Oh, God, Francy!"

"Francy. His wife?"

"Somebody's got to let her know," I said.

"We'll do that, Ms. Deacon."

"How? Knock on her door stone-faced, hat in hand? There's no telling how she'll react. She'll probably flip out all over you. You don't know Francy."

"Do you know her?"

"Yes. She's a friend."

"Perhaps you'd be willing to come with us then, to talk to her, when we get through here. She'll likely be needing someone she knows to be with her for support."

"Not likely," George muttered. I tried to elbow him to shut up, but it was too late. Becker turned quickly to look at him.

"What does that mean?" he said, sharply.

George had the grace to look sheepish, or goatish, which he does from time to time. His ears elongate, somehow, and his neck gets brownish-red when he says something tactless.

"Well. John Travers was a bit of a. . . not a good husband to Francine."

Becker looked at me. I hated to say it. Francy had just lost her husband, though she didn't know it yet, and even if he was a no-good son of a bitch who got drunk and hit her, she had told me that she loved him, most of the time.

"He was violent," I said. "Look him up, Detective Becker. There's probably some record of—what do you call 'em—domestics? John was a shit."

Becker's nice crinkly eyes narrowed and I swear his ears moved. "So, she might have some motive for shooting him?"

"Motive she may have had," I said, "but Francy wouldn't shoot anybody. She hated guns. Anyway, she just had a baby. Kind of hard to lug a body to the dump without bursting your C-section stitches and spewing your intestines." It was graphic, I know, and both George and Becker winced. What is it with men, that they can eat pepperoni pizza while watching a slice-and-dice Rambo film, but the merest mention of menstruation or childbirth and they go a sickly green colour?

The ambulance had pulled away from the dump hut, presumably with Spit Morton safely tucked away inside. I hoped he was okay. The fat cop drove back to the pit, pulling up just inches from Becker's left thigh. Becker jumped out of the way and swore, and the fat guy laughed.

A second vehicle arrived, painted a dark colour, very discreet. It had more class than Spit's hearse could ever hope for, and I knew that it was the dead-mobile. Suddenly, I really wanted to go home.

"Are we done?" I said.

"What? The little lady doesn't want to help us drag up

the nice, juicy body she found?" the fat guy said, poking his head out of the cruiser window, a greasy smile on his face.

"The little lady," I said, "is in shock." And I was, because suddenly everything went black.

Three

She's got her good dress on
and she's waiting like a bracelet
for his arm.
  −Shepherd's Pie

George drove me home after I woke up. I had never fainted before and I was mortified.

"Must have been because I didn't have any breakfast," I said, more to myself than to George, as the old truck bounced along the Dunbar sideroad. He was driving more slowly than usual, which I appreciated, but it didn't make much difference. The Dunbar road hasn't seen a municipal grader since the Great Depression.

"It is a good thing you didn't eat, actually," George said. "Bodies are best discovered on an empty stomach, I think."

"You have a point. Oh, shit."

George stepped on the brakes. "Are you going to throw up?"

"No, no. I just remembered that I was supposed to go with Becker to tell Francy about John. I don't want her to be alone when they tell her."

"The policeman Becker already thought of that. He said you should take it easy. He'll finish up at the dump and then come to pick you up. You should have seen him when you fainted. He caught you before you hit the ground, like one of those figure-skater fellows. I thought he would twirl you around a couple of times before he put you down."

"I really don't know why I chose that moment to black out," I said, disturbed by the thought of Becker's arms around me. Wish I'd been awake.

"It was good timing," George said. "It got us away from there. No more questions."

"True. Actually, I did it on purpose."

"Of course you did. What talent!"

"I feel like shit, George."

"Then I will make you some of that blood-cleansing tea you have been trying to make me drink. Set you right in no time. The policeman said he would call from the dump hut before coming out here."

George Hoito had lived alone in his old brick farmhouse for more than twenty years. He had emigrated to Thunder Bay in his thirties and found a safe home in the Finnish community up there. He'd married a Finnish woman, and stayed immersed in a culture that never changed. Then, when his wife died, he'd moved south. South, that is, as far as Kuskawa.

He had two cats and a tame raven called Poe, who strutted around belligerently on leathery black legs, just daring the cats to come within reach of his wicked beak. They very sensibly left him alone.

Poe's wingspan was too wide for indoors. He preferred a kind of flapping hop to raise himself up to his favourite perch—a bookshelf near George's woodstove. He was enormous and took some getting used to. I suppose it's instinct that makes a bird so watchful, so oppressively aware of everything. Aunt Susan had a budgerigar called Snubby which always stared at strangers, but being stared at by a budgie was not as off-putting as being watched by Poe. If a dog or cat looks at you, you can usually figure out what they're thinking. Fuzzy animals use body language and wear facial expressions. Birds just look judgmental, and Poe made me feel like carrion. He perched on George's shoulder sometimes, but he had never perched on mine.

Perhaps Poe resented the attention I paid the cats, whom George ignored completely, considering them working animals only, hired to keep the mice in line.

When I was comfortably settled in the guest chair at the kitchen table, a steaming mug of alfalfa tea before me, George's cats appeared out of nowhere like smoke and wrapped themselves around my legs, purring loudly. I lifted them both into my lap where they made a nice, comforting pillow of fur, and Poe, watching as always from his bookshelf, made a rude croaking sound and shook his feathers at me.

"Feeling better?" George asked. He had not made any tea for himself and was preparing to drive the truck out to the back field, where he would dig a deep hole for Dweezil.

"Much better, thanks. But I'm worried. Somebody shot John Travers in the chest and conked Spit Morton over the head. Why?"

"It was probably one of Travers's gambling friends," George said. "He was always getting into fights, you know that. Perhaps he refused to honour a debt. Or perhaps it was a husband. I have heard stories about John Travers and the ladies."

"Yes, but to leave his body at the dump? It's so ugly. So mob-like."

"Maybe it was Rico Amato. I always thought he had mob connections."

"Rico? Hardly." Rico ran a small antique store near the highway. He was a fastidious man, exceedingly well groomed and a well known supporter of local arts organizations. He played the violin, not very well, and gave fabulous parties.

"I don't think Rico has ever been to the dump in his life, George. And I don't think he's ever met John Travers. They don't travel in the same circles."

George looked at me oddly. "I was joking, child. Leave it to the police. They probably already know who did it, or Francy will be able to tell them. This is Cedar Falls, remember, not Toronto. We do not get mysterious killers hereabouts."

"But we did just find a body at the dump, George."

"And I guarantee that the police will arrest somebody by tomorrow morning. Now drink your tea. I'll be back soon." He headed for the door.

"I'll be gone before you get back," I said. "Becker, remember? He's coming to take me away in his cruiser. Maybe they'll arrest me, just to get the thing cleared up fast."

George smiled. "If they do, don't expect me to bail you out. I am just a poor old man."

"Poor, maybe. Old, never. Happy digging."

He left. At the last moment, just before the door closed, Poe swooped down from his shelf and settled on George's shoulder, going along for the ride. I imagined the tall, shaggy-haired figure seen from a distance, digging a hole, a raven perched on his shoulder and the lumpy sack containing Dweezil propped nearby. Gothic, very. I hoped nobody would be watching. That's how rumours get started.

It wasn't Becker who telephoned an hour later, it was the big guy. He identified himself as Constable Morrison and I recognized his voice—sort of greasy and self-satisfied. The last time I had heard him speak he had called me "little lady" and

I had fainted, plop, right into Detective Becker's arms. Maybe Morrison thought I had fainted with shock at his tone, because he was much more polite this time.

"Ms. Deacon?"

"That's me."

"Detective Becker is just finishing up here at the scene, and he asked me to call to inform you that we would be there shortly. It's the only house on the Dunbar sideroad, is that right?"

"Yes. Watch out for the potholes, Detective." I could imagine the frame of the police car groaning as Morrison's bulk jounced around inside. I caught myself hoping that he had eaten a huge breakfast (which was likely) and would find the trip as uncomfortable as possible.

After I hung up the phone, I felt a trifle disappointed. I had been looking forward to seeing Becker again, but I hadn't bargained on Morrison. I guess you can't expect Laurel without Hardy.

I ran my fingers through my hair and made myself sit calmly at the kitchen table, like a debutante waiting for her prom date. I was wearing chore clothes and I hadn't taken a bath recently. I probably looked like hell and anyway, developing a crush on a cop was really, really stupid. I counted the reasons.

One: Becker thought I was George's girlfriend, and the concept had obviously put him off—I saw the sneer. So he wouldn't be interested. More likely, revolted. Some people are like that about age disparity. Not me. Aunt Susan had a twenty-one year old boyfriend once and I thought it was incredibly hip.

Two: He was a police officer, which would mean that if we were to get involved, I would have to quit smoking dope.

Some people drink cognac, I smoke dope. No big deal, but I imagine it would be to him.

Three: I had not had a romantic relationship since Drew, the actor, had stormed out of my apartment after throwing a three-hundred dollar Audrey puppet against the wall. (The puppet bounced back. I didn't, and swore off men for life. I thought.)

Three strikes, you're out, I said to myself, as the cruiser pulled up outside.

There was no sign of George, but way off in the distance I saw a black bird, wheeling. Poe, doing the funereal raven bit.

Becker got out of the car to meet me on the steps. I glanced at the third finger of his left hand (oh, you idiot) and there was no ring. Great.

"You okay?" he said.

"I'm fine. Sorry about fainting all over you. I'm not usually so girly." I was babbling already. "You call Francy yet?"

"No, ma'am. There are some things you can't do over the phone."

"You sure this is okay? Me coming with you?"

"It's better this way," he said. "Informing families of a death is never easy, and I usually take a woman police officer with me if I've got to tell a wife about a husband, or a woman about a child. But there aren't any women available right now, so I'd appreciate you being there."

"As a woman-substitute?" Defensive. Real smooth, Polly.

He raised an eyebrow. "You know what I mean," he said. "No offense intended."

What was I trying to do? Get him to say "Oh no, ma'am, you're all woman. No question."

"I was joking," I said.

"Oh. Hard to tell these days, ma'am. Political correctness

seems to have killed humour dead." We both let the word "dead" just hang there.

"Anyway," he said, after a moment, "you'll be better in this situation than my partner. He doesn't do sensitive."

"So I noticed." We had reached the cruiser, where Morrison waited in the driver's seat, looking a little green. Good. The road had done its worst.

"I'm sorry, but you'll have to go in the back," Becker said. He opened the door for me, and I half expected him to put his hand on my head as I climbed in, like they do in the movies to protect the prisoner from getting bumped. It was not a pleasant feeling back there. There were no handles on the inside of the doors.

Morrison grinned at me in the rear-view. "You want to cuff her too, Becker?" he said.

Becker was no more amused than I was. He turned around in his seat to talk to me, his face distorted by the mesh separating us. I leaned forward to remove myself from Morrison's view. Our faces were very close.

"Tell me about Francy and John Travers," he said.

Four

The foam-choked howls of starving wolves
are background music—nothing more
when weighed against that drunken man
who staggers past my flimsy door.
—Shepherd's Pie

"I met Francy and John two years ago at the Shepherd's Pie barn dance in the village," I said. I didn't have to explain about the dance. It was an annual event, a local tradition. The Laingford cop shop always sent a couple of guys out our way on account of it, just to keep an eye on things. Becker had most likely been there himself at some point. Everybody went.

Ruth Glass and Rose Shelley are the lead musicians for Shepherd's Pie, the folk band that's been getting so much press lately. I've known Ruth since public school, when we were both considered a little strange. I wrote a lot of poetry back then, and Ruth started setting my stuff to music. When it began to pay off, Ruth hired me as her lyricist. I don't write as many songs for her as I used to, but I like to keep my hand in, because the money's good and it gives me a kind of second-hand glamour.

The band spends a fair amount of time on the road, touring, but every year around harvest time, Ruth and Rose throw a big party, opening up their barn and roasting a side of beef. They always bring in a couple of kegs of ale from the Sikwan Brewery and lots of people bring their own mickey of sipping whiskey. It gets pretty rowdy, sometimes, but it's Ruth and Rose's way of keeping in touch with the community and avoiding what they call the "uppity star syndrome". It works.

"I had only been there for half an hour or so," I said to Becker. "It was around eleven o'clock and the party was only just starting to cook. Shepherd's Pie usually plays a set after midnight, but before that all the local musicians take turns getting up on the platform to jam. Rico Amato was up there playing old fiddle music and there was a crazy square-dance happening, except that nobody around here knows how to do it and nobody was calling it so there was a lot of milling around. It should have been really good energy, but something was wrong."

"What do you mean?" Becker said.

"Well, you know how a crowd can turn ugly in a second? Like one moment everyone's best friends and the next moment there's a fight?"

"Been there. Done that," Becker said.

"Well, it was like I was watching it change in slow motion. I got there right at the crucial moment when things were okay, then a tension rose in the air, like a smell, near the back door. So I went over to see what was going on."

"Everybody loves a fight," Morrison said.

"It wasn't that," I snapped, although it had been, a bit. We've all got that morbid curiosity gene that makes us slow down when we drive past a road accident, even if we hate ourselves for doing it. Some people keep it in check, but most don't, including me. But I wasn't about to admit that to Morrison.

"I went to see if there was anything I could do."

"Like you've got a black belt, maybe?" Morrison said.

"Let her tell the story, Morrison," Becker said.

"We'll be here all day," Morrison said. Becker ignored him and so did I, although I took the hint and got to the point, describing the scene as best I could.

John Travers had been drunk. Really drunk, the blind, dangerous kind that makes some men seem twice as big as they really are. He was staggering around bumping into people, and some guy he'd bumped into had pushed him back. They were getting loud and people were starting to edge away, looking nervous.

I had seen John around—in the hardware store and the A&P, but I'd never spoken to him. He was very good-looking, sort of sulky and sexy at the same time, with a crazy, do-anything glint in his eye. I didn't know Francy then, but I'd heard of her. She was hovering in the background like a pale-faced angel, telling him to calm down, to get normal.

She was one of those women you can't help noticing. She had long, frizzy, white-blonde hair which bushed out from the top of a tiny, fine-boned body, and her skin was perfectly white, like wax. She wore a small diamond stud in her nose. But once you took a look at her, you sort of looked away and then looked back, because the whole left side of her face was a mass of burn scars. Once you see that, it's hard not to stare.

Everybody knew that something was about to happen.

"Stay back," some guy said to the people near me. "John's gonna snap."

John took a swing at the other guy, throwing himself off balance. He staggered and to make up for it, started roaring like a moose in heat.

The other guy hit back, clipping him on the chin and John went berserk. There was a screech like the sound a cat makes when you step on its tail, and then Francy was in there, clinging to his back and screaming at him to stop.

John acted like he was being bothered by a horse-fly. He shook himself, once, which made her lose her grip. Then he turned around, looked her right in the eye and belted her.

"I'll never forget it," I said. "It was the most gut wrenching thing I've ever seen. It was as natural to him as breathing. His fist just came round and whacked her. I stopped being scared because I got really, really mad."

"You waded in, huh?" Morrison said.

"Not really," I said. "I'm not the fighting type, but when John hit Francy, everyone kind of surged forward. Most people around here, if they see a couple of guys duking it out, they'll just move back and watch, but if a woman gets hit, they get angry.

"Suddenly I was next to Francy," I said. "I grabbed her arm and dragged her out of the way just as three guys jumped John. Her lip was bleeding. I asked her if she wanted me to call the—you guys, but she said there was no point. She said she never had the heart to charge him with anything."

"So this was not an isolated incident," Becker said.

"Nope. It happened all the time."

Francy had always been very tough about it. Stoic. I'd tried to do the caring-woman-friend number on her, but she wasn't interested. She insisted that she could handle it. She hated me butting in.

"So," I said, "she took me by the hand like a little girl and said 'let's get a beer.' But she stopped to tap some guy on the shoulder and say 'Don't hurt him much, just knock him out.' They did."

"Jesus," Becker said.

"I ended up driving them home. John was still passed out, so some helpful guys loaded him into the back of George's pickup, because the keys to John's truck had disappeared. Turns out that one of his buddies confiscated them because John was too drunk to drive. He meant to give them to Francy, but he forgot and left."

"It's nice to know that the message is getting through to some people, some of the time. There are responsible citizens out there after all," Becker said, pleased.

"Buddy with the keys put his own car into the ditch that night. Pissed to the gills. That's why he forgot to give the keys back."

"Oh."

"Anyway, I helped her drag John into the house, and she gave me a cup of coffee. We talked. Since then, we've been pretty good friends. John still flies—flew, I guess—into a rage now and then, but Francy always told me to butt out. You know how it is."

"I sure do, and it drives me crazy," Becker said. "You get called out on a domestic. Neighbours, usually, complaining about the noise. You arrive and there's some guy just whaling away on his wife, or girlfriend or whatever. She defends him, refuses to lay charges. When we do, because we have to, either she doesn't show up in court, or she recants the whole thing."

"I know. I read the papers. It's a syndrome or something," I said.

Morrison snorted. "What I can't understand is all you feminists saying it's the guy's fault when it's the woman who just stays there and takes it. Why don't they just leave?"

"Don't start on the feminist thing, Morrison," Becker said, quietly. I had a feeling they'd been through this once or twice before. Morrison didn't reply.

We had arrived at the Travers' place. The clapboard house was flanked by a row of derelict cars like a shabby bride with rusty bridesmaids. Some of the cars were on blocks, most had their hoods up.

Next to the house was a garage, a big quonset hut with filthy windows and a half open front, spilling car parts and unidentifiable slabs of metal. A beautifully hand-painted sign announced "Auto Repair and Body Shop—J. Travers, prop." Francy had painted the sign for John's birthday the year before.

A dog, chained to a doghouse a few feet from the front door of the house, began barking furiously.

"That's Lug-nut," I said. "John's hunting dog. The rule is he's not supposed to be touched, ever. He's kept hungry and he is not a happy puppy. Don't be patting him."

"Not likely," Becker said. "He's tied up, right?"

"He's tied up."

There was no sign of movement inside the house. Usually Lug-nut's welcome would bring someone out immediately, or at least prompt a twitch of the dingy curtains at the window.

"Are you just gonna sit there?" Morrison said. "Afraid of the puppy?"

Becker turned to Morrison in the first show of temper I had seen him display towards his bulky partner. It was long overdue, as far as I was concerned.

"Morrison," he said, "considering the fact that you have not moved your goddamn fat ass from that seat since we started work, and considering that you won't be moving it until the end of the shift, I would appreciate it if you would keep your stupid mouth shut." With that he got out of the cruiser and slammed the door shut with his foot.

"Geez," Morrison said. "I was only kidding."

Becker opened my door and handed me out with the manners of a highly-professional butler. He slammed my door too.

"Bravo," I said, very quietly.

We went to the door, giving Lug-nut a wide berth. The dog was almost hysterical now, and despite myself, I felt sorry for him.

"It's okay, Lug-nut. It's okay, boy." I always said that, using my most soothing voice. It probably didn't make a scrap of difference to Lug-nut, but it made me feel braver.

Becker had been knocking but there was no reply.

"That's odd," I said. "It's almost noon, and Francy usually puts the baby down for a nap around now and has a smoke on the porch." (I didn't tell Becker what kind of smoke she has on the porch at noon. I'm not stupid.) "You can usually set your watch by her."

"There's no car here," Becker said, "or at least no car you could drive. Maybe she's at a doctor's appointment or something."

"Francy doesn't have a car and she can't drive anyway," I said. "John's truck's missing, though. It wasn't at the dump, was it?"

"Nope. What kind of truck was it?"

"GMC half-ton. Beat up. Baby-poo brown. Don't know the year."

Becker went down the steps back to the cruiser to talk to Morrison. I supposed they would put out an A.P.—whatchamacallit for the truck.

"Try Kelso's Tavern in Laingford," I called. "He used to drink there practically every night."

Becker nodded, presumably passing the information along.

Lug-nut had stopped barking. In fact, he had stopped doing much of anything. He was lying with his head between his paws, ears drooping instead of the usual flat-against-the-skull signal to back off. His ribs stuck out. His water bowl was empty. He whined once, piteously.

I felt awful. Francy didn't like the dog, I knew that, but depriving him of water was mean.

"Are those crocodile tears?" I said to him. "If I come over there to fill your bowl, will you bite my hand off?" He didn't say.

Becker returned. "We'll be looking for Travers's truck," he said. "Now, what about Mrs. Travers? She got a neighbour she might have gone to?"

Then I realized that the pram was gone.

Francy and I had found the pram at the dump. It was an old-fashioned one with a high undercarriage like those monster trucks favoured by big men with small dicks. We had taken it away on a Spit day and it hadn't cost us a cent. Francy kept it on the porch because it was too wide to get in the door. When the new baby, Beth, was put in it, she looked like she was lying in a football field. I told Becker about the missing pram.

"She might have gone over to the Schreier's place, I suppose," I said. "It's the closest, and young Eddie sometimes helps John out in the shop. Francy's not particularly friendly with Eddie's mother, though. Carla Schreier's a holy roller, and doesn't approve of John or Francy."

"We'll go over there, then," he said.

"Wait, Becker." I had left off the "detective" part on purpose, because I wanted to know what his first name was. He knew mine, after all, and my hormones were way ahead of my reason. If he told me his name, I thought, it would be a step in the right direction. "Becker" was what

Morrison called him, and it sounded mildly aggressive. He stopped in mid-turn.

"Mark," he said. "It's Mark." Hah. I tried not to smile in triumph.

"Mark, listen, we have to do something about this dog. He's got no water and his master's dead, so he isn't likely to get fed any time soon. Francy will have enough to worry about after we tell her."

Lug-nut was listening half-heartedly. He wasn't a bad looking dog, really, when his ears weren't plastered to his head. Part shepherd, part black lab, and something else. Something mongrelly. His eyes were yellow, which was unfortunate, but it wasn't his fault.

Detective Mark Becker looked at me, then at the dog. Lug-nut knew we were talking about him and pressed his body further into the ground, achieving a kind of road-kill effect that was far from attractive. He whined again.

"Yeah, okay. You're right." Becker's eyes went to the hose attachment next to the porch. "We can fill his water bowl there, but unless his food is kept outside, he'll have to stay hungry for a while longer. We can't just break in."

"Why not?"

"It's against the law, Polly."

"Oh, puhleeze. Francy's my friend. I walk in all the time. I know where the food is. I'll do it."

"She keep her door unlocked?"

"This is the boonies. Nobody locks their doors here. You should know that, a country cop and all."

"I haven't been here very long," Becker said. "Where I come from, you don't go outside to water your lawn without locking your door." I didn't bother to answer. City people. Geez.

He walked towards Lug-nut and reached for the bowl. At once the dog sprang up from his abject pose and snarled, displaying an impressive set of fangs. Becker dropped the bowl and leaped back, swearing. From the cruiser came a high-pitched giggle.

"Morrison doesn't like you much, does he?" I said.

"The feeling is mutual. The dog's not crazy about me either."

"Let me try. He knows me, sort of." I moved forward, my hand out in the age-old Nervous-Human-Pretending-to-be-Friendly routine. "It's okay, Luggy. Okay, boy. Nobody's going to hurt you." I talked to him the way I talked to Beth, Francy's baby, who made me just as nervous as the dog did, for different reasons.

Lug-nut bought it. He sniffed my hand, then licked it and wriggled over on his back, presenting his belly to be rubbed. It was like winning a lottery. If only men acted that way.

Becker made a huffy, annoyed little sound.

"Want me to rub your belly too?" I said without thinking. He laughed aloud. A cop with a sense of humour. Curiouser and curiouser.

Lug-nut obviously wanted me to make up for his lonely years of never being touched, and I knew how he felt. But there was sad news to be delivered and I couldn't sit around playing Her Majesty and the Corgis all day. I picked up the bowl and turned to Becker, but he had walked back to the cruiser to talk to Morrison.

I filled the water bowl and put it within reach of Lug-nut, who drank most of it in one schloop. Then I took the food bucket and walked in the front door. Becker didn't follow.

The hall stank, as usual. It was full of sweaty, mud-encrusted boots and oily overalls. I headed through to the kitchen where Lug-nut's food was kept under the sink.

There had been a "domestic", I thought.

Chairs were overturned, there were beer bottles on the table, some smashed on the floor. The fridge door was open. I moved to close it and my foot slipped in a patch of wet. I looked down and saw it wasn't beer, it was blood.

"Becker!" I yelled.

Five

It's okay, Babe, if they hurt you,
God doesn't care how it's done.
God wants you there with a smile on your face
making sure that your man's having fun.
—Shepherd's Pie

"Did you touch anything?"

"Nope. Just got my tootsies in a little blood," I said and felt my face drain like a bathtub. Damn. Keeling over in Mark Becker's arms a second time just would not do. Especially since Morrison had shifted his butt out of the driver's seat and had come pounding in behind Becker when I called, or rather, screamed for help.

Morrison was really awfully big. How had he got on the force? Maybe he was regulation size when he was hired and ballooned afterwards. Some cops just get sucked into the Tim Horton's vortex and never escape, I guess.

I sat down on a kitchen chair and stuck my head between my knees, breathing deeply until the world stopped spinning. When I looked up, Morrison was standing there with a glass of water in his hand.

"Shock, right?" he said. He was smiling kindly.

"Thanks. Yup. Shock." I schlooped the water in a fair imitation of Lug-nut. Becker was making a phone call.

"...photographer, the works," he was saying. When he hung up, his face was grim. "Judging from the amount of blood on the floor, I'd say Travers bought it right here," he said. "You go wait in the car, Ms. Deacon. We don't want to spoil the scene."

Oh, so it was back to the formal Ms. Deacon, was it? What did he think I was going to do? The dishes? Still, he had blood to examine, and I had a dog to feed and my friend to find. I figured, accurately as it turned out, that this would plunk the crime directly in Francy's lap, and I knew she couldn't have done it. I had to find her before they did.

"Do you have any objection, Detective Becker, to my just getting a little dog food from that cupboard, or do you think that might constitute tampering with the evidence?"

He thought seriously for a full minute. Gone was the sense of humour, if it had ever been there.

"All right," he said, finally. I picked up the feed bucket and walked towards the cupboard.

"Wait," he said. He removed his nightstick from its sheath and used it to open the cupboard door. The bag of kibble was open, with an empty margarine container lying on top. I looked at it closely before touching it.

"No bloody fingerprints," I said. "I think we can safely assume that the victim was not bludgeoned to death with Kibbles and Bits." Morrison snorted, but Becker just glared at me. I filled the bucket and stalked out, trying desperately to remain dignified. I don't think it worked. Truth was, I wanted to stay and watch them detect, but I was too proud to say so.

Lug-nut greeted my arrival with so much exuberance that I had no choice but to sit down and bond with him. He wolfed the food and turned over on his back again, his tail wagging so hard his whole body jack-knifed in the dirt, sending up clouds of dust. I clung to him for comfort and thought about what to do.

The Schreier's place was only half a kilometre away to the east. It would take me ten minutes to walk there, less if I took the bush trail. If Francy was there, I could at least warn her that the police were coming. I had little doubt that she already knew what was going on, but Francy thought she was invincible. She led her life walking right on the edge of things. Without a friend there, this time, I was afraid that she would end up with more than bruises.

Becker had ordered me to go wait in the car. I looked at the front door of the house, which I had slammed behind me. Morrison and Becker were probably sifting through the debris, oblivious to everything but the evidence—the evidence which might send Francy to jail.

What had happened last night? I pictured John coming home from Kelso's tavern, liquored-up and horny maybe, or just spoiling for a fight. I knew how Francy felt about having sex with her husband when he was drunk. It was a battle every time, which she sometimes lost. We had been over it more than a dozen times. I would urge her to get out, go to the Women's Shelter in Sikwan, before it was too late. I urged her to get help, get counselling. She always said that John didn't mean it, that he always begged for forgiveness afterwards, and she was content with that. He would never do it again, she said. She also said that if I reported John to the police, she would hate me forever. I believed her. Now, when the police were well and truly involved whether she liked it or not, I discovered that I wanted to protect her from them. Go figure. Somehow, I felt that the whole mess was my fault. I should have tried harder.

Maybe, last night, the baby had been crying. Maybe the dog had been howling. Maybe something was said or done that made Francy lose her patience, her stoic "I can handle it" attitude. I imagined her grabbing the shotgun from its rack beside the kitchen door—I hadn't even looked to see if it was there. The cops would, though.

John kept it loaded, I knew that. It was his "protection", he said. From what, he never bothered to explain. Maybe, like Spit's gun, it was for the bears.

Maybe Francy blasted a hole through John as he reeled towards her with a smashed beer bottle in his hand, his eyes piggy and insane. I could imagine it and I didn't blame her one bit, if that's what happened.

What I couldn't see was Francy loading the body into the truck and driving it to the dump. She didn't drive, for one thing, and she would never leave Beth, for another. What I couldn't see her doing was whacking Spit Morton over the head to cover her crime. Somebody had, I was certain, but it wasn't Francy.

Although it was obvious that someone had blasted a hole in John Travers in his own kitchen, I was sure that Francy had not dumped the body.

"Hush, now," I said to Lug-nut, who whined once and then sat looking at me as I tore off on the woods path to the Schreier's place.

There are black bears in them thar woods. The dump attracts them, and they are not as afraid of humans as they ought to be. I had never met one, but everybody has monsters and bears are mine. After my parents were killed when I was ten, I woke up screaming night after night, chased by bears.

Black ones, grizzlies, polar bears, vaguely bear-like villains, and once, horribly, a sweet, murderous teddy-bear—the result of my well-meaning aunt's gift of a fuzzy Paddington to comfort me at night.

George had told me that the best thing to do if you meet a bear is to run away. Francy said climb a tree. Eddie Schreier said lie down and pretend you're dead, but I think he was kidding. Everyone has a different answer. Rico Amato, the antique dealer, assured me that bears in this part of the world are a myth, perpetuated by macho hunters who need an excuse to wander off into the bush and get drunk.

Aunt Susan advocates a calm about-face and a little song as you walk away. I can just see me coming nose-to-muzzle with a bruin, turning my back on it and humming "O Canada". Not likely.

This is why I took the woods path to the Schreier's place at a brisk trot. The sun had gone in behind a dark cloud, and the woods were gloomy. It was late autumn, and there was an added danger; not only were there bears, there were hunters, looking for deer, moose, or basically anything that was moving. I was not wearing the requisite orange jacket.

The woods smelled vaguely of cat pee, the way they do that time of year. It had been a wet season, and the piles of leaves were starting to decompose. After my recent brush with death, the smell was more than appropriate. It made the breath catch at the back of my throat, and as I was a pack-a-day smoker, my breath as I ran was not coming particularly smoothly.

I kept my ears open for snufflings or gruntings, but made it all the way there without meeting a soul.

There was smoke trickling out of the chimney of the sprawling bungalow, and Carla Schreier's old Dodge was in the driveway. There was no sign of the pram, but the Schreier place had a wide front door. Now that I was out of the woods, so to speak, I slowed down. No sense in arriving out of breath, especially as I had bad news to impart, and ought to deliver it with some semblance of decorum, as Aunt Susan would say.

The Schreiers, Carla, Samson and their son Eddie, were members of an obscure Christian sect whose purpose included the gathering of souls. Shortly after I arrived in the area, I was approached in a slightly nervous, albeit friendly manner by Carla Schreier in the A&P.

She was very pretty, with soft, shoulder-length hair which curled around her face. She wore too much make-up, but it was applied with skill. Her flowered cotton dress was all flounces and ruffles—rather young for her—and from a distance you might mistake her for a woman in her twenties. Up close you could see the slight sagging around her neck, indicating that she was probably closer to forty than twenty.

She had been staring at me while I was squeezing avocados in the produce section. I didn't know who she was, then. She was just a woman who was dressed for a party when there was no party in sight. Her eyes and the way she was trying to get my attention made me nervous. She came bouncing up and touched my arm.

"You're Susan Kennedy's niece, aren't you?" she said. (Susan is my mother's sister.) The woman's voice was breathy and child-like, the kind that makes people get all protective.

"Yes," I said.

"I thought so. You look just like her." This wasn't true. Susan is handsome, dark and strong. I'm plain and weedy.

"I heard you'd moved here from the city," the woman said. "Your aunt's a good friend of Samson's—my husband. We get all our feed from her, you know."

"Really. That's good of you." Later, Susan had some less

than friendly things to say about Samson Schreier, but I won't mention them here.

"Well, her prices are a bit higher than the new place on the highway, but her stock is always fresh and she delivers."

"I'm sure she does. Well, nice to meet you Ms...?"

"Schreier. Missus. Carla. And you're Pauline, aren't you?"

"That's right." Something made me not say "call me Polly," and I soon found out what it was.

"Well, Pauline, I just wanted to welcome you to the community and to ask you if you've accepted Jesus Christ as your personal saviour."

"I beg your pardon?"

"I just know you'd be interested in coming to our meetings. We have them every Sunday in the Chapel of the Holy Lamb, which is really not that far from where I hear you are staying." She was so enthusiastic. Reminded me of Lori Pinkerton, trying to get me to join the cheerleading team at Laingford High.

"Well, actually, I..."

"Oh, don't give me an answer now, Pauline. I know you'll want to think about it, but I want you to know that we would truly love to have you come and be a part of the glorious mystery of the love of our Lord. Ten o'clock sharp. See you on Sunday!" She retreated, trotting on her little patent-leather heels and making a quick left into the bakery section. She had pressed a tract into my hand and I looked at it, dazed.

"ARE YOU WANDERING, LOST, HUNGRY FOR MEANING?" A miserable-looking young person gazed heavenwards. There were little rays of light coming out of the clouds. Very artistic. "JESUS IS THE ANSWER," it said. I sighed.

When Jehovah's Witnesses or Mormons came to my door

in Toronto, I'd just usually tell them I was a witch—a Wiccan— but it didn't seem like a good idea to do that in Cedar Falls. It would get back to Susan, who would be derisive. Either that, or the zealots would burn down my cabin. The fact is, I'm not big on organized religion of any kind, and it's taken me a long time to shake off the residue of guilt left by my blessedly short career as a child-Catholic.

I shoved the tract deeply into my pocket and headed down the tinned vegetable aisle. I met Carla Schreier again in Dairy and she gave me a radiant smile. It was all I could do not to bare my teeth and hiss "six, six, six" at her.

I had never come face to face with her again after that. Although she was Francy and John's nearest neighbour, the Travers and the Schreiers were not friendly. Carla and Samson's son, Eddie, was interested in cars and liked to hang out in John's shop, but he did so against his parent's wishes. Francy had told me once that the Schreiers thought their neighbours were "ungodly".

"Probably because we show that kid a bit of fun once in a while," she had said, bitterly. "Carla's a bitch, and Samson's straight out of the Old Testament." Francy's venom was perplexing. Carla hadn't seemed like a bitch to me. A little over the top, maybe, but fluffy and warm. Just not my kind of warm.

Meeting Carla again after three years of careful avoidance was going to be tricky. I rang the doorbell and ran though a few opening lines in my head. A curtain twitched at a side window.

"Hi, Mrs. Schreier, remember me? The lost soul you tried to recruit a while back?"

"Hi, Carla. Can Francy come out and play?"

I had no proof that Francy was there, but where else could

she be? I was convinced that she was hiding, that she knew there would be trouble. But would Carla Schreier be the kind of woman to harbour a fugitive? It seemed unlikely.

The door opened. Eddie, looking guilty as sin, stood there with his mouth hanging open. He was tall for his age, which was sixteen. His body had run away with him in the past year, growing so fast he looked perpetually astonished by it. He was six-foot-two in his socks, his elbows and knees protruded from clothes which could never hope to keep up, and his feet were enormous. His hair, blonde and baby-fine, was cut fashionably short, which was imprudent, considering that his ears might have been happier with a little camouflage. His eyes were blue, his face tanned from outdoor work and his prominent Adam's apple bobbed up and down like a hamster caught in his throat.

'Oh. Hi, Polly. How are you?" he said. He made no move to let me in.

"Hi, Eddie. Is your Mom at home?" This threw him.

"Uh, yeah. Yes. She is."

"Do you think I could talk to her, please?"

"Sure. I guess. Let me check." He backed away from the door and only just managed to keep from closing it in my face. Eddie was normally very polite. It was one of the things I really liked about him. Something was definitely up.

"Mom!" I heard him yell. He hadn't moved far away from the door and was calling over his shoulder. "It's Miss Deacon, Mom."

"Ms." I said, out of habit. I heard a distant garbled murmur and then Eddie returned, opening the door wide enough for me to enter and casting a furtive glance past me out into the front yard.

"Come on in," he said.

As I moved past him into the hallway, he was still peering

out into the road. I tapped him on the shoulder. "Eddie," I said. He jumped.

"Huh?"

"When the police come, let your mother answer the door, okay? You're an open book."

"A what? How'd you know? Are they coming now?"

"They'll be a little while yet. Show me where Francy and your mother are."

Silent, he led me towards the kitchen.

Six

And every time the wind blows, she shatters.
–Shepherd's Pie

The interior of the Schreier home was, as Aunt Susan would say, "roped off by Sears". A spindly-legged hall table held a vase full of fake flowers whose buds matched the wallpaper. Above it hung a gilt mirror. Throw pillows and bowls of pot-pourri multiplied all over the place like Tribbles. There was God-stuff everywhere—embroidered Bible verses on the walls, stacks of tracts on every flat surface and an actual plaster Jesus bust, like a watchdog near the door. Francy's pram stood out like a beat-up Chrysler in the middle of a china shop.

A stack of sticky-looking squares on a decorative plate held pride of place in the centre of the kitchen table, and there were pretty napkins set out, as if company were expected. A silver coffee pot and rose-patterned cups and saucers stood at the ready.

Carla rose as I entered the kitchen. She was wearing a crisp, blue, Barbara Billingsley dress, and she smiled in welcome.

"Oh, Pauline, what a nice surprise," she said.

Francy was huddled at one end of the table, Beth in a snuggly-carrier against her chest. She held her coffee cup in both hands, as if the warmth of it were desperately important. She looked terrible.

Her skin, pale at the best of times, was almost blue-white, the scarred side of her face was livid, and she had been crying, lots. Her right eye was swollen almost shut and there was a cut on her cheek. I didn't have to ask who had hurt her. She looked at me once, as I came in, and then went back to staring into her cup. Her glance scared me. It was totally devoid of emotion—she had looked through me, not at me. The lights were on, as they say, but nobody was home. I felt the back of my neck prickle.

"Francy," I said, "good on you for getting out of there. You okay?"

"She won't tell you," Carla said, in a hushed, we're-at-a-funeral voice that made me want to smack her. "She's been like this ever since Eddie brought her in last night. She hasn't said a word."

"Oh, boy. She seen a doctor?"

"I tried to call one last night, but she went—well, she was quite upset. Pulled the phone cord right out of the wall." Carla gestured to a telephone on the counter near the back kitchen door. The phone cord dangled. Exhibit A.

I walked around to the end of the table and crouched next to Francy's chair. I put my hand on her arm, an experiment, and she didn't flinch, so I put my arms around her thin shoulders and hugged, hard. I could feel her vibrating like a small, cold animal, but she didn't make a sound.

"Is Beth okay?" I said. She nodded, still not looking at me.

Carla had poured me a cup of coffee and handed it to me, eagerly passing the plate of squares as she did so. Amazing, really, that kind of hostess training. Maybe it was so firmly ingrained in her psyche that she did it without thinking. I took a square, to be polite, and placed it on the delicate saucer next to my cup. What Carla Schreier would make of a tea party at my place, I didn't like to think. Mugs sluiced hurriedly in the water bucket, wood shavings and leather scraps swept from the guest chair, a bowl of pistachios plunked in the middle of the table, if you were lucky. Goat milk from a jar.

"Do you know what happened, Carla?" I said. "Was Eddie involved? When did he bring her over here?"

"I sent Eddie next door around six last evening to return a book Francy had given him," Carla said. "He didn't want to go. I insisted." What did that have to do with it? Carla was waiting for me to ask, so I did.

"Why didn't he want to go?"

"Well, the book, Pauline. I mean. I don't know if you've read it—you probably have—but I didn't think it was appropriate for a sixteen-year-old boy to read. Not at all. When I saw the cover I almost had a heart attack."

"What was it? That thing by Madonna?"

"Madonna? Oh, no, nothing like that. I don't have a problem with Catholics, although I don't hold with their practices. No, this was a book called *Lady's Lover*, or something. I've heard that it's absolutely disgusting, and I didn't want my son reading it."

"*Lady's Lover*? You mean *Lady Chatterley's Lover*? By D.H. Lawrence?" I said.

"Yes, that's the one."

I fought the urge to giggle and let my eyes flicker over to Francy to see if she got the joke, but she had not looked up. She wasn't even listening. Too bad. I would have given anything to see some light in those clouded eyes.

"*Lady Chatterley's* not really that bad, Carla. It was written a long time ago. People's perceptions have changed since then."

"Smut is smut. I must say that I didn't appreciate Francy giving Eddie that kind of thing to read. He's young for his age. And she must have warned him that I wouldn't like it, because he hid it under his mattress. I found it when I was cleaning his room."

I wanted to ask her how often she turned her son's mattress in the course of cleaning house, but I smiled instead.

"So, you found the book and asked Eddie to return it."

"She's loaned him books in the past, you know. I didn't mind that. We don't have a lot of books in the house, and I'm glad that he likes to read, but I feel they went behind my back, here." She darted a swallow-like, but resentful glance at Francy, and then back at me, waiting for my agreement.

I pictured Detective Becker on the porch of the Travers's place, wondering where I had got to. I didn't have much time, and this was neither the time nor the place to be getting into a heavy literary discussion, so I steered Carla back on track.

"And he went over there at six, you say."

"Yes. Well, he can tell you himself," she said. "EDDIE!" Her call was sudden and shrill, and I must have jumped about a foot in the air. Francy jumped too, and spilled her coffee. Beth began to whimper.

Eddie appeared almost immediately, and I guessed that he had been standing in the hallway, just out of sight. Carla looked pleased and surprised that he had come so soon. Perhaps her son normally made sure he was well out of earshot.

"Yes, Ma?" He cleared his throat and stood on one foot, then the other.

"Tell Miss Deacon what you told me about last night, sweetheart."

I didn't bother correcting my name to "Ms." this time.

Eddie stood to attention, like a kid auditioning for a part in a play.

"I took the bush path, eh? To the back door? Mr. Travers doesn't like me being over there when he's not home, and he wasn't because his truck was gone, but I didn't know that until later. If I'd went the road way, I wouldn't have even knocked. Francy, Mrs. Travers, I mean, said it was okay though. So I gave her the book back and then we had some tea and talked in the kitchen for a while."

"Tell her what you talked about, Eddie," Carla said.

"It doesn't matter what we talked about, Ma. Just stuff, okay?"

"It pays to be truthful." He glared at her and continued.

"Then Mr. Travers's truck pulled in and I said I had to go. Don't get me wrong. He likes me, eh? But, well, he has rules about stuff."

"What kind of rules, Eddie?" I said.

"Like never being alone with Mrs. Travers. Never touch his dog. Always ask him first before using his tools. You know."

"Yeah, Eddie. I know."

"Anyway, he came in before I got out, and I knew he would be mad. He was kinda drunk, and when he saw me he went for me like he was going to kill me. He hit me in the stomach and I fell down, but I didn't fight back or anything."

Carla was nodding her head and emitting little peeps of approval, as if she were following along in the script in her head. I wondered how many times she had made him rehearse.

"Did he say anything?" I said.

"No, he was just sort of growling. Crazy. Then he went for Mrs. Travers and started hitting her. I was real scared, eh, so I grabbed a wrench that was sitting there and sort of hit him over the head with it."

"That was brave, Eddie," I said. He looked uncomfortable.

"Mrs. Travers said it was stupid. She said when he woke up he would kill me and her both. So we grabbed the baby and got out of there. That's all really, except when we got in, Ma tried to call the cops or an ambulance or something and Francy ripped the phone out of the wall."

"Why did she do that, do you think?" I said.

"I don't know. I was in the bathroom and I heard a yell and when I came out there was Ma standing there with the phone cord in her hand, looking at Francy like she was crazy. Francy was crying. It was awful."

"Sounds like it. What time did you and Francy get here?"

"They came in about eight o'clock," Carla said. "I was so worried. Samson's away at a farming conference and I had to feed the stock all by myself. I don't like being alone in the house at night, and I'd told Eddie to come right home after dropping off the book."

"And what did you do after Francy pulled the phone out?"

Carla frowned, trying to remember. "I guess I served up dinner and tried to get things back to normal. Then I made up a bed for Francy in the guest room."

"Weren't you afraid that John would come over here?"

"John Travers would never dare come over here," Carla said. "Samson saw to that."

"They didn't get along?"

Eddie laughed. "That's an understatement," he said.

"Eddie," Carla said, a note of warning in her voice. Then she smiled at me. "My husband and Mr. Travers had a disagreement a long time ago," she said. "They don't speak to each other, and they both respect each other's property lines.

That's all. John knew better than to set foot in this house."
Her mouth was set in a prim, pink line. She looked like an
illustration for a story about the good girl who gets
propositioned.

"Besides," Eddie added, with a wry grin, "he was dead
drunk."

"So, you just all went to bed," I said. It made a weird kind
of sense. "What about now? Your phone's still out of order.
Haven't you tried to get it fixed?"

"Samson will see to it," Carla said. "He's coming back
today."

"And is this little coffee party in honour of his return?"
I said.

Carla looked hurt, and I immediately wanted to take it
back. She had gone to all this trouble, her eyes said. The least
I could do was to be polite about it. I didn't doubt that having
a near-catatonic Francy in her house was not something that
she would have chosen. Especially if Francy had been ripping
the place apart. People like the Schreiers prefer things to be
predictable.

"I know you're worried about your friend," she said,
apologetically, as if it were she who had been rude and not me.
"I thought she just needed things to be normal for a while,
that's all. We were waiting for the police to get here."

"Why are you so sure the police are coming?" I said.

"Well, John Travers will probably wake up with a nasty
bump on his head and sin in his heart," she said. She stood up
straight and clenched her little fists. "He won't come alone,
but he'll come all right, trying to blame Eddie for what
happened. Eddie's a good boy, but he did hit John Travers on
the head. He'll have to tell his side of the story to the police,
and policemen never say no to a cup of coffee, do they?"

It was a rhetorical question, and to fill the gap, I took a bite out of the pastry Carla had offered me. It was incredibly sweet.

"Why are you here?" Carla asked, while my mouth was full. "If you've come looking for Francy, well, you can see that she's in no shape to go herb-gathering." Her sarcasm surprised me. I wouldn't have though she'd had it in her.

I swallowed the sticky mass and cleared my throat.

"I came over here because I wanted to ask Francy what happened last night before the police did. I wanted to give her some support when they told her that John was dead." I stressed the last word and waited for a reaction.

Carla and Eddie gasped in unison.

Francy looked up. Her eyes cleared, and she began to laugh. It was just a chuckle at first, but it got louder and louder until she was howling, tears streaming down her cheeks. We all watched her, fascinated and horrified.

"Do something!" Carla said. I couldn't move. Then Eddie strode to the end of the table, lifted Francy's chin very gently with one hand and slapped her hard across the face.

"Jesus Christ, Eddie!" I yelled, going for him, but it had worked. Francy fell into his arms, sobbing.

"I can't allow blasphemy in my house, Pauline," Carla said, softly.

"I apologize," I said. "Violence of any kind makes me angry."

"Well, there's no need to swear," Carla said. "Eddie, you never, never hit a girl. You know that."

"You did say to do something, Ma," Eddie said.

"The police will be here soon," I said. "Francy, I'm glad they didn't see your reaction to the news, honey, but you've got to pull it together a bit, because they're going to want to ask you some questions. You too, Eddie. What you told me just doesn't tally with what we found next door."

"What do you mean?" Eddie said.

"Broken beer bottles, lots of them. Blood all over the place. You may have conked John over the head with a wrench, but I don't think that's what killed him. Someone shot him at point-blank range in the chest and dumped his body at the landfill site. Know anything about that?"

Both Eddie and Francy froze. Francy was definitely coming back to life. Her face wasn't empty anymore and a bit of colour had worked its way into her cheeks. Beth was quiet, amazingly, considering everything that had gone on in the past few minutes. Francy looked puzzled, and she turned her head to look at Eddie. She still hadn't spoken.

Eddie had gone very pale and was staring at me, his lower lip trembling.

"I didn't shoot him, honest. I just hit him on the head because he was hurting Francy. Is he really dead?"

"Very, Eddie."

"Ma?" He was panicking. "Ma, you said all I had to do was tell the police I hit him on the head. You said it was going to be okay. They'll think I shot him. They'll put me in jail."

Carla moved in and held him, pulling his head into her bosom and stroking his hair.

"They won't put you in jail, sweetheart. All you have to do is tell what happened, the way you told Pauline. Somebody else killed him. Not you." She sat him down at the table like a small child, took both his hands in hers and started to pray out loud.

"Dear Jesus, help us through this difficult time, Jesus, help the police to find the truth, Jesus, protect my boy from harm, Jesus..." in a gentle, soothing wave of sound which embarrassed me so much I had to leave the room.

I went to the front door to wait for the police.
As I stared out at the quiet road, I felt a touch on my elbow.
"Polly, get me out of here," Francy said. "Hide me."

Seven

Bear with me, he said
as his claws dug into my skin.
—Shepherd's Pie

It's hard being in Ontario cottage country without wheels. When the corner store is five kilometres away and you need a pack of smokes RIGHT NOW, having a car helps. If you have to go to the post office, it's a trip—an outing. The closest beer store to Cedar Falls is all the way over in Laingford, so locals either stock up or make their own.

I was auto-free—not by choice particularly. It was a money thing. So, when Francy tugged on my arm and asked me to rescue her, the first thing I did was curse the fates for not providing me with a getaway car.

If I'd had my bike, an old Raleigh I kept on the porch of the cabin with a seat wide enough for a sumo wrestler and his trainer, I could have taken Francy away by road. But I'd arrived by police cruiser, and that was not, at this point, the transportation of choice for either of us.

"You up for a hike?" I said.

"You don't have George's truck?"

"Nope. I came with the cops. They asked me to be there when they told you about John."

"Oh. They'll be here soon, I guess."

"Very soon, Francy. How come you don't want to talk to them? Is Eddie's story that much of a lie?"

"Let's just get out of here," she said. "I'll tell you later. Trust me, okay?"

"We'll have to take the old logging road," I said. "Are you sure you can make it?"

"I'm tough."

"Is Beth?"

"Like mother, like daughter," she said and gave me a pale smile, the first I'd seen. I didn't argue.

We had discovered the old road by accident, the previous summer. After we had become friends, we discovered a mutual interest in herbal remedies and had spent lots of time hacking through the bush together, stalking the wild asparagus. We nicknamed ourselves the "Falls Witches" and had gained a bit of a reputation in the community for pouncing upon anyone with a runny nose, diagnosing their symptoms and forcing herbal teas down their throats. We were often remarkably successful, which is probably why Carla Schreier, who was the kind of person who went to the hospital emergency room with a hangnail, was so snide about our "herb-gathering" activities. Alternative health practices, to some people, are Devil's spawn.

The old logging road meandered through the bush between the dump road and the Dunbar sideroad, and Francy and I often used it as a shortcut to each other's homes. It was a favourite of snowmobilers in the wintertime and was well-marked, though a bit rough in places.

"Let's go, then," Francy said. Carla was still praying up a storm in the kitchen, the sibilant hiss of her "Jesuses" seeping down the hallway like holy smoke. "Now, Polly, while she's on a roll."

"I've spent the whole day sneaking around," I said, as we slipped out the door, closing it softly behind us. I told her about the cloak-and-daggering with Dweezil, then how I took off on Becker and Morrison. "Now I'm escaping from the holy rollers," I said. "I should have stayed in bed."

"I'm glad you didn't, Polly," Francy said and squeezed my hand.

We knew the police car would be along at any moment, so we stayed on the woods-side of the ditch, keeping our ears open for the sound of an engine so we could crouch in the bushes if we had to.

"Shit. Car." Francy said. We dropped instantly, like they do in the movies. It was kind of fun, except that I whacked my knee on a stump going down, which hurt enough to bring tears to my eyes, but I didn't yell. Brave little me. I imagined John's fist in Francy's eye. That's what shut me up. Everything is relative.

As the car went by, I risked lifting my face to see, and it was the cruiser, all right. I caught a glimpse of Becker in the passenger seat, staring straight ahead and looking like thunder. My fault, I supposed, although he may very well have forgotten all about Ms. Deacon, now that he was hot on the trail of the prime suspect.

"It was them, wasn't it?" the prime suspect said.

"Yup. Let's move."

We found the entrance to the trail in a few minutes and struck right into the bush, relaxing as we got further in. Although the trees were still full of splendid gold and orange leaves, the foliage was thinner than it would have been in summer and I didn't feel safe until we were over the first rise in the ground. That safe feeling didn't last long. I'd forgotten. Bears.

"Hey, slow down," Francy called, and I realized I'd been doing the Polly-trot.

"Sorry," I said, waiting for her to catch up, "it's that bear thing."

"They don't attack on sight, you know," Francy said.

"Thanks. I feel a hell of a lot better now."

We trudged on, me feeling like a dink for being so self-centred and frightened about my own skin when it was Francy who was in real danger. Her husband had been murdered, and here I was thinking about myself.

"Polly," Francy said after a few minutes of silence.

"Hmm?"

"You ever think that maybe your bear-thing is a substitute for something else? Some other kind of fear?" I slowed down.

"Maybe," I said. I didn't know whether this was the beginning of some sort of confession on her part, or if she was actually talking about me. While I was ready for the first, I wasn't sure I could handle psychoanalysis in the bush, particularly because Francy, for all her own demons, was a pretty accurate judge of character. What amazed me was that she could switch like that, from her own private hell to my minor one. Still, I guess that's what friends are for.

"Remember that seminar we took?" she said. "The Vision Quest one?"

A few months earlier, we had attended a weekend retreat led by a Caucasian, New-Age shaman who called himself Dream-Catcher. (We ended up calling him Bum-Scratcher behind his back. These New-Age people get you in touch with your inner child real quick.) I had seen the ad for it in Aunt Susan's feed store and it wasn't very expensive, so we figured, why not?

Aunt Susan came too, but she only lasted one day.

"If I wanted to spend a weekend listening to other people trying to out-dream each other, I'd set up as a shrink and make them pay me for it," she had said. Which is more or less what Dream-Catcher was doing, I suppose.

The idea was to sit in a big circle, then close your eyes and try to envision going down a long tunnel, while Dream-Catcher played a drum. When you got to the end of the tunnel, an animal was supposed to meet you and take you on a journey of self-discovery. The meditations started out short, ten minutes or so, and by the end of the weekend they were running an hour or more.

After each meditation was over, Dream-Catcher led a talking circle, where everybody shared their journeys.

The problem was that, although your own little subconscious adventure might have been fun, the visions of strangers were about as interesting as a three-hour shopping-channel marathon. Some people went on and on, and we were all supposed to intone "good medicine, good medicine" after they'd finished. Francy and I didn't behave very well, although we stuck it out for the whole weekend. (There were no refunds.)

The animal who was supposed to have met us at the end of the tunnel was officially our "power animal", according to Dream-Catcher. He told us this before we started, his white beard trembling with emotion. This was significant. We were supposed to take the power animal with us in our hearts when we left the weekend.

The people in the circle got all sorts of neat spirit guides. Francy got a hawk, Aunt Susan was met by a wild boar, a woman with a voice like Shirley Temple on amphetamines got a king-snake and talked about it for so long I wanted to strangle her, and the young guy who works at the Petro-Can got a cougar. I got a hamster. Really. A hamster popped out of my subconscious on that first Vision Quest and bowed ever so politely, like the white rabbit in Alice. It had spots and stupid little pink eyes.

I was horrified, and although I tried to think up something impressive to tell everyone when my turn came around, I ended up admitting that my power animal was a hamster. They all laughed, in a good-medicine kind of way, and Dream-Catcher spent some time alone with me trying to put a positive spin on it. I could see that he was at a loss for what to say, though.

I didn't want to be reminded that my power animal was a domesticated rodent, particularly when I was tromping through a forest full of ferocious bears.

"Yes, I remember the seminar, Francy," I said. "How could I forget it? I've never felt so stupid in all my life. You tell just one hamster joke and I'll never forgive you."

"Oh, relax," Francy said. "I was just thinking that maybe the hamster-thing was your mind playing tricks on you."

"Huh?"

"Look. You dream about bears a lot, right?"

I nodded.

"They scare you, right?"

I nodded again.

"But you've never even seen a bear, so maybe the bear is really your power animal and your mind was just trying not to scare you, so it made it smaller. I mean, a hamster's pretty harmless, but it does sort of look bear-ish."

"Hmmm," I said.

"I think that if you'd been met by a bear at the end of your tunnel, you would have given up right there and left with your aunt. Instead, you learned all about Vision Questing—yeah, I know a lot of it was stupid, but it was cool too, right? So your hamster was sort of a substitute for the real thing, so you could learn."

"This is a good theory, Francy," I said. My mind was split between the notion that I was not of the hamster clan after all, which made me feel good about myself, and the realization that Francy was acting like Francy again. If talking about bears and hamsters could take her mind off the mess she was in, I was prepared to cope with it, uncomfortable as it made me feel.

"But if the bear is my power animal, my spirit guide, why the dickens am I so scared of them?"

"Maybe you're afraid of dealing with something which the bear-spirit can help you with," Francy said.

"Ooooh. Deep," I said. It was, actually. I knew that I was suppressing something—I had been for years. My parents' deaths, my grubby string of failed relationships with inappropriate men, my lack of ambition and my complicated vices were all probably bear-related.

Then, as if summoned, from out of the bush came a great big, black, smelly, grunting not-a-chance-it-was-a-hamster.

Eight

Truth's drowned in whiskey and water
bargain smokes and trying to keep clear,
truth can't speak after all these years
—Shepherd's Pie

The bear looked at us, we looked at the bear. Time, as they say, stood still.

I didn't do any of those things I'd been told to do. No climbing of trees. No singing. No playing dead. At that moment I couldn't have told you what my name was. I couldn't think, and I am certain that my heart stopped beating. I do know that I took a deep inward breath because the next thing I registered after my mind had stopped screaming BEARBEARBEARBEAR was an outrageous smell, as if a huge wet dog had burped in my face.

The bear shook its head, registered extreme annoyance and surprise (which, on a bear, is very funny to watch), then showed us his lardy butt and crashed off into the bush.

My legs gave out completely, quivering underneath me like a ruined soufflé. My heart started beating again, pumping hundred-proof adrenaline through my veins—I could hear it goosh, goosh, in my ears. The kind of hyper-awareness I usually only got from dope spread through my body like warm honey.

My vision became so clear I could see the veins of every leaf on every tree. I could have counted the pine needles beneath me, one by one.

"It was only a bear!" I said and started laughing. "He stank. He ran. He ran away!" It was the funniest joke in the world and it was a moment before I realized that I was crying as well.

Francy came over and kneeled down beside me, touching my shoulder.

"You okay?" she said.

I smiled up at her, and she helped me to my feet.

"That was fun," I said. "Sort of cleansing. I think I might have wet myself."

Francy giggled, the amusement in her eyes making me feel warm and human. "So, now the hamster is banished, right?" she said. "The bear rules. Got any beer at your house?"

"Yup." We hurried the rest of the way, not for fear, but for thirst and clean undies.

It was chilly in the cabin. I had banked up the fire in the morning, getting it nice and hot and then pouring a bucket of ashes over top, which usually kept the coals burning agreeably for hours. Not this time. The damn thing was out.

When you rely on a wood stove for heat, you develop a relationship with it, learning to feed and nurture it like a lover. Like most of my lovers, this one was demanding, temperamental and, unless it got enough attention, cold. There were times when I felt like whanging it across the damper with a two-by-four.

Francy stood in the middle of the room, shivering, as I started to shovel ash and lay a new fire.

"Beer's in the icebox," I said.

There's no hydro at my place, and so a fridge would be silly.

I got the icebox from Rico Amato not long after I moved in. He thought I was crazy when I said I wanted to use it for its original purpose. He had stripped it down to bare wood and varnished it (it was pine under the enamel paint) and the price tag matched its intended new life as a chic bar unit for some wealthy cottager.

I fell in love with it when I saw it in Rico's shop, nestled between an old steamer trunk covered in stencilled roses (five hundred bucks) and a vintage sled full of dried cattails (one fifty plus GST).

Rico knew his customers, kept on top of all the latest trends as laid down in *Architectural Digest and Country Home*, and the icebox was priced accordingly. The number on the tag was more than I'd made for the last puppet-building project, more than I had in the bank, and more than I would ever pay for anything smaller than a trip to Mexico, but Rico cut me a deal. I guess he liked me.

I get my ice in winter from the creek out back, hacking it out and storing it in straw in a small lean-to next to the cabin. It works, just like they tell you in *Harrowsmith*. The straw keeps the ice solid well into the fall.

Francy cracked a couple of cold Algonquins and sat down in my guest chair with a huge sigh. I was whacking away at a piece of kindling with my hatchet and making a big racket. I stopped and looked up.

"Is this noise going to upset Beth?" I said. Francy just shook her head. The baby, still wrapped in her snuggly and leaning against her mother's chest, was watching me with wide open eyes. I was amazed at how quiet she'd been throughout all the fuss.

"Does that kid have a larynx? Does she ever use it?"

"Oh, she uses it all right," Francy said. "She just never cries when you're around. Maybe you send out soothing psychic waves or something."

"More likely she recognizes that if she started, I'd join in," I said. Babies scare the crap out of me, and Francy knew it. She was always trying to convince me that there was nothing to be frightened of. That they were safe, really. But I still refused to hold Beth. I knew what would happen. I'd panic and drop her. Her skull would split open like a ripe melon and then I would have to kill myself. It was a kind of anti-maternal vertigo, and there was no getting around it.

"She will start yelling if I don't feed her, though," Francy said, opening her shirt and waving a breast, like an ice-cream cone, in her daughter's face. "It was hard to breastfeed at Carla's," she said. "As soon as I started, Carla would get real uncomfortable. She'd go red and sort of fidget, like she was itching to go get the holy water and sprinkle it all over me."

"Maybe she was afraid of how it would affect Eddie," I said.

"Oh, Eddie's seen it before. He's over at our place all the time. It doesn't bother him any."

"I'll bet Carla doesn't know that."

"She's such a damned priss," Francy said.

"Well, she's religious. Plenty of religious folks are hyper-modest, but that doesn't necessarily make her a priss, Francy."

Francy looked up at me, her face oddly blank.

"There's things you don't know," she said. "Take it from me. Priss is being kind." The blank look scared me, so I changed the subject. Beth was grunting wetly, making the kind of sounds I make when I'm knocking back an Algonquin on a hot day.

"What does that feel like?" I said. I'd always wondered, but the only other person I'd known well enough to ask was a girl I went to high school with who had a baby in grade eleven. We were too young to talk about that kind of stuff, then. Not too young to have sex, though. When I asked her, in a rash moment, why she hadn't used a condom, she told me that she hadn't known the guy well enough to feel comfortable asking him.

"Breastfeeding feels like heaven," Francy said. "It's sort of sexual, but not. Like she's pulling my soul out, if you know what I mean." I didn't. Motherhood. The great mystery. Count me out.

I finished getting the fire going and joined Francy at the table.

"You ready to talk about last night yet?" I said.

"Not really, but I will if you want me to."

"Why are you so scared of the police?"

She laughed. "I can't believe you're asking me that," she said. "You're the one who insists on hiding in the bathroom to smoke a joint. You're scared of them, too."

"Yeah, but possession isn't the issue here, Francy."

"Look, I didn't shoot John, if that's what you're worried about."

"I know you didn't. That's why I can't understand why you're afraid to talk to them."

"John wasn't dead when Eddie and I left. I'm sure the kid didn't hit him that hard, just enough to knock him out. We left him snoring on the kitchen floor. The only reason we got out of there is that I knew when he woke up he'd be loaded for bear. I didn't want either of us to be there."

"So who do you think shot him?"

Francy looked exasperated, and there were tiny white marks around her mouth. Maybe I shouldn't be pushing her so much, I thought. But still, her icy calm was getting to me.

"I don't know. There were plenty of people mad at him. There always were. John collected enemies like he collected trashed-out cars. He owed poker money all over the place."

"So maybe you could give the cops a list."

"No way. The point is, Polly, that I'm at the top of the list and you know it."

"Aren't you eager to find out who did it?"

"Oh, I'm eager, all right. I'll go right up to him and shake his hand, whoever he is. But I don't want to sit in a jail cell while the cops find him, Polly."

This was a new Francy, one I'd never seen before. In the time we'd known each other, she had always defended him, always underplayed the harm he did her. I stared at her for a long moment, and she looked back defiantly.

"Yeah, I know," she said. "The penny dropped, eh?"

"When?"

"When he started coming home smelling of perfume, just after Beth was born. When he went out for poker games that I found out later never happened. You know. I could handle the odd smack in the face, but there was no way I could handle not being the most important thing in his life."

"Geez, Francy. Why didn't you tell me?"

"I wanted it to be not true, I guess. Telling you about it would have made it true, you know?"

"So, who do you think he was seeing?" I said.

"God only knows. A stripper at Kelso's, maybe. Could've been anybody. He wasn't picky. He married me, didn't he?"

Francy had never talked like that before. The "poor little me" thing set off alarm bells in my head. It had to be an act. For the cops, maybe, and she was trying it out on me.

"So, back to last night," I said.

"What about it?"

"After Eddie gave you the book back, what did you guys talk about?"

"What?"

"I mean, Eddie said you had tea and talked. What about?"

"Oh, I don't know. The usual. His parents. School. Why?"

"How many beers did you give him, Francy? Was he drunk when John came in?"

Francy stood up, her eyes hot and angry. Beth's mouth slipped off her nipple with a little popping sound, like a cork coming out of a bottle.

"I don't know what you're talking about," she said.

"Oh, come on. There were beer bottles all over the place. No teapot in sight. If John was staggering drunk when he came in, and Eddie conked him out with a wrench, he wouldn't have had time to down the twelve or so I saw smashed in your kitchen, would he? I know you didn't shoot John, so why not tell the truth?"

Francy actually snarled at me. "Just who in the hell do you think you are, Polly? Nancy fucking Drew? So we had a couple of beers. So what? The poor little guy never gets any fun at home. None at all. It's Jesus, Jesus, Jesus from morning to night. What's the harm in a couple of beers?"

"None," I said. "None at all. That's what I'm saying. John is dead, honey. The police don't care about a sixteen-year-old drinking beer. They'll see that there's no teapot, though. No tea. They'll smell a lie right away and go looking for more."

Francy started pacing the floor. "It's not that," she said. "I'm not running because of that."

"Why, then?"

"It's because I can't remember. After Eddie and me left with Beth and headed for his parent's place, I sort of blanked out. I can't remember a thing."

"Oh, boy."

"Yeah. Oh boy." She was gulping in air. Beth was looking up at her, screwing her face up, getting ready to scream. I tensed. Francy popped the nipple back into Beth's mouth and sat down again.

"How's that going to sound, eh? We leave and I can't remember anything until you said at Carla's that John was dead."

"Nothing?"

"Nope. Carla said I pulled the phone cord out of the wall. Don't remember. Carla said I ate a hearty meal and slept in the guest room. Don't remember that either. Total blank, Polly. Until I get that back, I'm not talking to any cop."

"Okay. I get it," I said, getting really scared for her. I've heard that trauma can do that—wipe out whole blocks of time. What if Francy did go back and shoot John? What if her memory just wiped it all out?

"Do you think you went back?" I said, quietly.

Francy's face crumpled. "I don't know. Maybe. I feel like I could have. I'd decided to leave him. I was real mad. I was also ripped out of my mind, long before Eddie showed up. I could have done it."

"Could you have driven John to the dump, though? Could you have hurt Spit Morton?"

"Spit? God. Did someone shoot him, too?"

"No, but they whacked him over the head, Francy. You may have had something against John, but you like Spit, don't you?"

"Sure I do. And hey, Polly, I can't drive." With this

realization, she seemed to relax a little, but she looked awful. Her eye was still swollen, and her face had gone white again.

"I couldn't have done it," she said. "But if I didn't, then who the hell did?"

Nine

Judas sang a good song
right up until they paid the price,
then he felt awful.
—Shepherd's Pie

One thing I knew for certain, Francy and the baby couldn't stay with me for very long. To begin with, there wasn't the sleeping space. My bedroom was an add-on at the back of the cabin, barely enough room for my futon and a rack for my clothes. The bed was small and would have accommodated a friend only if our acquaintance were truly biblical. I didn't think Francy would be interested in spooning with me, and I wasn't about to suggest it. If Francy wanted to spend the night, I'd be sleeping on the workroom floor, which was part of the kitchen, which was part of the living room. In a place as small as mine, "open concept" just means there isn't any room for walls.

Also, there wasn't any plumbing. I had a pump outside, and when I wanted a bath, I heated water on the wood stove and bathed beside the fire in the zinc tub I got from Spit. There was no toilet, just an outhouse. On cold winter nights, I used a Victorian chamber pot. (I got it from Rico. When I told him what I wanted it for, he giggled, produced a lid for the pot and only charged me ten bucks.)

Francy had a baby, who would presumably need to be changed and washed occasionally, and after her recent ordeal, Francy would probably need a nice hot bath, but she wouldn't get one at my place.

Then there was Becker. He would be looking for both of us and we couldn't keep running forever. I was most likely in deep doo-doo as it was, scuttling away from the Travers place and then kidnapping the prime suspect. Did that make me an accessory after the fact? I wasn't looking forward to finding out.

Becker had probably already interviewed Carla Schreier and Eddie, and Eddie's statement would have made him even more eager to find Francy. He would discover that I had left with her, and he would drive back to George's place, expecting us to be there. George would make excuses for me, but it was only a matter of time before Becker figured out that I didn't live in the farm house. All he needed to do was ask one of the locals.

"Oh, you mean Polly? She lives in that old shack up on Hoito's farm. Been there some years now. What's she done? Always thought she was a weirdo." Becker would come screaming up the track to the cabin and that would be that.

I decided to save him the effort and give Francy a bit more time to get it together. I bullied her into lying down for a nap with Beth on the futon, and she was out like a light in less than five minutes. Then I made some ham and cheese sandwiches and left them on a plate on the kitchen table with a note, which told her that I was going down to see George and not to worry. I locked the door when I left, which is not my habit, but then people don't get shot around here very often, and leaving Francy and the baby alone gave me an uneasy feeling.

The October air was unseasonably cold, and I pulled my jacket around me, shivering. It was beginning to get dark already—those autumn nights closing in to warn the hapless Canadian that the snow would be flying soon. I had ten cords of wood split and stacked in my mind. All I had to do to make it a reality was to haul it out of the bush.

Leaves crunched under my feet and as I reached the end of the track which opened out onto George's hay field, I could see that we were in for a spectacular sunset. Fingers of pink and orange light were reaching tentatively out of a low cloud bank, touching the treetops like neon icing. I thought of John Travers. Had he ever enjoyed a sunset? Of course he had. He lived here, didn't he? Or had he been too unhappy a man to have ever looked up into the sky and felt glad to see what was there? He wouldn't be experiencing any more sunsets, now. Walking down the hill, bathed in those impossible colours, I threw out a kind of mental "sorry" to John, wherever he had gone. Not that I had liked him much, but knowing he couldn't see what I was seeing made me sad.

Becker's cruiser was parked next to George's truck, and I slowed to a saunter, putting off the inevitable. There were more lights on in the house than was usual. I guessed that the officer had decided to do a thorough search, maybe to see if the madwomen were in the attic, where they belonged.

I was about fifty metres from the house, fastening the gate which kept the goats out of the hay field, when Poe descended like a black bag of potatoes, landing so close to me that I gasped and jumped back.

"Dammit, bird. You scared me," I said. Poe cocked his head to one side and I swear he was grinning. He had something hanging from his beak which caught the light.

"What have you got there?" I said. He just looked at me. I stepped closer, softly so as not to startle him. He rarely came close to me and I felt honoured, albeit slightly nervous. Budgies and robins I can handle, but ravens are big suckers and their beaks are wickedly sharp. The thing in his beak was a pendant of some sort on a gold-coloured chain, and as it turned, it flashed pink and orange.

I knew better than to try and take it. Ravens are terrible thieves when it comes to shiny things; they snatch them and hoard them like dragons do. George raids Poe's stash every so often when he runs out of spare change, or if he can't find the key to something. Poe is very possessive, though, and will defend his property if it's threatened. George won't touch the stash unless Poe's outside, and even so, the bird notices right away and retaliates, usually by pooping on George's pipe stand.

"That's a pretty thingy you've got there," I said. "Snatch it off a dead body, did you?" Then I realized the gallows humour of what I'd said and let out a bark of laughter. The noise spooked Poe, who dropped the chain and took flight, passing so close over my head that I felt my hair move. He landed on the roof of George's house and started croaking at me, swearing in fluent Raven.

The thing was, he could very well have taken it off a dead body. After all, someone had left one lying around very recently, and Poe was a frequent visitor to the dump, often accompanying George by flying directly above the truck like an albatross.

I picked the thing up. The chain was heavy—solid gold, it looked like. The pendant was a crucifix, quite old and exquisitely carved, if you like that sort of thing. The tiny figure of the crucified man was lovingly detailed; anguished expression, nails and all. At the top of the cross was a little carved scroll, bearing the letters INRI.

I slipped it into my pocket, deciding to ask Francy later if it had been John's. I had seen him more than once with his shirt open to reveal gold, although I admit I'd never looked closely enough to check out his jewellery.

An image flashed into my mind—of Poe, circling above the ruined body of John Travers, lying there in the "wood only" pile at the dump. Poe swooping down, maybe aiming for the eyes, thinking "Hey, hey! Snacktime!" then snapping up the shiny necklace instead. It could have happened. I damned my imagination for the picture, which made my stomach hop a little. I straightened up and walked towards the house, sticking my tongue out at Poe on my way.

"Where the hell have you been?" Detective Mark Becker said as soon as I walked in. He was standing in the middle of the kitchen and the cats were twining around his ankles like fuzzy socks. George was sitting in his chair, calmly puffing on a pipe, his biggest one, the meerschaum that makes him look like Sherlock Holmes. He smiled and winked at me.

"Nice to see you too, Detective. Hello, George, darling. All well?" I breezed over to George and kissed him. I had decided, the moment I set eyes on Mr. Calm Policeman, that I wouldn't volunteer any information. I would just bloody brazen it out, as Aunt Susan would say. Nobody asks where the hell I've been and gets away with it.

George reacted to my less-than-subtle demonstration of our "domestic partnership" with a little pat on my behind. Good old George, I thought. He's playing right along with it. I stood behind him, using him as a shield and placing my hands possessively on his shoulders.

"What are you doing back here?" I said to Becker. "Worried that I stole some important evidence from the crime scene? A dog biscuit, maybe?"

"Cut the funny stuff, okay?" Becker said. "I know you don't live here. Mr. Hoito has admitted that much. What I want to know is, where is Mrs. Travers? Have you got her hidden away up at your cabin?"

I snatched my hands from George's shoulders and blushed heavily. I could feel George shaking with amusement. The pat on the behind had been gratuitous—a liberty, dammit. I would get him back.

"I don't know what you're talking about," I said.

Becker sighed.

"Look, Polly. We went to the Schreier's place. I know Francy Travers was there. I know you were there. You were both gone before we arrived, and you didn't exactly say goodbye to your hosts." I opened my mouth to tell another lie, but he kept on talking.

"I've been driving up and down the back roads looking for you two, and I don't appreciate being made to look foolish."

"You didn't leave your partner at the Schreier's, did you?" I said. "More than one of those squares of Carla's and he'll be going into sugar-shock."

Becker's mouth twitched a little, but he was still mad. "If you don't tell me where Mrs. Travers is, Ms. Deacon, I'll have to take you in for questioning."

"Do you guys actually do that?" I said. "I thought that was just a TV-thing."

"We do. You want to find out?"

"Would I get three square meals a day and a phone call?"

"The phone call's definitely a TV-thing," he said. "And we

only have one cell and a guy puked in it last night. I can't guarantee that anyone's cleaned it up yet."

Now, there's a lot I'd do for a friend, but staying in a locked room with stale puke is where I draw the line.

"You win," I said and sat down. Becker tried to, but he tripped on the cats, which were trying to climb up his regulation trousers. He stumbled.

"You must have had one of Carla's squares," I said. He just looked at me and didn't say anything. "Okay, okay," I said. "Francy's up at my place, asleep with the baby. She's not going anywhere—she's exhausted. The baby, in case you were wondering, is fine."

I got him with the baby line. He made a weary face and collapsed into a chair.

"Good," he said. "I'm glad about that. It's going to be hard for both of them, but we have to talk to her. You understand that, don't you?"

"Of course I do. She just needed to get away from, you know, the tension. It's not every day your husband gets killed."

"She tell you what happened?"

"As much as she can remember."

"What's that supposed to mean?"

"She sort of blanked out after... I suppose Eddie told you his side of it."

"We have his statement, yes."

"Well, after Eddie hit John, Francy says she sort of went away in her mind. Doesn't remember going to the Schreier's place. Doesn't remember anything till I showed up. She asked me to help her. How could I say no?"

"Easy. Like this: No."

"I'll remember that next time you need a favour."

"Polly, your friend Francy is the spouse of a homicide

victim. There's questions we've got to ask. Details. She wants to know who killed him, doesn't she?"

I remembered Francy's face as she told me that she would like to shake the hand of the murderer, but I didn't mention it.

"She's afraid you'll think she did it," I said.

"We have to suspect everybody at the beginning," Becker said patiently, as if he were speaking to a child. "It's the rules. Of course we suspect her. We suspect you. We suspect Mr. Hoito, here as well."

"George? You suspect George? Why the hell would he murder John Travers?"

"Polly—" George said, but I was building up a head of steam and kept on going.

"George Hoito is the gentlest, most loving man in the world. He rescues baby birds with broken wings, for God's sake. You're wasting your time suspecting him."

George patted my hand. "Thank you, Polly. That is the nicest testimonial I have heard in a long time."

"You're welcome," I said, glaring at Becker.

"All Mrs. Travers has to do is talk to us, give us a reason to believe she didn't do it, and she's fine," Becker said.

"What? What about innocent until proven guilty? I know that's not just a TV-thing. I think it's even in the Charter of Rights and Freedoms. Are you familiar with that document, Detective?"

George raised his hand like a grade-school kid asking to go to the bathroom.

"Excuse me," he said, gently. "I'm sorry to interrupt the debate, but Francy and her baby are up there in a cold, dark cabin, alone. Maybe she would appreciate some company about now."

"Oh God. That's right. Let's go." We said it together. Same words. Same tone. Weird.

"Follow me," I said. "George, can I borrow your flashlight?"

Ten

We prepared this banquet
to be eaten with our fingers—
no need to be polite.
—Shepherd's Pie

Halfway across the field, I asked Becker where Morrison was.

"Paperwork," he said.

"The kind that wraps around a jelly donut?" I said.

He laughed. He was carrying a flashlight of his own—a police-issue, beautiful black Maglight which can double as a club in a pinch, but he hadn't turned it on. The sky was magenta, the kind of colour which, if you saw it in a painting, would make you think that the artist had been doing some serious psychedelic drugs. Drugs. Oh God. This was my worst nightmare coming true. A police officer was coming to search my cabin. What if he smelled it? What if he had the nose of a German Shepherd and went straight for the little sweetgrass basket on the bookshelf? What, oh God, what if I'd left my alabaster pipe sitting on my desk? I tensed up and tried to think of a way to get in there first, leaving him outside, to give the place a quick once-over.

I had left the oil lamp lit on the kitchen table, turned way down. I hated doing it, being a fanatic safety nut when it

79

comes to fire (I own three fire extinguishers), but I didn't want Francy to wake up in total darkness. She wouldn't have been scared, I knew that. She had been on her own in the country enough for that to be a non-issue, but still, when there's no hydro, there's no comforting light at the end of a switch and fumbling around for a match in a strange place is no fun.

When we got to the door, I paused, thinking fast.

"Ummm, I'd better go in first," I said. He looked at me like I was crazy. Duh. Why wouldn't I go in first? It was my house.

"I mean, like, Francy sleeps in the nude, eh? And the cabin's open-concept. I'll just slip in and make sure she's dressed, okay?" I was glad it was dark. My face was burning.

"You won't slip out the back door and disappear into the woods, will you?" he said. He was kidding, I think.

"Not possible," I said. "There is no back door."

"Okay, then. Just don't coach her, please. I won't wait for long."

"You got it, officer," I said and walked in.

The lamp had gone out. I flashed the beam of George's flashlight around nonchalantly, hoping Becker wasn't peering in the window. Pretty stupid, really, coming in first and then pointing the light directly at my own mildly illegal activities, but there you have it. Cops. Paranoia. Dope smokers suffer from it and listen to it, or they get nabbed.

Luckily, the pipe was out of sight, and the place was such a pigsty that the sweetgrass box on the bookshelf was almost buried under a pile of stuff. No worries.

"Francy?" I said, softly. I re-lit the oil lamp and took it into the lean-to bedroom. The bed was empty.

"Francy?" I was being silly, seeing as there were only two rooms in the cabin and she was obviously not there. I realized then that the front door had been open, and I distinctly remember locking it when I left. Becker came in.

"Gone?" he said.

"Maybe she went for a pee," I said. "There's an outhouse." I dashed outside, calling her name. No light from the privy, no light anywhere. The sunset was over, the sky was overcast and the trees surrounding the cabin blocked out what little glow was left in the sky. I went back inside. Becker was reading the note I'd left on the table. The sandwiches were gone.

He handed me the note and stared into my face, waiting for me to take the blame. He looked really, really pissed off. On the bottom of my note was a scribble from Francy.

"We'll be fine. Thanks," it said.

"Shit," I said.

"That all you can say? Shit?" Becker said. "Where do you think she's gone? Out there? It's cold, dark. She has a baby with her."

"I don't know. Why are you asking me?"

"I'm asking you because you are plainly trying to engineer this situation."

"Me? Why would I do that?"

"Damned if I know. Maybe you're a control freak."

"A control freak? Me? Geez, Detective Becker, are you ever a poor judge of character. I can't even control my bladder," I said. He would not be put off by lighthearted quips.

"If I find that you've arranged it so that she's just hiding out there in the bush until I go away, I will personally charge you with obstruction of the law and haul your ass into jail," he said.

"Are you threatening me, Becker?"

"Yes, Goddamn it, I'm threatening you, Polly, you infuriating little...Deacon." We had been yelling. He stopped and we stared at each other for a tiny, electric moment and then fell apart laughing. Big laughs. The kind you only get once every few years. The more we laughed, the more we laughed, if you know what I mean. We'd stop, get it under control, and then catch each other's eye and start snickering and then be laughing again. It was like a cool shower on a blistering day. It was wonderful.

When we finally pulled ourselves together, the air had changed, as it does after a good thunderstorm. I was thinking more clearly and maybe he was too.

"Hey, look, I'm sorry," he said. "I'm not being very fair. To be honest, this is my first homicide and I'm trying to do things right. You are, according to the book, a hostile witness, and hostile witnesses aren't supposed to be so...well, never mind. Forget what I said."

"You mean you're not going to haul my ass into jail?"

"I didn't say that."

"Yup. You did."

"Huh. How level-headed of me," he said. "No, ma'am. No jail. But I would appreciate it if you'd be straight with me."

"I have been straight with you," I said. Well. Sort of.

"Why the big secret about where you live?"

"Oh, that. Well, I'm not supposed to be here. Zoning. Taxes."

"Polly, I'm investigating a murder."

"I know, but still."

"What about running out on us at the Travers' place? None of this would've happened if you'd just stayed put in the cruiser."

"I don't like staying put."

"Obviously. What about taking off with Mrs. Travers from the Schreier's?"

"Would you have stayed there? Really?"

He didn't answer.

"Look, Everything that happened today has been for Francy's sake," I said. "Her husband, who has abused her for years, goes berserk and her young friend Eddie beans him with a wrench. They get out of there and the next thing she knows I'm telling her he's dead. Of course she's running. I'd run too. You guys, you cops in uniforms, don't have the best track record when it comes to domestic violence. She was scared. I was helping her. End of story."

"But it's not the end of the story. You didn't arrange this little I-don't-know-where-she-is act? She's not out there hiding in the underbrush?"

"I left her sleeping off the horror, Detective."

"Swear?"

"Look, if I had a Bible, I'd take an oath right here, except that it wouldn't mean anything anyway. I could swear on Gray's Anatomy, if you like." I lifted the heavy book from the work-table where I'd been checking out the musculature of the human arm, prior to modelling a limb for the latest puppet.

He glanced around, seeing the chaos of my living space for the first time.

"What do you do up here, anyway?" he said.

"I'm a puppet maker."

"Not much call for that in these parts, is there?"

"Oh, you'd be surprised. I get an order every so often from the local municipal government looking for mayors. School boards looking for trustees. Police departments looking for chiefs. I keep busy."

"Very funny," he said. "Next time you make a police chief, call me. I'll soften up the stuffing for you."

"I'll do that."

"So, I'd better get going," he said. "I'll check her house again. She wouldn't be off lost in the bush somewhere, would she? Maybe we should get together a search team."

"Nah. She wouldn't have left without someplace to go. She's got Beth. Maybe she went back to the Schreier's."

"Would you go back there, if you were her?"

"I'd rather stick a needle in my eye," I said.

"Nice image. You'll let me know if she shows up." It was a statement, not a request. "You got a phone?"

"Nope."

"Are you one of those anti-technology people?"

"Not really. I'm just poor."

"Oh. So, send me a smoke signal if you hear anything, okay?" He gave me his card which read: Detective Constable Mark Becker, Ontario Provincial Police, Laingford Detachment.

"She can't keep running forever," Becker said. "She got relatives around here?"

"Not that I know of. She has in-laws in North Bay, I think, but they're not close. Her mother lives in the States somewhere."

"Would she head south?"

"Not a chance. Her mother's completely insane, according to her. She came up here to get away, she said. Doesn't talk about her family much." What Francy had told me of her family had given me bad dreams for weeks. I wasn't going to get into it with Becker.

"Well, tell her, if you see her, that we just want to talk to her, okay? No big deal. Just some questions. I know she's grieving. Well, I've got a killer to find."

"And you don't think it's her?"

"I don't know what to think, Polly. Not yet, anyway."

"I'll tell her."

"You're going to be okay up here by yourself?"

"I've lived up here by myself for three years. Of course I'll be fine," I said.

"Well, lock your door, okay?"

"Yes, officer."

"I mean it," he said. "Someone was murdered last night, in case you'd forgotten." I wasn't likely to forget John's dead eyes, like scummy boiled eggs, and the cavity of his ruined chest.

"I'll lock my door," I said.

"Good." I watched his flashlight beam disappear back down the path to George's, swinging from side to side. He was checking the bushes as he passed, still convinced that Francy was crouched somewhere, waiting. Cops. They never trust you.

When he was gone I went outside and spent an hour scouting around and calling her name, but I knew she was gone. Where, I didn't know.

Later, I discovered that she'd taken off with half my stash. I didn't begrudge it. There was a note. "Pay you back" it said, with a little happy face, so I knew she was feeling better.

I smoked a baby spliff and cracked open an Algonquin. The sweet smoke filled me, as it always does, with the urge to create. I picked up the arm limb I was working on and opened up a jar of modelling compound. The puppet I was building had not been commissioned. I was simply making it for my own pleasure, although I would probably take it in to the Artists' Consignment Depot in Laingford when it was finished. My stuff usually sold reasonably quickly, and money was always tight.

I was sculpting this particular puppet, a marionette-to-be, using the kind of clay which air dries and takes paint

85

beautifully. I was taking my time. The head was to be molded with clay on a papier-mâché base. The shell was ready, but the face had not yet come to me, and I didn't want to push it.

I began absently layering dabs of clay onto the mâché arm-shape, not really thinking about what I was doing. An hour later, I gazed at a little clay arm with interesting, ropy muscles and Becker's capable, slightly ugly hands. Then I looked at the unfinished head staring blankly from its stand and knew that I would model Becker's face there.

If I had been a witch, I would have cackled, looked up a spell and searched the floor for one of his hairs. I'm no witch, but I cackled anyway.

Eleven

Tonight thinking about you
I gave birth to a goat-kid
tremble-shanked and shivering in the dark.
—Shepherd's Pie

I am homeless and hungry, sifting through the garbage in an alleyway slick with rain and unmentionable filth. Strangely, the sounds I hear are not city sounds; I am surrounded by the secret, waiting stillness of the deep bush. A bird calls, and I hear the wind sighing through pine boughs, although there is not a tree in sight. I do not find this surprising, however, because I know I am mad. Homeless and mad.

Behind me there is movement and I turn to find a large, red-furred bear looking over my shoulder. I am not afraid, for once. The bear speaks with a cockney accent.

"You lookin' for 'Enry?" it says. The bear's teeth are very white, and its breath is curiously sweet.

"Yes," I say, as if the bear has stated the obvious.

"'Ere 'e is." The bear hands me a golden salmon, which I take solemnly but with some difficulty, as it is impaled on his claws.

"Thanks, mate," I say, and then notice that his other paw holds Francy's baby, impaled also and squirming like a hooked worm. I am instantly on the ground, curled up in a ball and gibbering with horror.

I woke drenched in sweat, my heart hammering. My dreams about bears usually ended up like that, but I never managed to get used to it. It took me a while to shake the fear, and eventually I got out of bed and lit the Coleman stove to boil water for coffee. It was five in the morning, but I was not going to risk going back to the alley for the sequel.

So much for my real-life, "everything's okay now" bear-experience. My monster was back, and if anything, bigger than ever. Why couldn't I dream about hamsters?

After a couple of cups of coffee and a cigarette to jump start my blood and bludgeon the last traces of nightmare induced adrenaline, I pulled on my overalls and headed down to the barn. The goats awaited, and I would surprise George by being early on the job for once.

George's goats are delightful animals. Don't believe that stuff you've heard about goats eating tin cans and butting humans in the bum. It's all hokum. They are affectionate, intelligent creatures, and very picky when it comes to their food.

There were fourteen goats in George's herd—there had been fifteen, but now Dweezil was frolicking about somewhere in heaven's clover patch. Maybe Dweezil and John Travers would get together up there and chat about what it was like to end up in the wood-only pile of the Cedar Falls dump.

Most of the goats were females, "does" in goat speak, never nanny-goats. A goat farmer would no more call a doe a nanny than a pig farmer would call the sows "mummy piggies". George kept two males, or bucks, for breeding purposes, and now that Dweezil was gone, he would have to choose one of the latest batch of kids to rear up to adulthood.

The male kids are normally sold for meat when they reach a certain size, as are all but the very best of the females. This is a part of goat farming that I find difficult to deal with, but if you're going to eat meat, I figure it's better to know where it comes from.

Adult goats aren't terribly cute, but the babies are adorable, like rabbits with long legs and floppy ears. George's herd is Nubian—the breed with ears like Basset hounds and liquid, loving eyes. Once you've fed a Nubian goat-kid from a bottle, you'll never think of the animals as smelly garburators again.

George runs a modest dairy operation, hence the preference for females, and each one is milked twice a day by hand, despite the fact that he could easily afford milking machines. It's my job to do the morning shift, and George milks the herd in the evening.

As usual, the goats heard my approach long before I reached the barn, and they started yelling as if their pens were on fire. A goat bleat is an odd sound, very human sometimes, especially when they're giving birth.

To make a realistic goat bleat, (make sure you're alone first), sit up straight, smile widely and call "Bleahhh!", starting on a very high note and dropping instantly to a very low one. Make sure your lips are relaxed for the "BL -" part, as if you were blowing a raspberry. Practice this. Amaze your friends.

There are other sounds, too, like the comforting "Uh-hn-hn" of a doe to her newborn kid, the outraged "Wlaaah!" of a kid getting butted by a sibling, and my favourite, the contented moan of a hungry goat tucking in to a bit of juicy hay. A goat moan is just like the sound your pillow mate makes when you give him/her a really good massage.

It was cold in the barn, and there was the thinnest skin of ice in the water buckets. I ran water from the main tap into a big bucket, plunked in the water heater, which looks like a giant potato masher, and plugged it in. Like most of us, goats appreciate a warm drink first thing in the morning.

I cleaned out the mangers, tossing the picked over hay into the pens so they'd have something to play with while they waited to be milked. Then I measured a couple of scoops of high grade, molasses-fortified grain into a feed pan and hooked it over the milking stand.

I milked Donna Summer first. She is the herd leader, a dignified old girl who has dropped triplets every spring for the past ten years. I opened her pen and she trotted out eagerly, conscious of her ranking as the first to get grain and the first to have the heavy pressure of a couple of pounds of milk lifted from her bulging udder. Milking her was like trying to milk somebody's forearm. She's old, and her udder has stretched like an overfilled water balloon. The younger ones are easier, but none of the others gives as much milk as Donna Summer does.

I leaned my head against her warm, hairy belly as I milked, humming a gospel tune to keep the rhythm. Donna Summer likes *Swing Low, Sweet Chariot* the best, although there are times when she responds quite favourably to show tunes.

After milking her out, I let her wander around the barn to make her morning visits while I weighed the milk and recorded it in George's book, along with the tune I had hummed. George's methods of record keeping are unorthodox, but if you discover that you get an extra ounce or two of high butterfat milk if you hum *Dixie* rather than *Feelings,* then why not be consistent?

I was nearing the end of the roster, trying to coax a thin

spurt out of Annie Oakley, a yearling who had got into Dweezil's pen by devious means and fooled around, later giving birth to a healthy pair of bucks that she hadn't told us she was carrying. Milking her was a trial—her teats were as narrow as ballpoint pens and she misbehaved when she was in the milking stand, fidgeting like the teenager she was.

"You're up early, Polly. Are you feeling all right?" George came in, carrying a pail full of vegetable scraps, the morning treat.

"Nightmare woke me," I said. Annie was trying to kick the milking pail over, and I was only half listening.

"Detective Becker dropped in again on his way back last night," he said.

"Hmmm."

"He runs hot and cold, that young man. Friendly one minute and stiff as a board the next. Seems to think you are trying to put one over on him."

"Yup. He sure does."

"You're not, I know that, Polly. But be careful around him. I don't trust him."

I started humming a Shepherd's Pie tune from their latest CD. I didn't exactly trust Becker either, but my reasons had more to do with chemistry than anything else. He was a cop investigating the murder of my best friend's husband, but he was also a good-looking guy who had already pressed more than a few of my buttons. Being a child at heart, I knew that if George told me to stay away from "that Becker boy", it would automatically make him even more attractive than he was. I had to keep my perspective, and it wasn't easy.

"You don't know where she went, do you?" George said.

I shook my head.

"Good. It is better if you don't try to find out. You were

never a very good liar. That policeman would have it out of you in no time."

I didn't argue, although I thought George was laying on the Finnish uncle routine a bit thick.

"George, we're going to need some more grain," I said, changing the subject. "It looks like we've got a raccoon again, and there's a couple of bags gone."

"I'll drive in and get some this afternoon," he said quickly.

I finished milking Annie and let her off the stand. "No need for you to go, George," I said. "That's always been my job. I have to go into town anyway."

"The truck has been misbehaving," George said.

"Since when?" I asked. "It was okay yesterday, wasn't it?"

"It coughs a bit. It might be an idea not to go all the way into Laingford, I was thinking. Maybe we could try that new feed store out by the highway."

"George!' I said. "How could you? Aunt Susan gives you a better deal than you could get anywhere else and she'd be so hurt if you bought your grain somewhere else."

He shifted uncomfortably and avoided looking me in the eye.

"Hey," I said, "have you two had a fight or something?" George and Aunt Susan were good friends, and I had been suspecting recently that the friendship might be turning into something a bit more serious. He had been over at Susan's a lot during the past month, having dinner and not getting home until late. Perhaps they had got too close, too fast. Precipitous relationships run in my family, and my aunt Susan's more afraid of commitment than I am. She's fiercely independent, and if George was pressuring her, I could understand why they were having problems. She can be pretty prickly when she's mad.

"I did not say that," George said. "You go if you want to, I don't care. Just be careful on the hills." He turned away. What was bugging him? He was usually perky and full of fun in the mornings. Maybe it was delayed shock after yesterday. He had coped with finding the body awfully well, but maybe he had had bad dreams about it, too.

"I'll be careful," I said to his retreating back. He just shrugged his shoulders. I weighed Annie's milk.

"Wow," I said. "Annie's outdone herself. George, you have to learn this tune."

Rico Amato grabbed both my hands and kissed me on both cheeks when I stepped into The Tiquery. He had left a message on George's machine, asking me to drop by. I knew why.

"Oooh, sweetie, you must be so upset," he said. "Here, sit down. Let me make you an espresso." I could see that he was dying to hear every detail. He was practically drooling.

The gossip grapevine works quickly in Cedar Falls. The day after John Travers's body was found, everybody knew about it, everybody knew who had found it, everybody knew that Spit Morton had been donked on the head, and everybody had a theory.

"Is it true there was an Italian stiletto sticking out of his chest?" Rico said, with great relish.

"No, Rico, he was shot."

"Oh. Thank God. They'd think I'd done it, wouldn't they? All those big policemen in my little shop." The concept was not without its attraction, judging from the way he was grinning. Rico's delicate olive features simply glowed with suppressed excitement. His natural taste for melodrama was seldom satisfied in sleepy Cedar Falls, and I could tell that he was planning to make the most of this episode, even if he hadn't been there.

"Have they found Francy yet?" he said. I shook my head, and he sighed dramatically. "So sad," he said. I noticed that Rico had finally sold the stencilled trunk. In its place was an old wash stand, also stencilled with roses and intertwining vine leaves. It looked vaguely familiar.

"Nice washstand," I said. "Did you do the painting?"

"All my own work," Rico said. "You see that table, too? It's new. Nice piece, eh?" Then his voice dropped to a whisper. "Just two days ago, that table stood in a house of tragedy." It was a pine kitchen table, lovingly hand-finished, with an unusual carved drawer in front.

"Hey. That's Francy's drawing table," I said. "The one in her studio. What's it doing here? Francy would never sell it."

"Francy didn't sell it to me," Rico said. "Her husband did. The washstand, too. I paid a good price for them."

"I'm sure you did, Rico, but they weren't John's to sell. At least the table wasn't. I helped Francy finish that table. She bought it at an auction a couple of years ago. That's where she did her work, right there. She kept her brushes in that drawer."

"I wondered where the paint stains came from," Rico said. "I thought they added authenticity to the piece." He was beginning to look uncomfortable. "Am I going to have to give it back?"

"I don't know, Rico. It's hard to imagine Francy agreeing to sell it, but I can't see John carrying the thing downstairs by himself. Francy's studio is on the second floor. Maybe they were short of cash."

"I gave Travers four hundred," Rico said.

"Wow," I said.

"It's a good piece, Polly. And the man seemed kind of... I don't know, pathetic. Desperate." The price tag said $1200. Rico noticed me looking and gave a little deprecating cough.

"Overhead," he said.

"So John just showed up with this stuff and you bought it, no questions asked?"

"You know me," he said. "Someone brings me something I like, I buy it. My turnover's pretty good. Nobody bugs me." What he meant was that sometimes his merchandise was a little warm. Everybody in Cedar Falls knew that, but Rico was generally careful to avoid what he called "local produce".

"If Francy wants it back, will you forget the mark-up?" I said. "For you, anything," Rico said, but he looked miserable.

I decided that, after I found Francy again, I would get to the bottom of the table question. I was sure she would want it back. What was more pressing, though, was to ask her why John was desperate for cash all of a sudden. It seemed to have, as Becker would probably say, some bearing on the case.

Twelve

With a breathtaking Doppler whoosh
your image spun in,
sleep-wrapped still,
and dangled perfect from my rearview,
spread-eagled like a plastic Jesus.
—Shepherd's Pie

Rico's espresso left me totally wired. After I said goodbye and climbed into the cab of George's truck, I could see that my hands were shaking.

Sooner or later, the health Nazis, who have marginalized smokers to the point of desperation, are going to turn on coffee drinkers. I figure that caffeine is the next frontier—they'll raise coffee-taxes, overwhelm our teenagers with anti-caffeine slogans (JUST SAY MILK) and then vilify the public health system for treating caffeine addicts with money from the pockets of clean living taxpayers. After that, they'll focus on television addicts. That's when I'll be dancing in the streets.

I stopped off at Gretchen's Petrocan Diner to fill up the tank before hitting the highway and nodded to Bert, the gas guy. He was the one who had attended Dream-Catcher's workshop and subsequently claimed the cougar as his power animal. He was a weedy young man, so thin you could see daylight through his wrist bones, and he kept his long, mouse-coloured hair pulled back in a pony tail. He was wearing those baggy trousers that are hip these days—the idea being to wear them so big that your butt disappears completely, leaving about a yard of wasted material. He was always quick with a hamster joke, but I didn't mind it coming from him. I figured he needed all the self-confidence he could get.

"Fill it up with regular, please, Bert."

"Hey, Polly. Got something for you." He poked the nozzle of the gas pump into the tank, scurried over to the secret glass booth, where only gas guys are allowed, and returned with something in his hand.

"What is it?" I said.

"I found it at the Lo-Mart last week. I couldn't resist." He handed it to me closed fisted, and I opened my palm to receive it. It was a small stuffed animal on a key chain, perhaps designed to look like a koala bear, but I could see why Bert had thought of me when he saw it. It was no koala, for all the designer's efforts. It was a hamster, and it was really cute.

"Oh, gee, Bert. A mascot."

He grinned, studying my face to make sure that I wasn't mad. "I thought you could, you know, hang it on the rearview or something," he said.

"It's adorable. Better than a St. Christopher medal. It'll protect me from the lumber trucks."

"What's a St. Christopher medal?"

"Never mind," I said. What did they teach them in those schools, anyway? "Thanks, Bert. I really like it." I handed him the Petrocan card (it's in George's name, like everything else) and waited, chewing my fingers, while he ran it through the authorization machine in his booth. George and I share a special relationship with Petrocan. We get into debt up to our eyeballs and skip the monthly payments, then Petrocan sends us a kneecapper letter and cancels our card. So we send them a small cheque, at which point they send back a note telling us we're a preferred customer and activate our account again so we can get deeper in debt.

We were, as it turned out, a preferred customer that week. I reminded myself to pay the bill soon, waved at Bert and chugged off to Laingford. The hamster mascot swung merrily from the rearview and I felt invincible.

The highway between Cedar Falls and Laingford is treacherous. It's a two laner, with sporadic passing lanes disguised as paved shoulders. Every six kilometres or so, there's a "keep right except to pass" sign, and if you don't move over, you'll get a lumber truck up your wahzoo.

George's truck was almost as old as me. I was born in nineteen-sixty-two, and his truck was pulled howling off the line in sixty-three. It "ran good," as they say around here, but it was not designed to gobble up the tarmac the way these plastic, Smartie-coloured compacts do. If I pushed it, the truck would do a hundred and ten clicks, but it would set up a whine like a dog who needs to pee, and I preferred to do the limit. Doing the limit on Highway 14 was not a popular tactic and driving to Laingford was always a lesson in self control. When you've got people passing you doing a hundred and thirty, it's hard to keep cool.

I was just huffing and puffing up the long hill before the exit ramp to Laingford when I saw the cruiser in my rearview, cherry-flasher spinning and headlights pulsating like a demented Christmas tree.

"Oh, terrific," I said aloud. Maybe I was going to get a ticket for loitering. I'd been doing seventy kilometres an hour on the upgrade, slow enough to warrant putting the hazards on, but it always embarrassed me to do that. I felt that if I did, the truck would know that I had no faith in it, and it would conk out in sheer disappointment. I pulled over and waited, trembling. Cops, as I've said, scare me, even if I've done nothing wrong.

I did a quick personal inventory. I was clean. I'd had not a drop of booze, not a puff of smoke, my license was up-to-date and the stickers on the plates were fresh that month. The insurance papers were in a plastic folder, paper-clipped to the visor. There were no empty beer bottles in the cab.

My pulse rate was still off the scale, and my palms were slicked up the way they used to get when I held hands with a boy in the Laingford Odeon.

I checked the mirror and cursed the hamster, who leered at me. Some mascot. Getting out of the cruiser was none other than Morrison the Large.

He took his time sauntering over to the truck. I couldn't see anyone else in the cruiser, so I guessed that Becker had managed to steal a few moments away from his partner.

"Afternoon, ma'am." He tipped his hat.

"Good afternoon, Officer. To what do I owe the pleasure?" My voice was shaking.

"You were going awfully slow, ma'am. I wondered if you were having some trouble with your vehicle. Stopped to see if you needed some assistance."

"You're kidding."

"Well, yes, ma'am. Actually, we've been trying to get in touch with you, and as you have no telephone in that shack I hear you live in, and Hoito never answers his, I thought I'd just pull you over. Give you the message myself."

"Mighty thoughtful of you," I said. I wasn't buying it. He pulled me over because he knew it would bug me. I was intrigued, though.

"We always try to be thoughtful," Morrison said, smiling cheerfully. "Mrs. Travers show up yet?"

"No, Constable Morrison, but I have reason to believe that she's safe and not wandering around in the woods somewhere."

"Now how would you know that, unless you've talked to her?"

"I found another note from her after Detective Becker left my shack, as you call it. She signed it with a happy face."

"So?"

"So, it's kind of a personal code. We write each other notes all the time. A happy face means everything's okay. So I figure she probably had a place to go, although of course I have no idea where that could be."

"Uh-huh. Well, if you find out, you'll let us know, right?"

"Of course. Can I go now?"

"Just a second. Becker was worried about that mutt at the Travers' place. He said that if Mrs. Travers isn't hiding out at home, the animal will probably starve. We could call the pound, but Becker thought you'd be willing to take it instead. I saw the way you acted with it. Real cute. Reminded me of that mountain gorilla movie."

"Oh, golly. I forgot all about poor Lug-nut. Yes, of course I'll look after him. I'll go get him as soon as I finish my errands in town."

"What errands would they be?" Morrison said. "Taking supplies to Francy Travers?"

I let out an exasperated breath. "Look, I've told you I don't know where she is," I said. "I can't lie. It's not in me." He narrowed his eyes at me. They were very blue, set deep in the fleshy folds of his face.

"As for my errands," I said, "I'm going to the Co-op to pick up some grain for the goats. Perhaps you'd care to accompany me. I hear they've got a special on pig feed." I don't know what made me say it. I was ashamed, instantly, when I saw the look on Morrison's face.

"Watch your mouth, little lady," he said. "You may think you have a friend in Becker, but I'm not such a pushover." He was talking big, but he didn't look angry, he looked hurt. Like Aunt Susan always said, retaliation only feels good while you're doing it.

"Hey, just kidding," I said. "Sixties flashback, eh? Won't happen again."

"Sixties? Hah. You couldn't have been more than six when the seventies started," he said.

"Seven," I said, doing a quick calculation. "My aunt took me to rallies, though." Aunt Susan was the one who had planted in me the notion that cops were, well, swine. Fascists. Nasty men. She had experienced their oppression, she told me, and she knew whereof she spoke.

"That would be your aunt that runs the feed store?"

"Yup."

"Figures. She ran for parliament a while back, didn't she? For the NDP?"

"More than twenty years ago," I said. "How did you know that?"

"My Dad ran against her. Victor Morrison, MPP."

"Tory," I said. "That was your Dad? You don't look like him at all."

Morrison smiled. "Nope," he said. "Don't think like him either."

He leaned against the cab of the truck. It looked like we were in for a chat, and what surprised me was that suddenly, I didn't mind so much.

In Laingford, if you get pulled over by the cops, it's all around town in two minutes. Traffic slowed as people drove past, craning their necks to see who was in trouble. I'd hear about it, later.

"You found John's truck yet?" I said.

"Nope. Still looking. Damn thing's disappeared off the face of the earth."

"Too bad. No luck at Kelso's, eh?"

"No point in asking," Morrison said. "He drove home before he was shot, remember?" I was surprised that he was talking to me about the case. I thought he and Becker were trying to keep me out of it. Still, I wasn't complaining.

"Are you sure he did that?" I said.

"The Schreier kid swears it. Travers died at home, with his truck in the driveway."

"So you think somebody used his truck to move his body to the dump, then drove it somewhere and left it," I said, carefully.

"You think so too, don't you?" Morrison said.

"Yes, but constable, Francy can't drive. So it couldn't have been her."

He winked. That was all. By now I was thoroughly confused. If he was going to start playing Good Cop, who would that cast in the role of the Bad One?

"Now, you hear anything at all, you let us know, okay?" he said. "And try not to get involved."

"If you don't want me involved, why are we having this conversation?"

"Insurance," he said, enigmatically. A Toyota buzzed by, way over the limit, honking loudly. Several young men wearing baseball caps leaned out and yelled something as they passed.

"Morons," I said. Morrison was squinting at the retreating car. "PZI 952," he muttered. Then he turned back to me.

"Mayor's kid," he said. "Gotta make a phone call."

I started the truck, then remembered that I had some new information. "Hey, Morrison," I said loudly, over the chugging of the engine. He looked back.

"John Travers was hurting for cash. He sold some stuff to Rico Amato and didn't haggle over the price. Wonder why, eh?"

Morrison grinned. "Atta girl," he said.

Aunt Susan's feed store was busy when I arrived. There were plenty of cars in the parking lot and a Co-op truck was backed up to the loading door, delivering the week's order. If I wanted to visit privately with my aunt, I'd have to wait.

Feed stores always smell wonderful, sort of a cross between a brewery and one of those brass and incense gift shops. Susan stocked hers with more than just feed. There were rubber boots and racks of work gloves, overalls and buckets, nursing nipples, milking pails, water heaters, bird feeders, tractor parts and tools.

If you were into agriculture, there wasn't a thing she wasn't happy to get for you, except American goods. She enforced a strict buy-Canadian policy, and although she would order items from the States if you insisted, she'd fill out the order form in icy silence and never look at you the same way again.

Theresa, her assistant, was at the cash desk, ringing in a big bag of low-priced, economy dog food for a man wearing a fur-lined coat. If Susan had been there, she would have made him buy a better brand. Cheap, high bulk dog food will make your animal poop twice as much as it needs to, without much benefit. The guy in the coat probably knew that already, though. Probably poured the cheap stuff into a bag of Martin's Best kept on display in the pantry. Rich people really bug me.

Theresa gave me a little wave as I came in, gesturing towards the back where Aunt Susan would be loading grain. Susan's five-foot-three and 68 years old, but she's built like a Massey Ferguson.

I excused myself past a woman and two small boys who were trying on rubber boots in the aisle, and headed for the door marked "Feed Bin".

Susan was slinging fifty pound sacks of feed around like down pillows, her short iron-grey hair standing up on end like the feathers of a startled rooster. Her hat was on the floor and her sleeves were rolled up to expose the kind of muscles that I only dream about.

"Hey," she said, "catch." A bag of feed came sailing towards me. Susan was always doing that kind of stuff when I was living with her, but I was in better shape then. Back then, I would have tossed it back. I had to catch it—or lose face, and I did both. The bag bowled me right over and I landed on my butt with the feed sack in my lap like a large, unwanted baby.

"Thanks, Susan," I said.

"Not at all. Toughen you up. You okay?"

"I'm fine." The feed truck guy had come around the corner at the moment of impact and looked mildly surprised, but very kindly did not laugh. I scrambled to my feet and put the feed onto a storage rack. I can't say I tossed it. Not really. But I tried.

"Can you give us a hand?" Susan said, and I spent the next twenty minutes acting stronger than I am, which I would undoubtedly pay for the next day.

It was just as I was easing the last sack into place and Susan was signing the invoice that I heard a noise from Susan's apartment upstairs. It was the cry of a baby.

Thirteen

Old man singing songs to a hairless child
lullabies in his eyes
and he wonders was he ever that damn small?
—Shepherd's Pie

I pretended I didn't hear that cry. I suspected
that Francy was up there with Beth. In fact I was surprised
that I hadn't figured it out right away, but I had promised
the cops that I would tell them if I found out where she was.
I wouldn't know for sure unless I asked, and I wasn't
planning to ask.

I didn't promise the cops I would report all my suspicions.
I could suspect that Francy was there without actually
knowing it for a fact. That little detail would keep me from
blushing like a tea rose the next time I saw Becker or
Morrison. The most important thing was for me to find out
who killed John Travers, before the cops got to Francy.

Aunt Susan heard the little Beth-cry as well and gave me a
sharp look, one eyebrow raised. Her eyebrows are bushy and
black and it's quite the effect. She taught me how to do it
when I was twelve, both of us practising together in front of
the mirror. I still can't do it as well as she does, although my
eyebrows are pretty severe, too.

I started whistling, picked her hat up off the floor, dusted it off and handed it to her with a smile. She handed the clipboard back to the feed guy, and we headed back out to the front of the store.

The woman and the kids were still trying on boots in the aisle and one child seemed to have its foot stuck. The dog food buyer at the counter was gone, replaced by Otis Dermott, one of the Cedar Falls holy rollers. I'd seen him handing out tracts outside Rico Amato's antique store. Theresa, Susan's help, beckoned us over.

"Afternoon, Susan," Otis said, touching his hat. He's bald as a baby and wears the hat all the time, probably even in the bath.

Susan gave him a curt nod.

"Donna-Lou's been thinking to install some more waterers in the chicken house," Otis said. His wife had a successful egg-business in Cedar Falls. She started out with a couple of laying hens for bingo money and found a big local market.

Otis still kept pigs the way he always had, but it was "Donna-Lou's Dozens" that kept the farm afloat. You could get them in Cedar Falls and a couple of places in Laingford, and people kept telling her to expand. Guess she was doing it, finally.

Otis saying something like that to Aunt Susan was like saying "Donna-Lou's been thinking to give you a couple of hundred dollars." She just had to pay attention.

"How many?" she said.

"Thirty," Otis said.

"Business must be picking up," Susan said.

Otis just grinned. "What have you got in stock?" he said.

Susan gestured with her head for him to follow her into the aisle where the water stuff was. I like agri-plumbing—it's unpretentious physics at its best, so I tagged along. We squeezed past the rubber-boot family and a mountain of small boots. They were having some disagreement about which colour to buy.

"We've got a couple of raccoons hiding out in the barn," I said, generally.

"That's awkward," Aunt Susan said.

"Real varmints," Otis said.

"The Boss-man is trying to trap them," I said.

"Of course. They're wily, though," Susan said. "Especially if it's a mother with her young."

"I haven't seen them, but I know they're there." I said.

"What kind of trap's he set?" Otis said. "If it was me, I'd just shoot 'em."

"Raccoons are survivors," Susan said. "They can elude a man with a gun, no problem."

"I hope so," I said. "You heard Dweezil died?"

"Who's Dweezil?" Otis said.

"Poor old Dweezil," Susan said. "Randy bugger though, wasn't he?"

I lost the subtle thread for a moment. "Randy? Susan, the poor thing had asthma. You know that. It wasn't his fault." Up went the eyebrow. Oh. Duh.

"Well, he did mess around," I said. "Probably got what was coming to him," I said. "Old goat."

"Who's Dweezil?" Otis said.

"At least we know what killed him," Susan said. "Now Otis, we have a full set of Grunbaum waterers and all the hookups in stock—look at this." She pulled a bunch of plumbing off a rack and started to talk business. I crept away, having got what I wanted.

As I passed the rubber-boot family, I leaned down to the smaller of the two children, who was crying.

"Excuse me, sir," I said. "Is there a problem here?" He was about three and looked up at me with some surprise.

"He wants the same kind as his brother, but they don't make them that small. They only have these," the woman said, holding up a very small pair of black wellies. The older child was looking smug and holding a pair of camouflage green rubber boots to his chest.

"Hey," I said to the small kid, "see these?" I was wearing my barn boots, size eight versions of the tiny ones in the woman's hand. The kid looked. Then he nodded.

"These," I said, "are the very coolest boots in the world. If Michael Jordan was a farmer, he'd wear these boots."

By the time I got to the counter, the older child was frantically searching for black wellies. I only hoped Susan had them in his size.

I bought and paid for a couple of bags of Shure-Gain and Theresa helped me carry them out to the truck.

"Polly," she said, "can you do me a favour?"

"Sure," I said. "What?" I didn't know her very well, but any friend of Susan's, etcetera.

"Well, my uncle's in the hospital, eh?"

"Oh, I'm sorry. Not serious, I hope."

"No. Just a head injury, they said. He's conscious, but I ain't been able to go see him yet and the hospital switchboard keeps saying he's asleep whenever I call."

"You want me to drop in on him for you, to make sure he's okay?" I said.

"Would you? He knows you, so it wouldn't be that weird."

He knew me? Did I know him? I barely knew Theresa, who lived in Laingford and came from, according to Susan, a huge family. I didn't even know her last name. Luckily, she was wearing her store name-tag. I let my eyes flicker over it.

Theresa Morton. Morton. Oh.

"Spit's your uncle?" I said without thinking.

Theresa frowned. "I heard some people call him that," she said. "He's Uncle Gerald to me. He says nice things about you."

"I'm sorry," I said. "It's not very polite, I know. But he likes it. The nickname, I mean."

"Not from me I bet he wouldn't," Theresa said. "So you'll go see him?"

"Sure. Is he allowed to have visitors?"

"Only family members, but I'll fix it. Just say I said hi, okay? Let me know how he is. Him and my Dad, they don't speak, eh?"

"Your Dad would be Hunter Morton, the funeral director?"

"Yup. He hasn't said a word to Uncle Gerald since they had that big fight about the hearse. So, like, he'd kill me if he knew I'd went there."

"I'll find out, Theresa," I said. "I'll call you." I got in the truck and headed for Laingford Memorial.

I am not, like some folks, squeamish about hospitals. When I was in to get my tonsils out, the nurses were great and I developed a hopeless crush on my doctor and wanted to stay for ever. Aunt Susan says I screamed and cried when it was time to be discharged, although I don't remember that part. Probably the best thing about being in hospital was that there were no chores to do and nobody was throwing sacks of grain at me.

I hadn't set foot in Laingford Memorial since George had been there for a cataract operation three years before. Someone, in the interim, had taken away the scruffy old lobby. In its place was a vast atrium with gleaming marble tiles and swish modern sofas upholstered in mushroom polyweave. The reception area was now protected by what looked like bullet-proof glass, and there was Muzak.

I went up to the bullet-proof glass and spoke through a little speaker-thing to a woman wearing a crushed-raspberry-coloured uniform. Why is it that medical personnel don't wear white any more? Has it gone out of fashion, or did someone make it illegal?

"Hi, I'm looking for a patient, Sp— Gerald Morton," I said.

The woman nodded and tickered away at her computer keyboard, stared at the screen for a moment and then looked up, checking me out. I was dressed in farm gear—overalls and my very cool, Michael Jordan rubber boots—not perhaps the most appropriate hospital visiting attire.

"You'll be a relative," the woman said. Would I? Okay. I guess I was.

"We're cousins," I lied, blushing.

"Right," the raspberry receptionist said, squinting at the screen. "Polly Deacon?"

"That's right," I said.

"Good," the woman said, satisfied that she had pegged me as one of the Morton clan. Theresa must have "fixed it", as promised.

"You can go up in a few minutes, Polly. Take a seat. I'll call you."

I sat down in the polyweave loveseat next to the reception desk and picked up a Cosmopolitan. The cover-girl was partially clad in a scrap of gold vinyl, her breasts rising out of the garment like warm bread-dough.

"DO YOU HAVE WHAT IT TAKES TO KEEP HIM HOT?" the cover shouted.

Probably not, I thought, looking glumly at my black rubber boots. Magazines like that depress me. Not because I waste my time trying to make myself look like an anorexic whore, but because there are advertising executives out there who think that I might want to.

I tossed the Cosmo back and picked up a National Geographic instead, entertaining myself with pictures of decimated tropical rainforests and endangered species.

A voice came over the loudspeaker above the sofa: "Ms. Deacon to reception." I looked up and saw the receptionist beckoning to me. She was within spitting distance and could have just rapped on the glass and I would have heard her, but I guess it was a new policy to go with the new intercom system.

I went over and peered through at her. "You can go up now," she said. "Your cousin's in room 402. The elevator's on the right, there." I could see where the elevator was. The sign was about ten feet high. I suppose they have to say that, but it struck me as awfully silly. I thanked her and walked to it, ten steps or so, straight ahead.

Spit was out of intensive care and in a semi-private room. He was hooked up to an IV drip, and his head was bandaged. Someone had given him a shave, and he looked pale and vulnerable lying there. The curtains were drawn around his room-mate's bed, but his were open. When he saw me he smiled broadly in recognition.

"Well, if it ain't the goat-girl," he said, wheezing. "C'mon in. Have a drink." He gestured to a pitcher of water next to his bed and winked. I had shared a slug or two with him one rainy Friday when I was feeling devilish. Spit drinks Rico Amato's homemade rotgut, so it was a bonding ritual only.

He got a kick out of calling me "goat-girl", and, seeing as I called him "Spit", it seemed like a fair exchange.

"How are you feeling, Spit?" I said, pulling up a chair.

"Big headache, girl. Big headache. But I'm alive, which is good. Gotta get out of here, though."

"How come?"

"Too many ghosts. Guy over there just died, eh? Heart case. He was talking to me plain as anything last night and when I wake up this morning, ain't no beep coming from behind his curtain."

"There's a body in there?" One dead body a week was about all I could take. Spit started laughing, then stopped with an inward gasp of pain and put his hand to his head.

"No, no. They took him away. But his ghost is flipping around the room like a trout, and I can't get any sleep."

"You see ghosts, do you?"

Spit's eyes narrowed and he studied me carefully to see if I was kidding him. I wasn't.

"Yup," he said. "Sometimes. Cops probably won't believe me either, when I tell them."

"Tell them what?"

"About Sunday night. They're on their way over here. To interview me, doctor says."

"The cops haven't talked to you yet?"

"Nope. Ain't talked to nobody but my roomie. And he's dead."

"When did you regain consciousness, Spit?"

"Last night, I guess. And they took away my damned tobacco."

I reached into my pocket, where I'd slipped the tin of Red Man I'd picked up on the way over. There was an honourable tradition to be upheld: Always bring tobacco when you visit an elder.

His eyes brightened.

"You're a good girl," he said, prising the lid off and stuffing some under his lip. "Now I got a use for that bedpan they keep shoving at me."

"So what about Sunday night?" I said.

"How'd you get in here, anyway? You a deputy cop or something?"

I grinned. "I'm your second cousin, twice removed. Theresa sent me to make sure you were okay."

He grinned back, his face distended by the wad of tobacco. "Little Terry," he said. "She's a good girl, too. Tell her I'm fine."

"Do you remember what happened Sunday night?"

"Sure do. But I'm not sure I should tell you before I tell the cops."

"I won't blab, I promise. It's important."

"Why? You and Freddy planning to get married or something?"

"What? Freddy?"

"I'm charging him with assault, eh? You shouldn't be pairing up with him, girl. He's not your type."

"Freddy was the one who hit you on the head?"

"Well, it wasn't the tooth fairy."

"But why? When?"

"We got into an argument about the dresser I gave to Amato last week. Freddy wanted to sell it for cash, eh? Like always."

"When? When did he hit you?"

"Why is that so important? What counts is that he did it." I realized that Spit probably didn't know about John Travers's body, or if he did, he was playing innocent.

"So why are the cops coming to interview you?" I said.

"Don't be foolish, girl. You know as well as I do that

Travers's dead body was in the wood hole. That's why you're asking me all these questions."

"Yeah, Spit. I know because I found him. But how do you know? You were out cold, and you said you only came to last night."

Spit spat. The glob hit the bedpan, four feet away and made a satisfying little "ping" when it landed.

"Small town hospital," Spit said. "Everybody knows. Got it from Pat, the nurse, who got it from Mack, the ambulance attendant."

"Oh. So you think Freddy did it? Killed John Travers?"

"Don't know about that. I was drinking with him in his hut from seven until nigh on midnight—the quart I got from Amato for the dresser. Freddy's usually a good drinking buddy, but Sunday night he was acting funny, and the wine made him crazy."

"So he hit you? Were you fighting, like, duking it out?"

"Nope. I turned my back on him after he called me a sneaking weasel and next thing I know, I'm here."

"But you were found in your hearse, Spit."

"I know that," he said. "He must have dragged me there after he done it."

"Why would he do that?"

"Probably thought he'd killed me. Put me there so he wouldn't be blamed, then took off. But after I tell the cops, he'll be blamed, all right."

"You said something about ghosts, Spit. On Sunday night. Before Freddy hit you?"

"That's the part the cops won't believe. They'll say it was DTs, like they always do."

"What part won't they believe?"

A flicker of fear passed across Spit's face, and he shut his eyes for a moment. "Could have been DTs, I guess," he said. "Could have been a dream. But I know a ghost when I see one."

"Where? When?"

"Sometime, girl. Somewhere. I was in that other place you go when you've been hit on the head after a jar of Amato's Triple X. One second I'm floating there with my head in a leg-hold trap and the next second I'm awake in my car and Travers is sitting next to me, real as you are."

"Alive?"

Spit shuddered. "Nope. He was covered in blood, his chest wide open like a butchered pig." I fought down nausea as the image of Travers's fly-covered body—the thing I had seen yesterday—came swimming back to me.

"But he was talking to me, see?" Spit said. "He was saying 'baby, baby, baby' over and over, looking straight at me. Then I blacked out again."

The hairs on my arms stood straight up on end.

"Geez, Spit. That's awful."

"You're telling me."

"You think the ghost was trying to tell you something?"

"Maybe. Don't know what, though. Could have been the words to a rock-and-roll song. Ghosts don't always talk sense."

"You're the expert."

"Wish I wasn't. Anyway, the cops won't take any notice of an old drunk like me. I may not even bother telling them. But I am gonna charge Freddy. Maybe the District will give me his weekend shift while he's in jail, eh?"

"Maybe. So he just whacked you over the head, then panicked and left, you figure?"

"I figure. Bastard."

"And he whacked you sometime after midnight."

"That's right."

I had to find out when John was shot, that was for certain. If he was killed after midnight, that made Freddy a prime suspect. I would have to talk to Freddy, too.

Just then, the door to Spit's room opened and Becker and Morrison walked in. They were not overjoyed to see me.

"What the hell are you doing here?" Becker said, striding towards me.

"There's no need to say that every time we meet, Detective," I said. "I'm visiting a sick friend. What does it look like?"

"It looks like interfering in police business," Becker said.

Morrison moved in, too. "I thought I told you not to get involved," the big cop said.

"I'm not..." I began, but Becker had grabbed my upper arm and was ushering me out of the room. When we got into the hallway, I shook him off.

"There's no need for that, Detective," I said. "I'll come quietly."

Now, I will admit this to you in private. When Becker took my arm, all sorts of lewd fantasy thoughts flashed across my mental movie screen. These thoughts had to do with handcuffs, uniforms and mildly kinky role-playing games. I don't know where they came from and I was so shocked by my unconscious mind that I lost control for a second. When I said "I'll come quietly," I immediately recognized the double-entendre, and the Aunt Susan eyebrow came up, I swear, of its own accord.

That would have been okay, I could have handled that and talked myself through it later over a joint at the cabin. The problem was that Becker's eyebrow went up as well, and a tiny, red-hot jolt passed between us that was pure, unadulterated sex. If I had been a Victorian maiden, I would have swooned.

"Quietly? I doubt it," Becker said. Lord help us. "What were you talking to Morton about?"

"That's none of your business."

"It's all of my business. Look, I know you want to clear your friend, who, incidentally, we have not been able to track down yet, but we will. I know you have an interest in this case, but you're getting in the way."

"How so?"

He sighed. "You know damn well. Interrogating witnesses before we get a chance to see them. You did it with Francy Travers, now with Morton. It's got to stop. For one thing, it's dangerous. Someone has been killed, unless you've forgotten, and if you happen to figure this mess out before we do, you could end up in the dump yourself. You ever think of that?"

"Which would leave you with another juicy murder to solve. Give you a chance to get promoted," I said.

"That isn't even slightly funny. You're playing in a game you don't know anything about, Polly. I don't want to find you dead somewhere. I really don't."

"Me neither."

"Well then, stop this. It's making life difficult for me, and you're putting yourself in danger, butting in."

"If I don't butt in, Mark, I'm afraid a mistake will be made, that's all."

"We're professionals. You're not."

"Yeah, and as a citizen, I should have faith in the justice system, right?"

"Right."

"What about Guy Paul Morin? Steven Truscott? Donald Marshall?"

"Those were..."

"Isolated cases? I don't think so. Listen. It's not that I don't have faith in you, but I know what kind of pressure you guys are under when somebody's been killed. I just want to make sure that Francy has the best chance, okay?"

"If Francy Travers didn't kill her husband, we'll find that out and find the person who did," he said, smiling with an assurance I just could not accept.

"I'm not so sure," I said.

Becker's smile vanished. His eyes (green with little gold flecks in them) got darker.

"Thanks. Thanks a lot," he said. "I'm glad you have so much confidence in me and in the system. You'd better just hope, in that case, that you never find yourself in court. You might, you know."

"That sounds like another threat, Becker," I said. "I just love your tactics. No wonder you guys get the wrong man so often. I can just see people falling over themselves in their eagerness to give you information." I backed away from him and poked my head around the door of room 402.

"See you later, Spit," I said. "I'm going to go save a dog, then talk to my fiancé. Mind you aim for the bedpan." With that I headed off down the hall, pausing for a moment to glare at Becker. He was white-faced, and I figured that he'd never want to speak to me again. A pity, really, but then he was a cop.

Fourteen

I drove that ramshackle rattletrap
hellbent for elsewhere
leaving you sleeping.
—Shepherd's Pie

When I let Lug-nut off his chain, he looked at
me like I was crazy. As usual, he had barked his head off when
I pulled up in the truck, and he kept on barking until he
recognized me, which was when I was roughly three feet away.
I wondered if he might be slightly myopic, which would
account for some of his aggression.

I had been trying to decide, on my way over to the Travers'
place, whether or not it would be a smart idea to take the dog
over to the cabin. After all, he was used to his own territory,
and I had no stomach for keeping an animal tied up. There
was no guarantee that he would be interested in sticking
around my place, except perhaps for the fact that I would be
feeding him.

When I pulled into the driveway, I knew immediately that
I would be taking him home, no matter what. He looked
impossibly lonely. The house was cold and abandoned, just
like Lug-nut, and there was a yellow band of POLICE LINE
DO NOT CROSS tape over the front door. Any territory
would be better than this.

I spoke to him softly, rubbed his tummy for a while and then unclipped his chain. That was when he gave me the "you must be crazy" look. The unexpected freedom confused the hell out of him. He made a sort of "chase me" dash for about a metre, then stopped, whirled around and cringed. I didn't say anything, just watched him. Then he came back to his feed bowl and sniffed at it in a hopeful way.

"Soon, soon," I said. I picked up the water bowl and filled it at the outside tap. Lug-nut inhaled it, and I had to refill it twice before he had enough. I had planned to feed him from the food bag under Francy's kitchen sink, but I didn't relish the thought of sneaking past the police tape. There might be a hidden camera in there or something, and they might decide I was returning to the scene of the crime. On the other hand, I didn't have much extra cash, and dog food is expensive.

"What do you think, dog?" I said. "Should we do a spot of B&E?" He wagged his tail, which I took to be permission from the only available resident. He followed me up to the door, which the police had very kindly left unlocked. I ducked under the tape, but Lug-nut refused to come in, although I assured him it was okay. He just sat there on the doorstep, whining and shivering. Maybe he had some sixth sense about what had happened there, or maybe he could smell the blood, I don't know.

"Hey, it's okay, Luggy," I said, patting his ugly head. "You don't have to come in if you don't want to, Just don't go anywhere, okay? Stay!" The word was obviously a recognizable command. He lay down immediately, his head between his paws, looking up at me. "Good dog!" I said. Great White Dog Wrangler. That's me. I went inside.

The kitchen was just as I had last seen it. The police hadn't done any friendly housecleaning, and the bloodstains on the floor had darkened to a rust-colour, which was much easier to cope with than the fresh puddles I had slipped in the day before.

There was a stomach-churning, coppery smell in the air, though, and I breathed through my mouth.

The beer bottles were still on the table, although there seemed to be fewer than there were before. Becker and Morrison must have taken some of them away as evidence. I knew that at least a few of the bottles would have Francy's prints on them, and I felt very afraid for her. The remaining few showed traces of a grey-ish powder, which I assumed was fingerprinting dust, just like in the movies. The whole scene was like a movie set, actually, as if the crew had just stepped away to go on a lunch break. It was spooky.

I glanced at the rack beside the door and John's shotgun was missing, but that didn't mean much. The police certainly would have taken the gun with them to do tests on, if it had still been there when we discovered the scene.

The teapot was dry as a bone, of course. I checked.

I tiptoed to the kitchen cupboard, uneasy in this empty, eerie house where John's violent death was still very much a reality. The house would probably never be the same, to Francy, anyway, if she ever got the chance to come back to it. I had spent a lot of time with her in this kitchen, sitting at the big table, sorting herbs and gabbing, talking about pregnancy and babies, Francy's commercial art business and my puppets. We never spoke about the past. We rarely talked about John, or about Francy's life before Cedar Falls. She was one of those people who lived in the moment, completely. I only hoped that the "moment" she was in now, presumably at Aunt Susan's, wasn't as awful as this kitchen was.

I opened the cupboard door with the edges of my

fingernails and hauled out Lug-nut's kibble. John had been obsessive about not letting anybody feed the dog but him, so taking the food was almost like stealing from the dead. He had been an uncomfortable man to be around—continually seething with some wrong, imagined or otherwise. I had always felt that he was on the very edge of exploding and had he been there I would not even have gone near the cupboard. I remembered Spit's ghost story and imagined John's spectre, enraged at my trespassing, flapping around my head like an angry vulture.

I was just standing up, with the heavy bag cradled in my arms, when I heard something upstairs. Just the creak of a floorboard, maybe, but it was enough for me. I beat it so fast out the front door, I forgot about the police tape and broke through it like Donovan Bailey winning a gold.

Lug-nut was right there where I had left him and wagged his tail as I burst through the tape, but he did not get up.

"Ummm, good boy, Luggy," I said. He still lay there like a coiled spring. John, for all his neglect of the dog, had certainly trained him well. There must be a magic word.

"Ummm... that's all right. You can get up now." Nothing. "It's okay, Lug-nut!" I said with some exasperation and he leaped about two feet in the air and started running in circles around me. That was it, then. "Okay." Simple enough. I would have to watch what I said around him, though. There was probably some secret command lodged in his doggy brain that would send him off into attack mode.

Now that I was outside, I laughed at myself for being spooked. If there had been anybody in the house, Lug-nut would have let me know. The overhead creak was probably just the old house settling on its foundations.

I walked sedately to the truck and after I had deposited the dog food in the back with the grain, I returned to the yellow tape to see if I could fix it. Either that, or I would have to call up Becker and tell him that I had broken in. If I didn't, he'd be off on some wild goose chase, further and further away from finding the real murderer.

The tape had been stapled to both sides of the door, and my dash outside had ripped one end away from the staple, which was still embedded in the door frame. I glanced over my shoulder to make sure that nobody was watching, then used my Swiss Army knife to wriggle the staple out. I lifted the tape back into position, poked the prongs through the plastic just to the right of the original holes and hammered it back with the butt of the knife.

Satisfied, I turned back to the driveway. The cops would have to study it pretty closely to know that it had been tampered with. I was betting that they wouldn't check to see if the dog food was still there, any more than they'd check to see whether there was still cereal in the cupboard.

Lug-nut had disappeared.

"Shit," I said aloud. I called his name, and immediately got an answering bark from the quonset hut next to the house. "Come, here, boy!" I said. I know my dog-wrangling techniques from reading Ted Wood's books. When Wood's cop-hero tells his wonder-dog Sam to Come, Stay, Keep, or Attack, the dog responds with impeccable, life-saving promptness and barrels full of loyalty.

Lug-nut did not come.

I went into the building to get him.

I'd never been in John's garage before. Like the dog, it had been his private domain—men only. It was like a mad mechanic's laboratory. The colours were muddy, all brown and black, and everything was covered in a thin layer of grease and dust. The floor-space was huge. You could have played baseball in there. There were two cars side by side, with open hoods, their guts spilling out and scattered as if some giant predator had been making a meal of them.

Tools were piled on top of one another on every flat surface, and from the ceiling hung chains and pulleys, rope and rubber hoses, like trailing fronds in some mechanical jungle.

I am a complete innocent when it comes to car mechanics, and so I found the atmosphere oppressive. If I'd known what it was all for, I would have felt better.

Lug-nut was waiting for me towards the rear of the building, where it was dark. I called him again, and he barked back, but stayed put. He was sitting in front of a vehicle which had been covered with a dirty tarpaulin and there was something familiar about the shape of it. I looked around for a light switch and found a trouble-light suspended from the ceiling in the corner. I switched it on and the naked bulb cast surreal shadows on the shrouded shape in front of me.

The tarp didn't quite cover the front bumper, and I'd know that hideous browny-green paint job anywhere. John's missing truck. Francy was always complaining about it, said it offended her sense of hue. Looking at that colour with an artist's eye was like listening to a beginner violinist if you had perfect pitch, she said. John had painted the truck himself, shortly after buying it from Otis Dermott. It had been purple, and John had refused to drive it until he got rid of "that faggy colour."

I lifted a corner of the tarp carefully so I could see into the cab. I don't know what I was expecting. Another body, maybe.

There wasn't one, which was a good thing. There was, however, a dark stain on the passenger seat, and the barrel of a shotgun poking up from the floor. I let the tarp fall back, switched off the light and headed for the open air.

As I left the garage, Lug-nut came trotting at my heels—obediently, now that he had shown me what he obviously thought was important. Then I caught a flicker of movement out of the corner of my eye. I turned to look at the house and saw a tall, painfully thin figure loping off into the bush. Lug-nut barked and lunged, but I managed to grab his collar in time to stop him from giving chase. It looked like Eddie Schreier. Nobody else in the world runs quite so much like a frightened spider. The door to the house was still shut and the tape was still up, but I guessed it had been Eddie upstairs, making that noise I heard. What was going on?

I walked Lug-nut to George's truck, still holding his collar, and put him in the cab. Maybe Eddie had returned to grab Francy's copy of Lady Chatterley. Maybe, but not bloody likely. I added Eddie to my mental list of people to have a chat with really soon, then fired up the engine and headed home.

Fifteen

Stuff gets born and lives and dies
like fire and sex and that look
in your chocolate eyes.
−Shepherd's Pie

I drove down to the barn to unload the grain and found George in the kidding pen with Erma Bombeck, who was in labour. Erma was five and an old hand when it came to giving birth, but George liked to be on hand anyway.

"Hey, George. I thought she wasn't due till next Thursday," I said.

"She wasn't. But I found her groaning and pawing at the ground around eleven, and she has had some discharge, so I put her in the pen. She was always stubborn. She is ready now, she says, not next week."

"You got towels and stuff?" George keeps a stock of "goats only" hand towels up at the house. Birthing goat kids is a messy business, and towels and hot water, trite as it may seem, are important.

"Yes, Polly. It shouldn't be long now."

The first time I witnessed the birth of a goat (triplets, actually; they nearly always come in twos or threes—sometimes four on a good day), I had disgraced myself completely. I'd thought, "Oh, wonderful. The miracle of birth. Let me in there." What I hadn't bargained for was the guck. I had crouched at the ready, a clean towel over my arm, having been instructed to take the newborn kid, clean it off and give it back to the doe to nuzzle until the next one came along. It had been a difficult birth. The first of three was trapped sideways in the birth canal and George had to reach inside to turn the little fellow around. That didn't bother me so much. I'd read James Herriot, and I knew this was sometimes necessary, but when George's arm emerged from the depths of Donna Summer, clutching a slimy, twitching thing, ropes of mucous hanging off it like, well, you know— my gag reflex kicked in, big-time.

"Get out of my barn," George had roared, hearing my preliminaries. I tossed him the towel and ran outside to be sick in the manure pile. We both apologized later. He said it happened occasionally to first-timers, and he should have been more sensitive. I reminded him that he had been up half the night with the pregnant doe and was tired and worried. All he needed was to have some city-girl throwing up in his nice, clean barn.

The next time someone kidded I was in there like a pro, grinning from ear to ear. I have even done the unspeakable "reach in and tweak" trick one New Year's Eve when George was out late carousing with Susan at the senior's club and Julian of Norwich had delivered early.

Erma Bombeck was in deep labour now, lying on her side and pushing, yelling with each push in an outrageously human voice.

"*Puske vaan*," George said, softly. Finnish for "push like hell," I guess. He always muttered in his mother-tongue during a birth. The goats seemed to like it. "*Anna tulla vaan.*" The first kid made its appearance, popping out so fast that

George had to catch it. He quickly cleared the matter away from its mouth as Erma turned her head to inspect her offspring. It was a very pretty kid, almost completely white, with caramel-coloured markings on its back and caramel-coloured ears.

"A male," George said with satisfaction. Dweezil's heir, maybe. Two more followed in quick succession, were cleaned, and arranged in a squirming, bleating row at Erma's side. Two does and a buck, all healthy, and the buck was quite large.

It always made me a little teary-eyed, being in at the birth. There's something extraordinary about new life—the incredible tenacity of it. Goat kids start bleating only minutes after being born, start trying to stand up almost immediately. By the time we left the barn, one was already trying to get her tiny muzzle around Erma's enormous teat.

Outside, in the thin autumn sunshine, Lug-nut was having a staring contest with Poe, through the window of the truck cab. The raven was perched on the grain sacks, peering in the back window, and Luggy was not barking, just sitting quietly on the seat, his nose only inches away from the bird's beak. The only thing separating them was the glass.

"Think I should let him out?" I asked George.

"Well, he isn't being very aggressive," George said. "Did you not say he was a watchdog?"

"He's supposed to be, but I don't think he's got great eyesight, and when he's not tied up, he's a pussycat."

"He's ugly."

"He is not," I said. "Well, he's maybe homely, but he grows on you." Obviously, some kind of nurturing, maternal instinct was kicking in. Children never affected me that way, but Lug-nut seemed to.

I opened the truck door and Luggy bounded forth, tail wagging, and licked George's extended hand.

"Friendly to me, anyway," George said. Poe had not moved from his spot on the grain-sack. When I let down the tailgate, Lug-nut jumped up into the truck bed and moved slowly towards the bird, tail still wagging. Poe bristled to make himself look bigger, but he did not fly away.

"Do they know each other already, you think?" I said.

"Perhaps. Poe is often at the dump, and the Travers place is nearby. I have never seen that bird remain so calm around a four-leg, though. Maybe he's waiting for your dog to get close enough so that he can get a peck in."

I tensed, ready for a nasty flurry of feathers and teeth. It didn't happen. The dog and bird were close enough now to touch each other. Lug-nut whined once and Poe croaked, then the dog sat. Poe croaked a few more times and took off in a leisurely fashion, sailing over our heads and making for the farm house. Lug-nut, ignoring us, jumped out of the truck and followed.

"What was all that about?" I said.

George was shaking his head in amazement. "Never seen anything like it."

We unloaded the grain and drove back up to the house. The dog was sitting waiting for us on the porch, the bird perched on the railing a few feet away.

I got the dog's feed bowl out of the cab and filled it from the bag of kibble.

"Lunch," I said, putting it down. We left dog and bird, happily sharing the feast, and headed for the kitchen. I had to use the phone.

Before I called Becker, I told George about finding the truck in John's garage.

"That is a very strange story," he said.

"Yup. What's even stranger is that the cops didn't find it first. Aren't they supposed to go over everything with a fine-tooth comb when someone gets murdered?"

"You would think so," George said.

"Still, Becker told me this was his first homicide. I guess he's making it up as he goes along."

"This news is going to anger him, Polly."

"Yup. Sure is. Not only because he overlooked the obvious, but if there were any tell-tale tire tracks in the driveway, they'll be gone by now."

"What do you mean?"

"Well, let's say the killer arrived, shot John, then used John's truck to take his body to the dump and then drove the truck back and hid it in the garage. That would mean the killer's car would have been standing there for a while. It might have left, I don't know, tire tracks. Oil-stains. Something."

"Unless the killer arrived on foot," George said.

"Where from? You mean he parked on the road?"

"I mean he, or she, might not have been very far away."

"You mean a neighbour?" I said. "Who? You think Eddie did it? Or...oh, no, George. If you think Francy did it, I'm going to be really, really pissed off."

"You did say that she can't remember what happened," George said.

"I can't believe you're saying this. I thought you liked Francy."

"I do like her, Polly. All I'm saying is that she had every reason to do it, and she's the most obvious choice. I think you should prepare yourself for it to be so. Francy was most likely the only one to know there was room to hide the truck in Travers's garage."

"Everyone else is prepared for it to be so," I said, trying to keep my temper. "I seem to be the only one who is willing to entertain the possibility that she didn't do it."

"What would happen if her memory comes back and she admits it?"

"You mean when hell freezes over? I'll be too busy trying to keep warm to care." I turned my back on him and reached for the phone.

A woman answered the Laingford Police line and I asked if Becker was in. He wasn't, and I left a message to have him call me as soon as possible.

George had made tea for both of us, so I sat with him and tried to swallow my disappointment in him. It wasn't easy—particularly because he started in on Becker's favourite theme: Stay out of it.

"Look, I can't drop this now," I said. "Look at the truck-thing for instance. If I wasn't involved, the cops would still be scouring the back roads, wasting their time. All I'm doing is giving them a little boost."

"But, as far as they're concerned, the truck hasn't been found yet. They may still be scouring the back roads," George said. "Why did you not just leave the information over the phone? Why did you have to speak to that policeman personally?"

There was a little pause.

"Ah," he said. "Like that, is it? I thought it was so."

My face went hot. "Like what? What do you mean you thought it was bloody so?"

"Which is why I didn't tell you where Francy Travers is. I knew you would not be able to lie to that big, handsome policeman."

"What? You know she's at Susan's? You knew already?"

"How do you think she got there? She was in no shape for walking. I drove her, after your policeman left."

"He's not my policeman. You mean she was there when we were all talking here before Becker came up to the cabin?"

"She was hiding in the barn. She followed you down here, Polly. She knew I was safe, she only had to wait until you and the policeman were out of the way."

"Until I was out of the way? Why? Doesn't she trust me anymore? God. I'm the one who's been defending her all this time."

"She knows that," George said gently. "But she knows you better than you think. Something you said, perhaps, when she was with you. She knew she had to get away, so she came to me and I took her to your aunt. Don't look so betrayed. It was all for the best."

I was devastated. My best friend didn't trust me. After all I had been doing to try and clear her name, she was trying to get away from me.

"So why are you telling me now?" I said.

"She decided to turn herself in."

I stared at him, my mouth open.

"You mean she did do it?" Impossible.

"Not necessarily. She still can't remember, but she wants to go home, and Susan told her that to speak to the police would be the quickest way for it. Susan telephoned a short while ago. They were headed over to the police station together. She's probably there now."

I couldn't speak, I was so angry. I felt like the kid that everybody has labelled a tattletale, not to be trusted with any secrets. I felt left out. I felt like a jerk. But was it true, what George was saying? What Francy had told him? That I was so transparent I was dangerous? Then I remembered that I had told Becker she was up at the cabin. I had led him to her, in fact, except that she wasn't there. That made me feel even worse.

"I still think she's making a mistake," I said.

"It is hers to make."

The phone rang and I answered it. It was Becker.

"We've got Mrs. Travers," he said.

"I know."

"I know you know. You could be charged with obstruction, Polly. You and your aunt."

"I didn't know where she was for sure until a few moments ago, Becker."

"Who told you?"

Oops. "Uh . . . you just did."

"No, I didn't. I just told you we had her."

"Never mind that. Anyway, you don't 'have' her—she came in of her own accord, right? That should weigh in her favour."

Becker sighed. "What do you want, Polly? Is there something else you 'only just found out' that you want to tell me?"

"As a matter of fact, there is, Mark. I found the truck."

"What? Where?"

"It's sitting under a tarp in John Travers's garage. There's a bloodstain on the seat and I think there's a gun in there, too."

"Holy Toledo."

"Holy Toledo?"

"I'm trying not to swear around you."

"Oh. Thanks. So, how come you didn't search the garage when you were detecting the scene of the crime?"

"Oversight," he said.

"I'll say."

"When did you discover it? What were you doing over there?"

"I went to pick up Lug-nut, remember?"

"Who?"

"The dog. The one you were afraid might starve."

"I have no idea what you're talking about," he said, after a pause.

I exhaled loudly into the phone. "When Morrison pulled me over this afternoon on the highway he said you said I should go pick up John's dog because there was nobody to look after him."

"This is all news to me, Polly. You sure you're not just making this up?"

"You have a wonderfully retentive memory for a cop, don't you?"

"No need to get nasty. So you went to save the dog and did a little snooping around, did you? What did I say not long ago about getting involved? Don't you listen?"

"The dog went into the garage and wouldn't come out, so I went to get him and I found the truck. No snooping. A baby could have found it if he'd thought to look."

He ignored the dig. "Thanks for the tip," he said. "We'll go check it out and I'll have to come out to get a statement after we're done. Don't go anywhere."

"You know where to find me," I said.

After I hung up I thanked George for the tea, but didn't stick around. I was still mad at him for holding out on me and mad at myself because I understood why he had done it. I borrowed a wheelbarrow to haul the dog food up to the cabin, called to Lug-nut and headed home.

sixteen

Old Rebecca's telling me
leave them bugs be,
let them bugs mate and live and die
their day or two,
part of the plant that's healing you.
 —Shepherd's Pie

There are a lot of things to be said for living alone, not the least of which is that you only have to do the dishes when they start moving around in the sink by themselves. I hadn't had lunch yet and I was starving. I wanted to fix myself a big tuna and lettuce sandwich, but I had to clean up first because a bunch of ants was trying to make off with the bread knife.

I am not a bug-killer. When I see an ant, I do not shriek and whack it with a magazine. The only bugs I kill are the ones who are biting me, which limits my insect murder to a few hundred thousand every spring and summer, during blackfly and mosquito season.

I really like the concept that the fluttering of a butterfly's wings in Fiji affects the air-flow of the world just a tiny bit, which affects something else, etc. So, generally speaking, I don't kill things. Especially not ants.

I put my nose down to the counter, coming face-to-face with

a burly worker-ant who was carting off a breadcrumb the size of a Mack truck, in Ant. He stopped, waving his antennae in distress.

"It's okay, buddy. No fear," I said. "I just wanted to ask you to tell your work-crew that I'm about to do the dishes, so you'd better clear out or somebody's going to get drowned by mistake." He scuttled away, escaping from my monstrous breath, which to him was probably the equivalent of standing downwind of a week-old massacre.

It worked, like it always does. By the time the water was boiling, there wasn't an ant to be seen.

Lug-nut had been reluctant to come indoors, but had finally agreed after I put his food and water bowls inside. I knew that the local squirrel population would treat his kibble the same way they treated the seed I put out for the birds, and though I tolerated squirrels, I wasn't willing to contribute to their winter larders any more than I could help. Let them get their own stuff. There were plenty of pine cones around.

The dog spent his first half hour at my place just sniffing at things. I hoped he was sensible enough to know that crapping or peeing indoors would not endear him to the management, but apart from that, he was welcome to make himself comfortable anywhere he liked. Anywhere, that is, except the futon. I showed him the bed.

"Lug-nut," I said, pointing, "this is a NO. Got that? Anywhere else, you can sprawl and sleep, but NO on the bed." The word NO he certainly seemed to get. His ears flattened against his skull and his eyes rolled in his head like two ping-pong balls.

I had a big, ugly cushion which I had inherited from an old room-mate in Toronto, and I dragged it from the closet and arranged it in the corner beside his food.

"This is yours," I said, patting it. He came forward and sniffed it, then pounced on it, kneaded it with his forepaws, turned around three times (why do they do that?) and flumped down, taking one corner of the cushion into his mouth like a pacifier.

"Okay," I said, "just don't rip it apart." I felt suddenly smug and protective, at the same time. My dog. My god. I had acquired a dog. How prosaic.

I washed the dishes quickly, vaguely aware of an unusual compulsion to clean. Then I attacked the work table, straightening the scattered tools, dusting and putting things away. I swept the floor, pausing only for tea and my sandwich, then getting right back at it. I went outside to chop wood, discovering in the process that Lug-nut had never played fetch before, which I found heart-breaking. It was like meeting a child who has never had a birthday party.

He gambolled about like a puppy, trying to help, until I was forced to place him off to one side and tell him to sit. Chopping off his paw at this point would have been a great pity, seeing as we were getting along so well.

When I tossed him a piece of bark, the perfect size for fetch, he just looked at it, dumbfounded.

"It's okay, Luggy," I said. "Okay." He whined and nosed the bark, perhaps wondering if I expected him to eat it.

I put the axe down and picked up the bark.

"Fetch!" I cried and threw it. He stood there, his tail waving just a little.

"Okay. Wait a sec." I retrieved the bark myself, wondering if he knew perfectly well how to play the game, but was making the damn human go get it for once. I brought it back and let him sniff it.

"C'mon, Lug-nut. This is supposed to be fun." He

grasped it tentatively between his teeth and tugged.

"That's it." I whipped it away and threw it. "Fetch!"

The mental block in his furry mind gave way all at once. He leaped to his feet and fetched. And fetched. And fetched. I abandoned the woodpile and devoted myself to Lug-nut and the first recreation he had probably experienced since puppyhood. I felt like a Big Sister. Or a hospital volunteer. There should be big brownie-points for stuff like that.

I stowed the wood in the closet behind the stove and then got to work on the puppet. The arm I had made was dry now, and I made a second one, forming the hand in such a way that it could be made to hold something. A nightstick, maybe, or a gun. Or my thigh.

I didn't want to sculpt the face yet, not until I saw the subject-model again and firmly implanted his looks in my mind. As I sat working, I realized that my uncharacteristic cleaning binge had been brought on by the knowledge that Becker would be coming up to the cabin at some point to take my statement about finding John's truck. This was embarrassing. I might just as well have put on an apron and baked a cake. What was I trying to prove? That I was actually a little Suzie Homemaker in waiting?

It was an old story. Despite Aunt Susan's influence, despite my life-long struggle for independence, despite what I thought was my deeply ingrained feminism, I had still absorbed the Cosmo-Imperative.

"To get a man, impress him with your femininity. Ask him questions about himself. Be interested in his answers. Always be well-groomed and keep your living space immaculate."

In reality, I was, not to mince words, a slob. I always would be. I had made myself seem what I was not, many times before, in order to attract the interest of a particular man. It had never worked. Pretending was always exhausting and invariably ended in disappointment as my cover slipped. I would find myself tiring of the charade, and the man I had struggled to impress realized, poor sap, that I was not girly after all. I don't know why I did it, but every time the hormones kicked in I would start playing the same old game.

I suppose, looking back, it just never occurred to me that my problem lay in the kind of man I was attracted to. Beefy macho dudes don't generally want to get involved in romantic relationships with beefy macho women. End of story.

I had worked myself up into a lather of self-loathing by the time Becker showed up. Lug-nut was asleep on his pillow by the door and didn't even notice the man's approach until he knocked. The Great Watchdog woke up, shook himself, inhaled and commenced barking.

I grabbed Luggy's collar and opened the door, inviting Becker inside. The policeman eyed the dog apprehensively and remained standing near the exit until things calmed down. I didn't blame him. Lug-nut, in full bark-mode, was pretty convincing. I managed to convey to the dog, through a series of gestures, then sharp words, then soothing, "good-boy" type rubbing behind the ears, that our visitor was persona grata. Lug-nut subsided and returned to his cushion, where he sat, keeping Becker under close surveillance.

"Well," Becker said. "You're well protected."

I smiled. Protected up to a point, I thought. "Thanks for reminding me about him," I said. "He seems to like it here. Better than the pound, anyway."

"That was Morrison's doing, not mine," he said. "He was the one who remembered the dog. I've been too tied up with the case to be thinking about animal welfare."

"Oh. He said you suggested it."

"I know. I asked him about that and he mumbled something about you not wanting to hear it coming from him. He has a dog of his own, eh?"

"A pitbull?"

Becker chuckled. "Don't tell him I told you, but it's actually a poodle. A little fuzzy white one."

"Holy Toledo."

"My words, exactly. There's a lot about him that makes no sense."

"I noticed that," I said. "Hey, can I offer you a cup of something, or a beer, even?"

"Coffee would be good, if you have it."

"You don't drink, eh?" I should have known. A teetotaller. We were incompatible. It was hopeless.

"I don't drink on duty, that's all." He sounded defensive.

"I thought that was a TV-thing."

"It's also a regulation-thing."

"Too bad." I meant it. I wanted a beer myself, but having one if Becker was going to have coffee wouldn't be very ladylike. Of course, offering him a beer wasn't particularly ladylike either, but I wasn't thinking clearly. He was wearing aftershave and it was driving me crazy.

"You trying to corrupt me?" he said. I held his gaze. We had one of those moments again, and according to the rule-book, he had just issued Opening Flirtation Gambit Number One. Golly.

"Oh, no, Officer. I wouldn't dream of being so forward." I practically danced over to the kettle. "It'll take a while, though. There's no electricity and I have to boil water the old fashioned way over a candle flame."

"I'm in no rush," he said. "Now, talk to me about this truck. When and how did you find it?"

I told him the details, leaving out the bit about going into the house to get the dog food and neglecting to mention Eddie Schreier's appearance and retreat. I liked Eddie and I didn't want to get him into trouble, at least not until I'd talked to him myself.

"You said you thought you'd seen a gun in the cab of the truck, right?"

"Right. I just saw the barrel, sticking out a couple of inches. It was on the floor, I guess, leaning against the seat."

"But you didn't touch it."

"God, no. After the way you acted in Francy's kitchen, I almost didn't look at it at all. Didn't want to mess up the evidence, eh?"

"It was dark in there, wasn't it?"

"Yes, but I switched on a trouble-light and brought it with me to the truck."

"Why did you do that?"

"Because it was dark, of course. I wanted to make sure it was John's truck, first, before reporting it. I lifted up the corner of the tarp with my fingertips and shone the light in."

"Could you describe the gun?"

"Well, I figured it was John's gun from the kitchen. It's an old shotgun, I think. I don't know much about them, but that's what it looked like. I really only saw the barrel."

"You sure it was a gun barrel and not just a stick or something?"

"Of course I'm sure. It was long and metallic and—wait a second. You didn't find a gun in the truck?"

"Nope."

"Oh, great. Well, I didn't touch it."

"Somebody did."

"Who would do that? Why?"

"That's what we want to know. Having the murder weapon would have moved the investigation along. So now it's gone."

"It was there. I swear."

"Right. I'll have this statement typed up so you can sign it. In the meantime, you keep your door locked. Whoever shot John Travers and dumped his body, also hid the truck and the gun, which you found. He was probably watching when you went in there. Then he panicked and grabbed the gun, and he knows you saw it. You should probably plan to stay with Mr. Hoito for a while, Polly."

"This doesn't make any sense. I mean, hiding the truck in the garage was just a stalling measure, wasn't it? It would have been found eventually. There's no reason for the killer to think that finding the truck and the gun would necessarily lead to him, is there?"

"Sure there is. We've got DNA testing now. Even if he wiped the gun, there's still hair and fibre samples we can get from the truck. It's not as easy to get away with murder as it used to be."

"Still, how come he would be after me, just because I found the truck?"

"People who murder other people don't think straight. If some guy shot Travers in his kitchen, moved the body in the man's own truck, then hid the truck in the man's own garage, I don't think he's the kind of criminal who's going to find it illogical to attack a woman who sticks her nose into his business."

"It doesn't sound like you suspect Francy anymore, anyway."

"I haven't ruled anybody out. I talked to Mrs. Travers today and she's cleared up some of the personal details, that's all. We would be progressing quicker if you and your aunt hadn't decided to play Underground Railroad, though."

"Have you talked to Freddy yet?"

"I'm on my way to do that now," he said. "You haven't, have you?"

"No. I was going to have a chat with him after talking to Spit at the hospital, but then I stopped off at the Travers' to get Lug-nut and I found the truck instead. I can't do everything for you."

He frowned. "You're not involved with him in some way, are you?"

"Freddy? Hardly. Why?"

"Just something you said. Never mind." He fidgeted and looked at his notebook.

I cast my mind back to our heated conversation in the hospital corridor. Then I laughed, remembering.

"Oh, you mean my fiancé? That was a joke. A Spit-joke. He knew what I meant."

"You're always joking about things like that. First Mr. Hoito, then Freddy. You're one very confusing lady."

"I like to be unpredictable," I said. "I like to play with people's expectations of me. What amazes me is what people will believe, once they decide you're different. It's fun."

"It's fun being different, is that it?"

"More or less. The problem is, once you get a taste for the unconventional, the normal becomes absurd."

"Like having a phone or electricity? Or co-operating with the police? You find these things absurd?"

"If you can manage without them, yes," I said.

"If you co-operated with us more, we'd be solving this thing quicker," Becker said. "And if you had a phone, then we could call to check on you instead of me hiking up here every damned day."

"Why does everyone suddenly have this thing about me being okay?" I said. "I've been living alone for three years with no trouble at all, and now everyone suddenly thinks I'm this soft, fluffy, vulnerable little cream-puff. What is it with you guys?"

"And if you had a phone," Becker went on, ignoring what I was saying, "I could call to ask you out instead of having to do it in person."

"What?"

"But that would probably be too conventional for you and you would just write me off as another one of those absurd normal guys you joke about."

"Are you asking me out?" I said.

"Well, yes."

"Are you allowed to do that?"

"Not really, seeing as you're involved in the case. If you'd just keep out of it, it wouldn't be so far out of line."

"Oh. That's why you want me to mind my own business? So you can ask me out? Holy shit."

"Watch your language. How about tomorrow? I'll pick you up."

"Tomorrow? I—well, sure. Yes. Thanks. What time?"

"Seven-thirty. I'll bring the statement for you to sign and I won't come in a police car, unless you think that might be fun and different."

"No police car."

"Right. Thanks for the coffee. See you." He almost ran out of the cabin, his face crimson. He left his pen behind. It was a nice pen, a Shaeffer. It was still warm.

Seventeen

Edge of the forest you lose your breath
trip over a sliver of bone
flat-nosed to the cinnamon loam
you laugh at death.
—Shepherd's Pie

Mark Becker and I are wading hand in hand through a spring meadow on soft-focus. We are looking for a secluded spot to spread out a blanket and have thumping, roaring, unprotected sex. I am so hot I am holding my crotch. Suddenly we are surrounded by a herd of large, ferocious white poodles, all snarling. Their teeth are long and yellow. Mark reaches for his gun...

I sat upright, totally bewildered, interrupted by a nightmare in the middle of a wet-dream. Lug-nut was hysterical, throwing himself against the door of the cabin and I was frozen solid in bed, one hand still glued to my privates, the other stubbornly refusing to respond to my command to grab the matches and light my bedside candle.

Becker had been right. I should have gone down to George's for a couple of nights. Now I was about to be raped and murdered and Becker would find me first. Or George.

I stayed in that horror-movie mode for what seemed like

hours, but was probably only a couple of minutes. Lug-nut was making too much noise for me to be able to hear what was outside, but I felt it—a presence, and I just sat there, hoping it would go away. I said "please" a couple of times, but I don't know who I was addressing or if I said it aloud. When the presence went away I was too frightened to say thank you.

The dog finally moved away from the door, still whining, and I lit my candle, slipped out of bed and tiptoed into the kitchen area, lighting every candle and oil lamp I could find. No phone, eh? No electricity. No gun. "I can take care of myself," I'd said. Well, that only applied for as long as I was certain that nobody was out to get me. I looked around the cabin. The only weapon I could find was my hatchet, a beautiful little Estwing with fine balance and a leather handle.

I picked it up and hefted it. Solid, yes, but with a reach of about eight inches. I supposed I could bonk an intruder on the head with it if he got close enough, but it would be a messy business. If I lived till morning, I resolved to ask George if I could borrow his shotgun—not that I know dick about guns, but a firearm would make me feel a hell of a lot braver than the hatchet made me feel.

I made a big fuss of Lug-nut, praising him for scaring off whoever it was—I had no illusions that it had been a raccoon.

Then I made coffee and settled in for the seige, propping myself up in the armchair next to the stove, cradling the hatchet.

When I woke up, I was stiff and sore. The hatchet had fallen to the floor and Lug-nut was guarding it with both paws, as if it might escape.

I groaned and stretched, discovering a nasty ging in my neck which prevented me from turning my head to the right. If somebody tried to sneak up on me from behind, I was dead.

I lit the burner under last night's coffee and sat at the kitchen table, whimpering. I have never been good with pain. Aunt Susan once told me never to go into the spy business. She said that the enemy would be able to get secrets out of me just by threatening to cut my fingernails.

Lug-nut was padding around the cabin with a distressed look on his face. I finally realized that he had to go out to do the thing that dogs must do, and I hauled myself upright and opened the door, following him to get a bead on the morning.

While the dog peed against the porch steps, I examined the dead squirrel nailed to the front door.

It was a big one. It had been shot in the head with what I guessed was a pellet rifle, then its belly had been split open. The guts spilled out artistically in a nice cascade of yuck. I threw up over the railing before going back to read the note, which was stuffed into what was left of the squirrel's mouth.

I handled the paper carefully, by the edges. "STICK TO YOUR GOATS," was all it said. It was made with cut-out newspaper letters pasted onto a piece of lilac-motif notepaper, slick with squirrel bits. Becker, I hoped, would be able to find fingerprints and maybe even find a pack of lilac notepaper in someone's desk.

I went back inside, poured coffee and was on my third consecutive cigarette before I noticed that my hands were shaking. It's all right for some people, I suppose, finding a gruesome body on a Monday, meeting a bear on a Tuesday and getting a maimed squirrel tacked to your door on a Wednesday, but it was way too much for me. I went sort of crazy. First thing I did, even before breakfast, was to roll a really big joint and smoke the whole thing.

According to my herbal remedies guide, dope is an analgesic, anti-asthmatic, antibiotic, anti-epileptic, antispasmodic and anti-depressant. It's a tranquillizer, an appetite stimulant, oxytocic, preventative and anodyne for neuralgia (including migraine), aid to psychotherapy and agent to ease withdrawal from alcohol and opiates. It's also great stuff in a crisis.

When I smoke dope, the clarity is wonderful. I see the veins in the leaves, the roughness of tree bark, I smell the earth and ideas flow like blood. The negative side of dope is that whatever is uppermost in your mind assumes a paramount importance. So, when Lug-nut and I went down to the barn a little later to do the chores, I carried the image of a dead squirrel on my back like a throbbing emotional hump.

I'd removed the corpse from the door. It had been jammed onto the nail which lives there holding up a scrap of paper and a pencil on a string. When I go out, I usually scrawl a note telling where I've gone and when I'll be back, just in case someone drops by. In the boonies, this is not interpreted as an invitation to burglary, but rather as a pleasant and neighbourly practice. It had been, in this case, abused.

After I pulled the squirrel off the nail, (it made a faint sucking noise which almost made me throw up again), I dumped it into a big plastic baggie and put it into the top compartment of the icebox, next to the block of ice. I put the note into another baggie and slipped it into my desk. Exhibits A and B.

In the barn I did the chores quickly, feeding the kids a bottle of warm milk stripped from Erma Bombeck's teat, in case they weren't getting enough the regular way. I doled out hay and grain with more than half my mind on who the hell had sent me the squirrel. I was so distracted I forgot to sing while I was milking, and production was down by several ounces, which made me feel guilty.

After the barn chores, I went up to George's place and slipped in to use the phone. George was up, bustling around the kitchen.

"Are you all right, Polly?" he said. "You look terrible."

I told him about my night-visitor and the squirrel, then asked him if I could borrow his gun.

"You are joking, yes?" he said.

"Nope. I don't want it loaded or anything, George. I just, you know, thought it would be a good thing to have. To wave around if I needed to. Sort of a talisman."

"Huh. A talisman for trouble, maybe," he said. "You don't have a firearms certificate, for one thing. It is registered to me, and if you were caught with it, I'd get the blame. Considering that you are spending all your time with that policeman, I think you are better off without it."

"Okay, okay, I was just asking." It was a stupid idea anyway.

"Maybe you had better stay here for a few days," George said, "until this mess is all settled." It was daylight now. I wasn't scared any more. I was angry.

"The cabin is my home, George. I'm not going to be harassed out of my home by some nutbar who likes to dismember squirrels. Besides, I've got Lug-nut and he did a pretty good job of scaring the guy away."

"Well, just keep him with you all the time, then."

"I was planning to."

I called the police station and after I sat on hold for five minutes, Becker picked it up.

"What is it, Polly? I'm in the middle of a meeting."

"Someone came up to the cabin last night."

"Who?"

"They weren't invited, Mark. I don't know. It was the middle of the night."

"Are you okay?"

"I'm fine. The dog went nuts and whoever it was went away, but he left a message behind that I think you should see."

"He left a note?"

"In a way. It said 'stick to your goats'."

"It said what?"

"And the piece of paper it was written on was shoved into the mouth of a dismembered squirrel nailed to my front door."

"Jeez. We'll be over. Don't go anywhere."

I said I wasn't planning to, and Becker hung up.

I accepted a cup of strong, black coffee from George, who had looked hard at my face as I was dialling, concluded that I was stoned and turned on the coffee-maker. George knew I smoked, disapproved, but considered it my business. He didn't lecture me, just asked me to acknowledge that this was no time to be on a different planet.

While we were waiting for the cops, Francy called.

"I'm back at home now," she said. "The place is Polly, they left it all like it was. The cop who brought me back last night just took down the tape and said it was okay to go inside. The kitchen is—oh, God. I went to sleep on the couch, just curled up in a little ball."

I remembered the state of things when I'd been in to get the dog food. Not a pleasant welcome. "That sucks, Francy. They should have warned you. Could you use a hand cleaning up?"

"Oh, yeah. Would you? I know it's a lot to ask, but I can't stay here without some sort of, you know, exorcism. Maybe we could burn some sage or something. If I don't stay here, I'll have to go stay with my in-laws in North Bay, and we kinda don't get along. I'd rather stay at home, but right now it's like I'm living in a haunted house, you know?"

I told her I would try to get over there in a couple of hours, that I had an appointment first, though I didn't explain what it was about. I figured she had a big enough case of the creeps as it was, and there was no reason to add to it. The cops had told her that Lug-nut was with me and she thanked me for taking him.

"That dog's never liked me, and the feeling is mutual," she said. "And now I'm scared he'd hurt Beth. You can keep him if you want." I told her that I'd be glad to, and that I would see her soon.

I went out to the porch with my coffee, where George was sitting on the steps with Lug-nut. The dog was sort of leaning against him while George scratched him behind the ears. Lug-nut turned his head as I came out and looked at me. Somehow, he knew he was mine, now. Or I was his. Whatever.

"How come Francy hated you so much?" I said.

"Huh?" George spun around.

"Lug-nut, not you."

"Oh. Well, he was John's dog," George said.

When Becker and Morrison arrived, I told the whole story again, and then the three of us hiked up to the cabin to collect the evidence. I was surprised that Morrison wanted to go— maybe he was curious about where I lived, or maybe he was aware of something starting up between me and Becker, and just wanted to be in the way, like a little brother. Anyway, the hike cost him and he was wheezing by the time we got to my front door.

I was sure that there was still the faint smell of grass in the air, but the cops didn't seem to notice it, or, if they did, they didn't comment. I opened the icebox and brought out the baggie with its grisly contents. Becker peered at it for a moment, then handed it to Morrison, who took it delicately between thumb and forefinger.

"Ugly," Becker said. I passed him the bag with the note and he shot me an approving glance. "You didn't handle it, then?"

"Only by the edges. Maybe you can get some prints from it."

"Maybe, maybe not, but it was good thinking, Polly."

Morrison sneered at Becker's tone and looked away. Then he laughed, a short, sharp bark. I followed his gaze and found he was looking directly at the puppet-head I had finished the night before, after Becker had left. It was a pretty accurate portrait, if I do say so myself. I had been proud of it up until then, but now I would have done anything to have it disappear off the face of the earth.

"What's your problem, Morrison?" Becker said. He hadn't noticed the head yet. When he did see it, I knew he would be uncomfortable—maybe flattered, but more likely just embarrassed. It would be like seeing your name scrawled in someone's math notebook in high school. Your name ringed with hearts and flowers and mottoes. I cringed.

"No problem, Becker. None at all," Morrison said, surprising me no end. He moved his bulky body between Becker and the work table, blocking his partner's view. I could have kissed him. I owed him one and he knew it, too.

Becker brought his gaze back to the baggie with the note inside, and Morrison caught my eye. He winked.

On the way back down to George's, Becker again tried to convince me to shack up with George for a while. I answered him the same way I had George. Both cops seemed to think I was just being stubborn for the sake of it.

"It's not like you have to prove anything, Polly," Becker

said with some exasperation. "We all know what an independent, self-sufficient woman you are. But this..." he shook the squirrel-baggie, "is proof that someone wants to hurt you. Being up there in that place with no phone means you're a sitting duck."

"Maybe she's holding out for some twenty-four-hour-a-day police protection," Morrison said, an innocent smile on his face. I shot him a look, but he let it slide right over him.

"I don't need protection," I said. "I have the dog, okay? Just drop it, would you please?" Becker dropped it, but, while Morrison was stowing the baggies in the trunk of the cruiser he tried again, very quietly.

"Be extra careful, please. I don't want to pick you up in a body bag tonight."

"Charming image."

"Charm is my strong suit, eh?" He smiled in a way that left my knees feeling funny. "I'll see you at seven-thirty, with another statement for you to sign. You're creating too much paperwork. Cut it out."

"Okay. I'll wait until you catch up," I said. "See you later."

I watched the cruiser bounce and swerve its way down the potholed sideroad and then went to ask George for the truck. Francy was waiting for me, and after visiting her, I planned to look in on Freddy at the dump. Not to do any detecting, mind you. Just to pass the time of day, that's all.

Eighteen

*I should have known
the shufflings of strangers
would unhinge me.*
—Shepherd's Pie

Blood sure stains, eh?" Francy said. She was on her knees scrubbing the kitchen floor. We had argued over who would actually do the dirty work. I thought it would be too much for her, emotionally speaking, if not physically, but she insisted. With both of us doing it, it wasn't so bad, like we were spring-cleaning before a visit from relatives.

"Yup. It's the protein," I said, then wished I hadn't. Protein meant meat and I suddenly saw John's body again. I was collecting beer bottles and sweeping up the broken glass. The morning sun streamed through the window and Beth sat in her carrier in the sunlight, playing with the dust in the air, batting at it with her tiny fists.

"Of course, any woman with her period knows that blood stains, I guess," Francy said. "Once something has blood on it and it dries, you can never get it out." It felt like we were in a Pinter play.

Cleaning up the kitchen didn't take us that long, once we got started. Francy poured bleach over the remaining dark patch on the floor-boards and I made tea while we waited for it to soak in, staring at it like it was a Polaroid we had just taken.

"How are you feeling, Francy? Were the police hard on you?"

"I'm okay. The police were very nice, actually. The big guy especially."

"Really?"

"He was the one who did most of the questioning. I was a real mess the last time I saw you, you know. Still in shock, I guess. But your aunt, she straightened me out."

It still hurt that Francy had sneaked away from me to be with Aunt Susan instead, but I didn't say so.

"Susan's good at straight-talk," I said. "Did you remember what happened?"

"Not really. At least, nothing more than what I already told you. I was drunk and pretty high when Eddie came over, and we had a couple more beers before John came home and started beating on me. Then we took off to the Schreier's place after Eddie clobbered John over the head. God, Polly. You should've seen Eddie go for him. It was like a scene in one of those Kung-Fu movies where the nerdy guy goes nuts. When John went down—I said this to the cops too, so don't worry— I did wonder if Eddie hit him too hard. Just wondered. Maybe that's why my head went blank after that. That's still all I remember."

"And you told the police all this."

"Yup. They didn't push it. It was a relief to know that Eddie didn't kill him with the wrench, though. The big cop said if he hadn't been shot he would've needed a few stitches, but the head-wound didn't kill him. I'm real glad about that."

"Did the cops ask you any, you know, leading questions? Anything that might incriminate you?"

"I don't know. I don't know what might do that. They asked about money. About how we were doing financially and if we owed money to anybody. Of course we did. We owed money all over the place, but not to anybody who would kill for it, I said."

"Was there anything pressing, though? Like a gambling debt?"

"They asked that, too. I told them about John selling that stuff to Rico. John said he wanted to get some new piece of machinery for the shop."

"You let him sell your table for a piece of machinery?"

"He said it was important. "

"Did you believe him?"

She looked at me and smiled a little. Her face was still swollen, the eye still half-closed. "It was never smart to show him you thought he was lying," she said. "Best thing to do was take him at face value. I told you I was planning to leave him anyway. That table didn't mean anything to me anymore. I was gonna be out of here."

"What about now?"

"Now? Dunno. Now maybe I'll stay. We'll see."

"How much money did John say he had to raise for his machinery?"

"Four hundred, he said. He got it, too, for the table and that old washstand that was in the hall. Amazing what old furniture is worth these days, eh?"

"So did he buy whatever he was going to buy, do you think?"

"I doubt it. He probably drank it or gambled it away or paid back whoever he owed four hundred bucks to. Unless he hid it somewhere and it's still here. Hey. You think it is?"

"Could be. We could look."

Francy stood up quickly. It was the most animated I'd seen her in a while. "Let's do it. I could use that money real bad right now."

We looked. It turned into a weird kind of treasure-hunt, opening all the drawers and checking behind pictures and under loose floorboards. Francy got it into her head that the police had looked for it already. She said that there were things that were a little bit out of place, a little wrong, but I explained that the cops hadn't even known about the money-thing until yesterday, and they hadn't had time. Then I remembered Eddie and the noise I'd heard upstairs. Had Eddie searched the house? Had he been looking for the money? Why? How could he have known about it?

I didn't tell Francy this. I only had the barest suspicion, and it still seemed likely that Eddie had come back to get the D.H. Lawrence book. It was confirmed a moment later when I asked Francy where it was and she couldn't find it.

"I put it back right here," she said, pointing to an empty space on the bookshelf. Francy had a lot of books, She bought them at garage sales and scavenged them from the dump. She was crazy about them and knew exactly what she had. If she said the book was missing, I believed her.

"I guess Eddie must have snuck in and grabbed it," Francy said. "Good for him." That explained that. I could cross him off the list. After all, there was no way Eddie could have been mixed up in a gambling debt. He wasn't even allowed to look at a deck of cards.

After about an hour of searching, we admitted defeat and went back to the kitchen. The house was very quiet, but it had lost its previous eerie feeling. It felt lived-in again, and now that the kitchen was back to normal, it was just a house.

We had another cup of tea and as I pulled my smokes out

of my jacket pocket, something else fell out and landed on the floor. We both bent to pick it up and narrowly missed knocking heads. We came up laughing and I opened my palm to show Francy what I had dropped. It was the golden crucifix I had taken from Poe. I had completely forgotten about it.

"That's pretty," Francy said. "Not your style, though."

"No kidding," I said and explained how I'd come to have it. "I thought maybe it might have been John's. He wore stuff like this, didn't he?"

"Yeah, but this wasn't his. It looks familiar, though. Like one I had once a long time ago." She reached out a finger to touch it. "It's solid," she said. "You think it's worth anything?"

"You'd think so. Here," I put it into her hand, "take it. Rico might give you a decent buck for it, eh?"

"You bet," she said, grinning. "I'm going to wear it first, though. My grandmother gave me one like this when I was thirteen or so. I lost it and she totally flipped out and then died. Maybe if I wear it for a while her ghost will toss some good luck my way." She fastened it around her neck and the heavy gold cross hung down between her breasts. It made her look pious, which I didn't think quite suited her, but I just grinned back.

"Sister Francis," I said. She lifted the pendant and looked at it closely.

"INRI," she read. "I always wondered what that meant."

"I think it's Latin, or Hebrew," I said, showing off my Catholic background. "Jesus with an 'I', of Nazareth. Rex, which is king, and Jerusalem, spelled with an 'I' too, or Judea or something."

"Oh. I thought it was somebody's name. Sort of like Henry."

My dream came back to me like a whack in the face. The

big red bear, the golden salmon. "You looking for 'Enry?" the bear had said. My unconscious mind must have been punning—putting the salmon in there because it was a fish, the symbol for Christ. (More Catholic stuff.) Cute. It had been an ugly dream, full of ugly foreboding. I was all at once certain that the crucifix was enormously significant and dangerous.

"Maybe you'd better not wear it until you're sure that someone isn't looking for it," I said, carefully.

"How come? You think someone's going to accuse me of stealing it? I don't think so," Francy said. "I'll just say I found it at the dump."

"That's what I'm afraid of."

"Don't be paranoid, Polly. Poe probably just found it in the road or something. Anyway, you gave it to me, right? I like it. I'm wearing it. Okay?"

"Hey, no sweat. Okay. Maybe it'll work as a talisman to ward off Carla and the Holy Lambers," I said.

Francy laughed bitterly. "It would take more than a gold cross," she said. "Try garlic and holy water."

Before I left I made sure that Francy was comfortable about staying there alone. She assured me that she was, explaining that she was used to it, because John had spent most of his time out partying or in his garage. We hadn't talked about his death much, but she certainly didn't seem to be wallowing in grief. I asked her if she needed anything in the way of groceries, seeing as she didn't have any transportation. She scribbled out a list which she handed to me along with a crumpled twenty-dollar bill.

"I really appreciate all you're doing for me, Polly," she said. "The sooner I can get things back to normal the better. I have to figure out what to do with myself now that John's out of the picture. Maybe you can teach me to drive, eh? He would never let me."

"I'd be glad to," I said. "Soon as the cops bring John's truck back."

She grimaced. "From what I hear, I'll have to bleach the inside of it before I can use it, anyway." I'd forgotten that. There had been bloodstains in the cab. It would be a long time before Francy was able to erase the memory of John's death from her life. I just wished, a little, that she wasn't so happy about it. It looked so suspicious.

"Well, we can always re-upholster," she added, brightening. Her smile pulled the skin tight on the scarred side of her face, where it reflected the light from the window like a piece of stretched plastic. For a moment, her eyes flashed almost red.

Lug-nut was waiting for me in the back of the pick-up. He had stayed there when I drove up to the house, and when I got out, he had eyed me nervously as if he were afraid I had brought him back for good. He seemed to have no interest in jumping out and checking up on his old territory. I didn't blame him. His life at the Travers' place hadn't exactly been puppy heaven. I backed out and headed for the dump.

I had prepared for my chat with Freddy by slinging a couple of full green garbage bags in the back as an excuse for going there. I wasn't sure just what I was planning to say, and I didn't know what I wanted from him. If he knew anything about what had happened after he had clobbered Spit over the head, Becker and Morrison would have wormed it out of him by now. Freddy might not even be at the dump. He could be locked up in a cell at the Laingford cop-shop, facing assault charges. Still, Freddy had always been reasonably friendly to me and if he was on duty, there was a chance that he might tell me something he wouldn't tell the cops. It was worth a try.

He wasn't in his shack when I drove up to it. I saw him off in the distance, poking through the "wood only" pile with a stick. I waved and he came over quickly, as officious as ever. As soon as he was close enough, he hollered, "Whaddya got?"

Freddy was a bean-pole, well over six feet tall, with enormous hands and feet and ears to rival Prince Charles's. He looked like an older version of Eddie Schreier, same sticky-outy Adam's apple, same gangling walk. It was probably something in the local water.

"Hey, Freddy," I said. "Just a couple of bags of household. You know. Food stuff. Unrecyclable plastic."

He squinted at the dog standing guard over the garbage bags in the back of the truck. Lug-nut was growling, his hackles raised, which surprised me. Freddy was about as menacing as an old shoe. He kept his hands to himself for once, though. Normally he would have reached out and sort of felt up the bags, trying to guess what was inside, making sure that they were what I said they were.

"That's Travers's dog, ain't it?" he said.

"Mine now. Francy didn't want to look after him any more, after what happened." I could have said she'd always hated the dog because it was John's, but that would have been telling.

"Ugly, ain't he?"

I laughed. "Well, head-on he is, but if you catch him in profile, he's not so bad. Sort of noble, if you work at it. Hush now, Luggy. That's enough."

Freddy waited until I removed the garbage from the truck, out of Lug-nut's reach, then he took them from me and started to carry them over to the household garbage pit. I followed him, desperately trying to come up with a way to get a conversation going. Usually, Freddy was the one with the opening gambit, but this time he was as tight-lipped as a Tory senator.

"It must be weird being here alone after a body was found here, eh?" I said. He grunted and kicked at a chicken bone with his foot. I tried again. "Lots of people coming around trying to get you to talk about it, I'll bet."

He looked at me slant-wise. "Nope," he said. "You're the only one. You and the cops."

"They talked to you, did they?" Here was an opening. It was just like the women's magazines. Draw him out. Get him to talk about himself.

"They interrogated me is more like it," Freddy said. "Nazis, both of 'em. Specially the fat one. They came in here with some damn fool story Morton cooked up to explain the lump on his head. He blamed me, eh?" Freddy was looking at me carefully, gauging my reaction.

"He did??" Surprise. Outrage.

"Yup. Said I hit him. That's a crock of shit if I ever heard one."

"I saw him at the hospital yesterday," I said. "He's doing fine, but he did take quite a knock to the head. I guess he's confused. Maybe his story is a little exaggerated, eh?"

"Huh. I'll bet it's mostly from the hangover. He drank most of a jug of Amato's hooch on Sunday, then he fell down outside the hut." Freddy pointed. "Knocked his head on the cement step there. Out cold. I dragged him over to his hearse and put him inside to keep warm while he slept it off. Did him a favour and that's how he pays me back."

It could easily have happened like that, I supposed, but I must have looked sceptical, because Freddy turned nasty.

"That's what you wanted to know, ain't it? You talked to Morton and he told you his fairy-tale, and then you come nosing over here to get my side of it. Just like the cops. Meddling."

"Freddy, I just came to drop off some garbage, that's all."

"Two measly bags fulla paper, more like. I know my business, and you, Missy, should know yours. Meddling in what doesn't concern you. You should stick to your goats."

I froze. A vision of the ruined squirrel swam before me and I tottered a bit, remembering.

"What did you say?" I said.

"I said you should mind your own business. I got no quarrel with you, and I don't want to start one." He was standing very close to me—close enough that I could smell the musty coat he was wearing and see the blackheads on his skin. It was very still and there was nobody at the dump but me, Freddy, Lug-nut and a couple of seagulls. I backed away, slowly.

"Okay, Freddy. I'll stick to my goats. You bet."

"Atta girl. That way you don't get hurt."

I hopped in the cab of the truck and beat a hasty retreat, my heart pounding. That had been a threat, no question. What I couldn't figure out was what Freddy had to do with the whole thing. Was he the one John owed money to? Was he the murderer? As far as I knew he had no connection with John or his friends, but I was fooling myself if I thought I knew everything that went on in Cedar Falls. It seemed the more clues I found, the more confused I was becoming.

If John had been shot before midnight, as I believed he had, Freddy couldn't have killed him, because he was drinking with Spit at the dump. Was Freddy an accomplice? Was it all set up beforehand? I doubted it. Although there was a phone in the dump hut, the killer would hardly have called Freddy while Spit was there and said: "Knock him out. I'm coming over with a body I want to dump." Would he? I would have to ask Spit if there had been any phone calls while he was whooping it up with Freddy.

I was quite sure that Freddy had been responsible for my scare of the night before, though. He had as good as admitted it. The question was, should I tell Becker about it or keep it to myself?

If I told Becker, would he search the dump hut, maybe find a package of lilac-motif notepaper and a newspaper with letters cut out of it? I decided it was probably best to drop it. I had told Freddy I would mind my own business, and around here, if you say you'll do a thing, people generally believe you. I'd just have to be more discreet, that was all.

On my way down the dump road, I saw a tall figure walking slowly along the gravel verge, head bent, shoulders hunched. It was Eddie and as I slowed to give him a ride, he looked up mournfully. He had a black eye, a fresh one, as ugly as the one Francy had been wearing on Monday. What was this, an epidemic? One thing was certain, this bruise at least had not been caused by John Travers.

I reached over to roll down the window on the passenger side.

"Hey Eddie. Want a lift?"

"Sure. Thanks." He climbed inside.

"Don't tell me. It was a doorknob, right? You walked into a door." It was tactless, I know, but I'm like that.

He grinned. "Yeah, that's right. Late at night. You gotta pee. You get up and smack! Right into the bathroom door." Back in theatre school we called that "follow-up"—when you take a suggestion from a fellow improviser and run with it. Eddie would have been good at improv.

"You okay?" I said.

165

"Yeah, thanks. You should see the door." His jokey tone sounded hollow.

"Your dad back from that conference yet?" It was a shot in the dark, and it earned a bull's-eye. Eddie winced, as if he had been shouting "Dad" loud enough for me to hear it. So it was Samson who had hit him. Figured. Samson was short and mean as a weasel.

"Yeah. I mean, yes," Eddie said. "He came back yesterday. Why? You want to talk to him?"

"Not especially. Listen, Eddie. I saw you over at the Travers' place yesterday. I mean, we saw each other, right?" He blushed. Welcome to the club, I thought.

"Maybe," he said.

"Maybe nothing. I saw you. It's none of my business what you were doing over there, so I won't even ask, okay? It's between you, me and Lady Chatterley."

Eddie smirked. "I don't know why my Mom's all upset about that book," he said. "It's pretty tame, really."

"Read on," I said. "It gets better. What I wanted to ask you though, is, did you tell anyone you saw me over there? I was wondering if you'd mentioned to someone that you saw me."

He seemed grateful that I wasn't probing—I guessed he got enough of that at home. If he wanted to tell me he went back for the book, and if he wanted to say who had whacked him in the eye, he would. It didn't matter. He thought for a moment.

"Well, I might have mentioned that you took the dog, eh? I thought that was cool. John never treated that dog right and Francy never liked him either."

"So your parents knew I was over there. Was anyone else at home when you mentioned it?"

"Well, no, but we had adult Bible class at our place later,

and the text was Lazarus, so we got to talking about dogs and I might have said something again then. I don't remember. I just thought it was good that you took him. Real Christian. Mom thought so too. Real Christian charity, she said."

Great. So most of Cedar Falls probably knew I'd been over to the Travers' place to get the dog, and somebody was suspicious enough to go check to see if I'd found the truck and the gun. They'd taken the gun and told Freddy to nail a dead squirrel to my door. Charming. I was no closer to the truth, though.

"Eddie," I said. "Someone's trying to scare me off asking questions about John's murder. Do you have any idea who that might be?"

"Heck, no. I don't know nothing about it. I was just over there for a minute, honest. I hardly saw you. I was just getting that book. I went in the back way and when I heard you downstairs I got out of there. Please don't tell my parents, okay? My Dad'll kill me. I'll read it and then I'll give it back. I wasn't stealing, I swear."

He was freaking out and totally missing the point. It seemed cruel to ask him any more questions, so I let it go. "I know you weren't stealing, Eddie," I said. "Francy wants you to read the book. Don't worry about it."

"Are you, like, helping the police or something?"

"Sort of," I said. "Just asking questions." I glanced sideways and saw his face turn wooden.

"Questions are dangerous," he said. "Sometimes, you get hurt."

"Everyone keeps saying that," I said, "but isn't the truth worth getting hurt for?"

"I don't know. Mostly, I think the truth is stupid. You can let me out here, Ms. Deacon. Thanks for the ride."

I pulled over just outside the entrance to the Schreier's driveway. Samson Schreier's pickup was parked near the door and there was smoke coming from the chimney. Home sweet home. I watched Eddie unfold his gangly limbs from the cab. I liked the kid, but there was definitely something amiss in Jesusland. I hoped that he would be able to cope with it, whatever it was. He was too old to hope for Children's Aid protection. I swallowed hard. When an adult suspects child abuse, what do we do when the kid is out of the jurisdiction of the act? Pray?

I headed back out to the highway, digging Francy's grocery list out of my front pocket. Here was something pro-active I could do to make the world a better place. I could help out my friend. I had a few things to buy for her, and I decided to pick up a bottle of brandy just in case Becker turned out to be interested in coming back up to my place for a nightcap later. Hope springs eternal, and all cops like brandy. I knew this was true: I had read it somewhere.

Nineteen

The shape of your skin,
The smell of your bones,
the sound of your hair when you're
dancing alone...
—Shepherd's Pie

The extremities of the puppet were finished. The head, hands and feet were complete, sculpted to resemble Mark Becker's. I had molded a small pair of regulation police boots and I'd made one of the hands curl around thin air, ready for grasping weapons or food, like a G.I. Joe doll. The head, I have to admit, was dead on. Now I just had to make the body, and to do that correctly, I had to do some research.

In order for a marionette to work the way it is supposed to, the person building it must have a reasonable grasp of basic anatomy. If you make a knee joint the wrong way round, the finished puppet will walk funny. If you miscalculate the distance from shoulder to hand, your puppet's knuckles will drag. But even the most anatomically correct puppet will remain lifeless until you give it character. Character comes from how the joints are fitted, which way a puppet leans when it walks. No human head is fastened squarely in the middle of the shoulders. If the head sprouts from a point close to the chest, the puppet will slouch. If you attach it towards the back, the puppet will strut. To get the character of the body right, I had no choice but to study the life-model, preferably in the nude.

I started to get ready for my date with a policeman by heating the water for a bath. While I waited, I picked up a stray lump of clay and started rolling it absently between my fingers. Five minutes later I had a perfect little puppet penis, testicles and all. Nothing monstrous. Just lovingly detailed. I felt shy for having made it, but I couldn't destroy it, so I hid it in my stash box. Maybe later I could wire it up with the rest of the bits—just another moving part.

After my bath, which I had in the zinc tub in front of the fire, I ached with indecision about what to wear. Apart from the fact he was a cop, what did I know about him? Here I was planning to jump him and all I knew was his name and profession. How could I possibly jump him if I was wearing the wrong clothes?

I tried on everything I had, which took about four minutes, then I repeated the process a couple of times.

There were three ensembles to choose from. First, my "please, at least try to look respectable" outfit, a sober, black wool suit circa 1948, which had been my mother's. It was perfect for weddings, funerals, and anything official which required a skirt. Outfit number two was for parties at which I wanted to look sleazy. I hadn't worn it since Toronto. Narrow black jeans, a cropped, skin-tight tank-top and a jacket which was meant to be undone when it got too warm. Wearing it in Cedar Falls or Laingford would be reputational suicide.

Outfit number three was for meetings with people who wanted me to build puppets for them. It included a clean item from my shirt collection, a pair of trousers which weren't stained and my city boots. I went with number three, but the shirt was silk and I accessorised, even. (My earrings and belt buckle were both silver.)

I don't own any make-up, so it wasn't an option, but if I'd had some it would have meant another half hour wrecking my complexion with three increasingly disastrous applications and three scrubbings off.

I put on chapstick, though.

I got down to George's at seven and found a note on the door.

> "Gone to the harvest dance at the Community Hall with your aunt. Join us? Will run past midnight.
> George.
>
> P.S. Night chores are done. Will be back tomorrow."

Tomorrow? Aunt Susan and George were having a pyjama party? Oh God, if Aunt Susan married him and moved to the farm it would mean I'd have to go. My aunt was close enough in Laingford.

I let myself in and borrowed a shot of single malt scotch from George's bottle of Glen Lach (clear your throat and mumble the next bit) Flanghlahlyn. I'd had a shock. I'd suspected that there was something up, but staying overnight? Was it wise? Or perhaps he would be sleeping on the couch. That was it. They'd stay up late playing cribbage and he'd fall asleep on the couch. Susan would cover him up with a blanket and make cocoa. Hah. No way. They were doing it.

Becker arrived in a black Jeep Cherokee. It was spit-polished and very big. Lug-nut stood on the porch, barking, and wouldn't stop until I got in front of him and held his mouth shut. Becker stayed in the truck.

"Lug-nut, no. Friend. Hush." I let go of his muzzle and he

gave me a look straight out of a cartoon. I called to Becker.

"It's okay. He just doesn't recognize your vehicle."

Becker got out and came over to where I held Lug-nut's collar just in case. He was wearing designer casuals, expensive cowboy boots and that dizzying aftershave. I couldn't help thinking that he must be making good money for a policeman. I mentally reviewed what I was wearing and thought about going back to change into the party outfit.

"Hey, Lug-nut," Becker said, reaching out to the dog with a friendly hand. "We're pals, remember?" Lug-nut sniffed his hand and relaxed, then wagged his tail, so I let go of his collar.

"I imagine, like me, he thinks you might be a different person, out of uniform," I said.

Becker held out his hand again, this time to me. "Mark Anthony Becker, ma'am. I work for the government."

"Pauline Deacon," I said, taking it. "I work for food."

I invited him in for a scotch, and he came, willingly.

I always kept another bottle of Glen-thing stashed up in the cabin and when the one at George's got low, I switched them. George pretended it was his magic bottle. It was our own private Santa Claus game.

"Thanks," Becker said, as I handed him one. "And where is your chaperone this evening, may I ask?"

"He's with a lady at the harvest dance down in the village hall," I said. "I thought we could drop in, maybe."

"I can't dance," Becker said.

"You wouldn't need to. I just want to give George something," I said. I had a condom in my pocket that I wanted to give my old friend, just to let him know that I was aware of what was going on.

"Sure. No problem. So he's gone out, eh? You house-sitting?"

I stared at him. He was wearing exactly the same expression Harold Finley wore in grade eleven whenever he asked me if I was babysitting. Harold used to come over and we'd neck.

"I do have my own place," I said, "but yeah, I guess I am."

"Do you have to feed the animals as well?"

"The goats? Not till tomorrow morning. George did the evening milking before he left."

"You have to milk them too?"

"Yup."

"By hand? Like a cow, right?"

"Hey, Becker, don't tell me you've never seen a goat."

"I've never seen a goat."

"I said don't say that. Really?"

He grinned and knocked back his Glen-alcohol. "Show me one," he said.

We threw on barn coats and I gave him the grand tour. He liked the goats, I think. They can be enchanting en masse. When a visitor comes to the barn, the goats don't say much, but they all start watching. If they're chewing cud, they'll be too relaxed to get up, but they'll crane their necks to keep you in view. The young ones will slip out of their pens (the gaps in the fencing are wide enough for kids to pass through) and prance around, acting cute.

I introduced him formally to each goat.

"Donna Summer, Julian of Norwich, Erma Bombeck, Annie Oakley, Kim Campbell, Rose Marie, Vicki Gabereau, Loreena Bobbitt, Princess Diana, Susannah Moodie, Cher, Saint Bernadette and Mother Theresa," I said.

"Hi," he said and got right in there, scratching faces and touching noses.

"This is Pierre Trudeau," I said, guiding Becker down to the pen at the end where Old Pierre, a mournful, testosterone-driven love machine with a face like a muppet, waggled his stinking beard and moaned in welcome.

"The sire of the herd. Don't touch him," I said, but it was too late. Becker drew his hands back gently and looked at me.

"He pisses on his beard when a doe's in heat," I said. "Mother Theresa is raring to go and poor old Pierre can smell it. He's been nuts all day." The musk glands behind Pierre's horns would have been giving the old goat a twenty-four hour, hot oil treatment.

Becker put his hands to his nose and sniffed.

"Whoa. Does this come off?"

"Soap and water, no problem," I said. "Just don't wipe your hands on your pants."

He lifted his hands like a surgeon after a scrub. "I won't."

I caught a flying goat kid as it leaped up into Pierre's manger. "This is Keanu. The new stud. He's only a week old and he's already sucking up to his dad."

"Pleased to meet you," Becker said, shaking its small hoof and rubbing its head. "I hereby anoint you with the body odour of the holy goat. Now can I wash my hands?"

We walked back up slowly, not saying much, enjoying the silence of the evening. I showed him where the bathroom was, then went back to the kitchen to rinse our glasses. He came out a few moments later, still holding his hands upside-down in the air.

"There was no towel in there," he said. I found one in the hall linen cupboard and draped it ceremoniously over his hands. He smiled, then gasped, crossed his eyes and went stiff.

"Dr. McCoy," he said, "that goat-poison. It's—it's got me. I can't move!"

"I'm a doctor, Jim," I said. "Not a spin dryer." However, I moved in and dried each of his fingers carefully one by one. Then I took the towel away with a flourish. "Voilà. You are healed."

He sniffed his hands. "I can't smell anything? Can you?"

I sniffed in his general direction. "Well, there's a strong smell of Ivory soap, overlaying a more subtle, yet lingering odour—" a worry line appeared between Becker's eyebrows "—of something male, some particular—"

"I'll wash them again," Becker said.

"I've got it. Old Spice, is it? Or Paco Rabanne?"

"Obsession for Men," Becker said. "My ex gave it to me."

"Oh. Well. I like it."

"She hated it. It was a divorce-iversary present. I sent her sexy underwear. It's a thing we do every year."

"A weird thing."

"Yeah, well, you gotta keep laughing, you know."

"Any kids?"

"Bryan's with his mom," Becker said. "I get him alternate weekends. He's seven."

"Anything else I should know about? You have a Doberman, too, right? She's in your Jeep."

"No Doberman. I do have a fish, though. Called Wanda."

"In the Jeep?"

"Yup. There's an attack tank in back. Watch her like a hawk. She's the jealous type."

We were standing very close.

"You didn't, you know, touch your stinky goat hands anywhere else, did you?" I said.

"I might have rubbed my face."

I started sniffing.

"Maybe over to the left. Yeah. About here."

He was a pretty good kisser, for a cop. There was no hurry, just a mutual and leisurely reading of the lips.

"Umm, Bkrr?"

"Mm?"

"You got plans for tonight?"

"Mmm. I was thinking of taking this interesting woman I know out for dinner and a game of pool in Laingford."

"Lucky her. Anyone I know?"

"Well, she's about your height, got a tiny scar on her chin just like that one . . ."

"You're dating my evil twin sister, Hydra? You deceiving cad."

We tussled. My hair got mussed, and he popped a button on his designer shirt. It was very satisfactory and we both hit pause at the same moment, which was better still.

"Let's drop off whatever at the village hall and then go have dinner," he said. Lug-nut knew I was going, and as we left, he settled down agreeably on the porch to wait. Life was working out just fine.

There were dozens of vehicles in the Cedar Falls Community Hall parking lot. Lots of Jeeps, pickups and 4x4s, although very few of them were new. Lots of junkers, too. The people of Cedar Falls aren't rich. If they were, they'd be living in Laingford.

Becker squeezed his SuperJeep between a dented Ford van and a rusty pickup with wide tires, splattered with dried mud. I hoped the pickup boys didn't leave before we did, or we'd find rude things scrawled on the Jeep windows when we got back. The pickup boys were trouble. They were four young guys from the Cedar Falls Chairworks, renting a house together in the woods. They'd been rowdy in the village and were locally suspected of having had a game or two of mailbox-baseball along the River road.

Frankly, they scared the heck out of me, but they weren't doing much more than being obnoxious. They were of drinking age and they had jobs, which made them cocky and often really stupid. Still, I would have been happier if Becker hadn't parked right next to them. I didn't say anything, though. I figured he probably recognized the truck and parked there on purpose, being a cop and all.

The hall was fairly crowded and very dimly lit. The music was live and too loud—it always is at community dances. The bar was doing a brisk business, and there were plenty of people on the dance-floor.

"Polly! Nice to see you here. Who's your friend?" It was Donna-Lou Dermott, the egg-queen. Donna-Lou, who still hand-delivered to a few select customers, also kept the Cedar Falls grapevine in working order.

"Hi, Donna-Lou. This is my friend Mark. Mark? Donna-Lou." They shook hands. Becker had gone pink.

"From the city, ain't you? Nice boots."

"Thanks," Becker said.

Otis Dermott, well oiled, came up behind his wife and draped an arm over her solid little shoulders. I knew that the holy rollers generally didn't approve of drinking and dancing, but maybe Otis and Donna-Lou were an exception. Otis seemed awfully pleased to see me. In the state he was in, he was probably awfully pleased to see anybody at all.

"It's Susan Kennedy's Polly. Hello, girl. With a man, eh?"

"Otis," Donna-Lou said.

"You look familiar," Otis said, squinting at Becker. "I seen you before?"

"I'm not from around here," Becker said.

"Ain't I seen him before?" Otis asked his wife.

"Nice to meet you both," Becker said and moved away into the crowd.

"Yeah. See you later, eh?" I said, then followed him.

"I'd rather not stay too long," Becker said.

"We're just checking in to say hi. George invited us. Courtesy call, that's all. I take it you don't want to be recognized."

"That's right. I may need to question some of these people later."

"Wouldn't they be more likely to talk if they knew you out of uniform?"

"Let's just find Mr. Hoito and his lady, okay?"

I picked out George and Susan, sitting at a table crowded with empty glasses near the band. Their heads were close together and their gazes were locked. They just had to be doing it.

The band started playing an old country favourite, suitable for stomping around to, and the dance-floor filled quickly, blocking my view.

"We might as well have a beer while we're here. You want one?" Becker's face was very close to my ear, and it startled me. "Hey, you okay?" he said.

"Yup. I'd love a beer. Thanks. Shall I meet you over there?"

"Where are they?"

"The table next to the band on the right. George's hair is directly below a blue stage light, so he's kind of glowing. You can't miss him."

"I'll be over. You know where the washrooms are?"

"Downstairs in the basement. Make noise going down, eh?"

"Why. Are there snakes?"

"Sort of. You're off duty, right?"

"Absolutely."

I waded through the crowd, dodging the twirlers and stompers as best I could. When I reached George and Susan's table, they were gone, but their jackets were still there, so I guessed they must be up jumping around. I don't care for dancing, myself. I always feel cumbersome and very aware of how silly we all look.

Then George and Susan danced by the table, laughing and looking radiant, not the least bit silly at all. I guess it's how you feel when you're doing it that counts.

When the music ended they returned to the table, holding hands. When they saw me they smiled and didn't let go, so it was out in the open, at least.

"Where's the fellah?" Susan said. "George said you might drop by with a gentleman caller. He wouldn't tell me who it was." I glanced at George, surprised.

"Why not?" I said.

"He just said you had a date with a government man," she said. "Who is he? It's not like I have anything against civil servants, not that I have any say in the matter anyway. Incidentally, George has told me that you know that we hid Francy's whereabouts from you. I'm sorry about that, Polly, but you must remember that we're dealing with the police. They're a nasty, brutish, impolite lot, and it's best to have no dealings with them at all."

"One round coming up," Becker said, setting down four beers. "Ms. Kennedy, good to see you again. Mr. Hoito, how are you?" My aunt had been speaking loudly, in order to be heard above the music. Her eyebrows did a beautiful double-take, but she recovered quickly.

"Why, Detective Becker. What a surprise. Drinking on duty are you?" I think she meant it as a joke.

"I'm not working right now, ma'am," Becker said. "Here. It's Canadian." He handed her a plastic glass of beer.

"Oh. Thank you kindly. But I must excuse myself for a moment first. Polly? Coming?" I came. I know a summons when I hear one. I plunged through the crowd after her, and she slipped her arm through mine.

"What on earth are you doing? This is your gentleman caller? An Ontario Provincial Police officer? You must be off your head. No wonder George wouldn't tell me."

"He's a nice man, Susan," I said.

"Hmmmph."

Susan started hissing at me after we'd peed for appearance's sake and were washing our hands at the sink.

"I think it's very foolish, considering your lifestyle, to think for a moment that you'll have anything in common other than sex. He's good-looking, I'll give him that, but he's a policeman, Polly. A copper."

A young woman burst into the washroom at a run, followed closely by three or four friends. She made a bee-line for the wheelchair toilet and proceeded to vomit loudly into the bowl.

"What about you?" I said, turning back to Susan after assessing the situation and deciding that the girl didn't need another witness. "You and George don't have much in common either. Yet it's obvious that you're getting physical. What's wrong with sex?"

"Nothing at all. With the right person."

"And do you think that George is the right person for you?"

"Why? Do you think he isn't?"

"I bet you fifty bucks the guys are having the exact same conversation right now," I said.

They weren't. We came up to find that the bar and the

dance-floor had emptied. The musicians had stopped playing and were standing together behind the lead microphone, as if they were discussing whether or not to join everybody else outside in the entrance way.

There was a fight going on, and it sounded big.

Twenty

When you want to know the colour of the night, girl,
ask the band.
–Shepherd's Pie

"**What's going on?**" I called over to the band.

It was loud outside. One of the musicians answered, but I couldn't hear him.

"Sorry?"

The guy stepped up to the mike and spoke into it. The sound-technician had left the setting on reverb, and it sounded like the voice of God.

"We just finished a song and someone screamed real loud over by the door and then all hell broke loose. People swinging punches. Place cleared like a loose bowel. Pardon me, ma'am." Behind him, the rest of the band snickered manfully. We headed for the door.

A wall of people jammed the exit. There was the smell of adrenaline in the air and the crowd was pressing in to get a look-see, chattering away like greedy gray squirrels at a city picnic. It was first come, first served, and we were late. We joined the jam, at the very back.

"When I heard that gun go off, I spilled my beer on my wife," one man said. "She'll kill me for sure when we get home."

"That was no gun," the man next to him said. "Someone threw a chair."

"Oh? Geez, so I spilled it for nuthin, then. Well, I'll get hell anyway. Who screamed? You see?"

"Some woman. I was over by the bar. Fight broke out, four or five guys, right about where we're standing." Both men immediately looked at the floor, possibly for blood.

"Excuse me," I said. "Can we get by, please?" The man who had spilled his beer on his wife glared at me.

"Wait your turn, dear," he said.

Susan tapped me on the shoulder.

"Window," she said, pointing.

We couldn't see much because it was dark outside and the windows hadn't been washed since Trudeau's reign, but there was definitely a brawl going on. Lots of inarticulate profanity and what looked like some unpleasantness with fists.

"Do you think anyone's called the cops?" I said.

"There's a policeman there already," Susan said. "There he is, look. He just pulled the little one off the big one."

"Oh, God. Becker. I have to get in there."

"Why? You the cavalry?"

"No. The girlfriend," I said. "Is there a back way?"

Susan gave me an eyebrow, then made for the washrooms again. I followed.

Next to the ladies' room was a door marked FIRE EXIT ONLY—ALARM WILL SOUND. Susan pushed it open. I'm more Canadian than she is. I gasped. She chuckled.

"The alarm's never been connected," she said.

It was cold enough outside to see our breath. We walked along the side of the building, around behind the kitchen-extension and out to the front, where a set of stairs led up to the foyer of the old building.

The exterior lights were on, and it looked like a stage set, the brawlers front and centre, with a Greek chorus made up of Cedar Falls citizens, grouped artistically on the steps, beer glasses in hand.

We stuck to the bushes, finding ourselves a bit closer to the ringside than was comfortable. I've never been big on violence, and while I may have jumped in a time or two when Francy was in danger, I certainly had no intention of getting involved for Becker's sake. He was holding his own.

The six guys fighting were the pickup boys, whose names I didn't know, versus Becker and Vern, a giant, simple man I'd seen occasionally in the village. It was four against two, but three of the pickup boys were stagger-drunk. The other was right out of his mind with rage about something, but he was tiny, shorter than Susan is, and thinner than a winter birch.

Vern was easily identifiable as the focus of the trouble. The pickup boys were trying to kill him, but they weren't having much luck. Their opponent stood his ground like a front-end loader, baffing them away with hands the size of dinner plates. Whenever two or more went for the giant at once, Becker stepped in and pulled them off, which meant a battle every time. Vern's fists had dealt some stinging blows, but this just seemed to enrage the boys, the same way a rolled up magazine enrages a wasp.

They were all yelling.

"Back off now before somebody gets hurt."

"Fucking touch my motherfucking girlfriend fucking asshole?"

"Neil, fucking help us, man."

"Fucker smacked me right in the face."

"Fucking kill him!"

From the giant came a low rumbling sound, like a semi out on the highway, getting closer. His eyes were half-closed and he had a serene, beatific smile on his face. His tweed cap hadn't budged from his head.

Susan and I had crept round to where George and Otis Dermott stood near the front steps. Otis toasted us with his plastic glass.

"Vern'll blow any minute now," Otis said.

"Why isn't anybody helping?" I said to George. "Surely three of you guys could go in there and help pull them off?"

"They started it," Otis said. "Vern won't get hurt none, although your cop friend may get hurt if he don't stay out of the way."

I raised an eyebrow, Susan style. "Cop friend?" I said.

Otis leered. "I remembered him," he said. "I seen him talking to Freddy at the dump. You go for a man in uniform, eh? I should have wore my army coat." He wheezed with laughter and swigged at his beer.

I looked at George and Susan. They gazed blandly at the fight, avoiding my eye. When I looked back at Otis, he was doing the same thing.

"It's like this, eh?" Otis said, after a moment. "Them boys have been making trouble since they got to Cedar Falls. Everybody knows, but nobody's been able to catch them at it."

"This fight could be classified as trouble, couldn't it?" I said. "Grounds for arrest?"

"What good would that do? They wouldn't get a court-date till God knows, and there'd be worse trouble in between. Listen up. Them boys were stupid enough to pick a fight with Vern, they should take their medicine here and now. He won't kill them."

Vern's rumble was getting louder. The little guy was still

calling him a motherfucker and poking at his underbelly with a pair of pointy little fists.

"Why's that little guy screaming about his girlfriend?" I said.

"Vern felt her up, eh? I seen it. She was staggering around and she bumped into him and almost fell over so he caught her. He held her wrong and she screamed and ran for the bathroom and the boys went for him. Vern broke a chair getting outside, eh? He knows he's not supposed to fight."

Becker was bleeding from a cut over his left eye. Every time he pulled a boy off Vern's back, the boy lashed out with wild punches and kicking feet.

"That guy should get out of it," a young, bearded fellow said to Otis.

"He's a cop, eh?" Otis said. "Probably feels obliged."

"I guess that's why he's not hitting back. If he gets decked, I guess we should go in there, eh?"

"If he gets decked," I said, "the guy who decked him will be charged with assaulting a police officer." Both men looked at me.

"He should be minding his own business," Otis said. I gazed back at them. They were grinning.

I looked over at Becker. He was wiping blood away from his eye.

"Becker! Hey!" I said, raising my voice. He looked up, frowned and hurried over to me. The pickup boys, sensing a void, moved in on Vern.

"You should move away from here," Becker said. "You could get hurt."

Vern blew. It was like a Marvel Comic.

Biff! Blowie! Splat! Ka-boom!

Four pretty pickup boys, laid in a row. The crowd went

wild, hooting, cheering and stamping their feet. Vern swept the cap off his head with a flourish, bowed gravely to the audience and shambled away into the night. The crowd started moving back inside, while three or four big, strong fellows stepped forward to check on the boys. They were conscious, but groggy.

Becker stared wildly at the four prone figures on the grass, turned to see the last of Vern as he disappeared into a thicket of fir trees and then turned back to me.

"Jesus," he said.

"You're bleeding," I said and handed him my backup hanky.

George and Susan came up, arm-in-arm, as if they'd just returned from an evening at the opera.

"You may need a stitch or two," Susan said.

"I'm fine," Becker said.

"You did well, son," George said. "Just leave them be, now."

"I've got to make a phone call," Becker said.

"To the station?" I said.

"Where do you think? There's been an assault."

"Becker," I said, "you're off-duty, remember?"

"It was just a little misunderstanding," Susan said.

"They've learned their lesson," George said. "Kevin, there, will drive them home. He knows where they live."

Becker was breathing through his nose. He was very pale and his hands were clenched into fists at his side. There was a nasty little pause.

"Jim?" I said. "James T. Kirk? Speak to me. Is it? Oh, God! Not . . . the goat poison?"

The corner of his mouth twitched.

"Who's James T. Kirk?" Susan said. Becker said nothing,

kept on breathing. His eyes were bugging out. I stepped in closer.

Becker's breath hissed loudly through his clenched teeth. Susan moved in as well, worried now.

"Relapse," Becker said softly into Susan's ear. "Tell McCoy to beam us up."

"Is he all right?" she said, turning to George.

"Nothing that a Deacon can't fix, I think," George said.

"Who's McCoy?" Susan said, turning back to Becker, who hadn't moved. Susan had never watched much TV.

I reached into my pocket for the condom-packet, which I slipped into George's hand. "Dr. McCoy says play safe," I said.

He handed it right back. "Dr. McCoy should teach her grandmother," George said.

Becker and I headed for the parking lot.

I drove. I told him I didn't think he should be behind the wheel after receiving a blow to the head, and he agreed. Gosh. Jeep Cherokees sure go fast.

"Hey, slow down," Becker said, "or I'll have to pull you over."

"Show me your flashing lights."

"I think they got punched out." He laughed, a little wildly.

I pulled over to the side of the road and turned on the overhead.

"What?" Becker said.

"Detective Mark Becker, what you did back there was noble and totally right-action, but I want to thank you for not arresting anybody."

"Well, I was off duty, right?"

"Right. So. I guess dinner and pool in Laingford's out." The cut over his eye was still bleeding. "How hurt are you?" I said. "You want to go home? Are you dizzy? Should we go to the hospital?"

"I think sick bay would be better."

"Sick bay your house or sick bay my house?"

"You're the doctor."

"You got gauze and disinfectant at your place?"

"No."

"The Deacon residence it is. Anyway, when you're suffering from goat poisoning, you have to return to the source."

I headed for the Dunbar sideroad and home.

Twentyone

Move me I'm steel pipes
bashing demented in the gale
—Shepherd's Pie

I handed the keys over reluctantly. It had been a nice ride. Driving the Cherokee after three years of molly-coddling George's cranky old pickup was like a snort of fine brandy after years of drinking lemonade. It would never do to own a vehicle that powerful. No wonder that the men who drive those things act like teenagers with painful erections.

"I can feel the testosterone just pumping through me," I said.

"What?" Becker said. He slammed the passenger door and winced as something in his arm reminded him that he had been rough-housing with the locals.

"The Jeep," I said. "Getting behind the wheel turns you into a seventeen-year-old boy with his baseball cap on backwards."

"Not me, ma'am," Becker said. "I drive like a cop." Lugnut jumped up and put his paws on Becker's chest, wagging his tail.

"Down!" I said, but it was too late to save the shirt. "Sorry. He likes you."

Becker patted the dog's head. "It's only a shirt. So, medicine woman, you got the cure down here or in your cabin?"

"Are you up for the hike?"

"No problem. I'm tough. I own a Jeep, remember?"

He slowed down halfway up the hill. The stars were out, in a navy blue sky.

"Hey, Polly, come here a sec," he said.

It was dark where he was. There was moss and bracken on the ground. We stayed there a while.

"Mmm, Bkrr?"

"Mmmmn?"

"You're still bleeding."

"How come you're still calling me Becker?"

"I hardly know you."

"Oh. You have a thing in your hair. Wait."

"Mmmmn."

Later, we finished the climb. At a trot. I lit the lamps and put the kettle on.

"You cleaned up in here," Becker said.

"Yeah, well. Sit here where the light is. We'll fix that eye."

"Now?"

"There's clean pillowcases," I said. "I don't want blood on them." It was a lie, but still. Tending to the wounds of a devastatingly handsome officer by lamplight has got to be the biggest Florence Nightingale wet-dream in the world.

"Don't move." I washed the cut with a goldenseal solution to disinfect it, then mixed up a bit of myrrh and goldenseal into a paste.

"What the hell is that?" he said.

"If we had gone to the hospital, they would have given you a couple of stitches. This is cheaper, and you won't have a scar."

I used a couple of tiny strips of surgical tape to close the wound, which was a split just above the eyebrow. Then I dabbed a bit of herbal paste on, added a scrap of gauze and a band-aid.

"I did this a while ago when I slashed my finger with an Olfa knife," I said. "It works. Trust me. Just don't wiggle your eyebrows for a couple of days."

"Whatever you say, ma'am. As long as I don't wake up with three eyes in the morning. Some kind of spell involved here?"

"You're not religious, are you?"

"No."

"Thank heaven for that," I said and poured a couple of brandies.

"It's quiet up here," Becker said. "How do you stand it? You listen to music at all? Have you got a CD player? Tunes?" There had been CDs in his Jeep. I hadn't thought to look at them.

"There's no hydro and batteries are expensive," I said. "I do have a radio that winds up like clockwork, though. It gets the CBC."

"You're kidding. Clockwork?"

"Yeah. They were designed for the third world. I figure we'll all be third world soon enough, so I bought one."

"Where? Is this it?" Becker walked over to the clockwork radio which held pride of place over the sink, by the window. "How does it go on?"

"Crank the handle at the side, then press the ON switch. Don't worry about over-winding it, they're indestructible."

Becker turned the crank until the coiled spring inside was tight, then pressed the button and Margery Doyle's genial Newfie drawl came on, introducing a string quartet.

"Perfect," I said.

"You like this stuff?" Becker said.

"Don't you?"

"I listen to MEGA FM most of the time. This is fine, though."

He returned to the table and started to massage the back of my neck.

"I feel like I should be wearing a suit and tie," he said.

"Why? The music?" There was a long pause. The cello spoke of caramel passion and the violin sang like spring.

"It's kind of high-brow," he said.

"We could turn it off. Nobody says you need music."

He turned it off, then came back to me.

"Mmmn. That feels wonderful," I said. "Cop fingers. Strong."

My shirt melted off.

"Aren't you cold?" Becker said.

"Come this way. It's warmer under the covers."

He had a body like sculpted granite, but his skin was soft and smelled wonderful. We lay there, staring at each other, nose to nose, just grinning. It was the kind of shyness that occurs when two people, who have chosen to act on a mutual attraction, are finally confronted with a delicious expanse of willing, unexplored flesh. It's dizzying. Where to begin?

Going to bed with someone for the first time is nerve-wracking. I've never been thoroughly engulfed in the moment, the way the heroine is in romance novels. There's no "suddenly they bonded together like liquid fire, she opened herself to his throbbing manhood and their passion exploded so that she swooned with pleasure" stuff.

That isn't to say that it wasn't good, but rather than Bolero, ours was an intricate Slavonic folk dance, where every gesture held particular meaning.

Everybody has a specialty or two and our moves were

introduced one-by-one, like characters in a play, presented with bashful pride. After all, the audience had never seen the show before.

I've never believed that sex was an entirely mutual act. There's a certain selfishness to it that requires tiny, electric moments of wordless negotiation. If things are going well, the back-and-forth pleasure is seamless and wonderful. With Becker, it was. We kept our eyes open. We fit. We even managed the absurdity of the condom with dignity and humour. After the first tentative rehearsal, we didn't need to ask each other for an encore, it just happened.

When first sex is satisfying, you feel like you've just won a medal for your gender—there's no other way to describe that "I've still got it" glow. You've just represented womanhood, or manhood, and you got the gold—no faking it, no failure, no need to apologize and blame it on the booze. You've just proved that there's something deep and profound that men and women can do together beautifully, without messing it up. It makes you really cocky.

We lay together in the classic "her head on his chest/his arm around her/their legs tangled together" position. We were warm and wet and panting happily.

"Mark? I'm sorry. I really have to pee," I said. "You want another brandy while I'm up?"

"Mmmmn." He began a caress he knew would make me not want to leave.

"Unfair, Becker." I retaliated with a move of my own. Later, my bladder screaming for attention, I slipped out of bed, then found myself tucking the duvet around him, a curious feeling of warmth spreading out just below my rib cage. He was quiet, his breathing even. Asleep, the crinkles around his eyes relaxed, and he looked a little sad. I kissed him gently, and he smiled in his sleep.

The outhouse was freezing cold. When I got back, I poured myself a splash of brandy and put the kettle on for a quick wash. I was too keyed-up to go back to bed. Whatever I was feeling—and it was a new one for me—I wanted to savour for a bit.

Lug-nut had looked at me reproachfully when I came out of the lean-to bedroom. He'd accompanied me outside, guarded the outhouse door and stuck close on the way back. Could he be jealous? Great, I thought. No male attention for years and then two guys at once. Go figure.

After my sponge bath, I rolled a small joint and smoked it outside on the porch. The moon was nearly full and the outlines of the trees and the grey ghost of my breath and the smoke swirled together in a comfortable, smug spiral. There was a lot to think about. The evening's scenes played again in my mind's eye, from Vern, the pickup boys and the puking girl in the bathroom to Becker's heroics and inevitably to the last few hours. It was odd to be sad about John's death, Francy's pain, Eddie's black eye and Spit's getting whacked and at the same time to acknowledge the bubbling excitement I felt at the back of my throat when I thought about Mark Becker.

Then suddenly he was there, zipping up his pants, dressed again. I reached out my hand, and he squeezed it, then dropped it as if it had burned him.

"Are you smoking dope?" he said.

"Yup." I handed the joint to him in a friendly way.

"I can't believe you're offering me a joint."

"I was being polite." It was terribly funny, and I started laughing.

"Polly. I'm a cop. Don't you have any sense at all? I could bust you right now."

There was a nasty little pause. Oh God. He meant it. He was serious.

"They might want to know what you were doing here at four in the morning, Officer," I said, punching him playfully on the arm.

He didn't laugh. He didn't even crack a smile. "Did you grow it yourself? A little patch out back?" It was a complete transformation. He was utterly furious, and his anger frightened me.

"Just try it, Mark. It's very mild. Better than brandy."

"Just put it out, would you? Please?" He slumped over the porch railing and stared out at the moon.

I touched his back. "It's only a little grass," I said. He shrugged my hand away.

"I gotta get going," he said.

"Let's just go back to bed," I said. "We can forget this. I won't smoke around you if you don't like it, Mark. This doesn't have to be a big deal."

He turned to look at me. His hair was rumpled, and there was a faint shadow of stubble around his jaw line.

"Lots of people smoke the occasional joint," I said. "It doesn't make me a bad person, does it?"

He just stared at me. Something passed behind his eyes, some kind of internal battle. The Mark Becker who won wasn't the Mark Becker I'd just been falling in love with. It was someone else, and the cold, sorrowful look he was giving me made the bottom drop out of my stomach.

"You're not a bad person, Polly," he said, "but you are breaking the law. In a way, I am the law. That's my job, but it's also my duty, and I care about it. If someone's smoking marijuana at a party, I may not wade in there and arrest everybody, but I sure as hell leave. Right away."

"You can arrest me if you want," I said.

"I'm not going to arrest you." His voice was full of bitter disappointment. Everything had gone down the toilet in a lightning moment and I would have given anything to put the whole thing on rewind.

"It's not like we don't have anything happening between us," I said, then hated myself for saying it. I was pleading and it wasn't pretty.

"We did," he said. "I'm sorry about that. It was a mistake. I should have kept a lid on it. I'm leaving now." And he did.

Twentytwo

She's waiting for me, fathoms down,
where light's a rumour
death and pain the only game in town.
—Shepherd's Pie

I **have an old-fashioned** alarm clock. It winds up. it's brass. It made a lot of noise when it hit the wall, and the glass front made a satisfying shattering sound just before the ringing stopped.

Lug Nut barked at it for two minutes as it lay dying on the carpet.

"Leave it, Lug-nut. It's toast." My head pounded. Too much brandy. I'd killed the bottle after Becker left. At least I think I did. It was empty, anyway.

I heated up some coffee and sat carefully, trying not to move too much. Perversely, my mind told me that if only I had left some hooch in the bottle, I'd be able to have some in my morning coffee. The thought made me retch. Lug-nut, sensing my discomfort, shut up and started tiptoeing around, which was wise. I was not in the best of moods.

The goats were yelling their hairy heads off as I approached the barn. I banged around a bit, muttering. If I was in a lousy frame of mind, there was no need for anybody else to be cheery.

I was carrying the milk up to the dairy room off George's house when he pulled up in the truck. He positively scampered out of the cab. Scampered. I growled.

"So," he said, stretching as if he'd just got out of bed. He probably had. "Lovely day, yes?"

I glowered. He stopped in mid-stretch and stared at me.

"Oh. Oh, dear." He didn't say anything else for a while, just fell into step beside me and followed me into the dairy.

I strained the milk while George set up the pasteurizer for me.

"Thanks," I said. "Had a good time last night, did you?"

"It was fair to middling," he said, backtracking. "The beer was flat."

"The entertainment was pretty good, though. Local cop in bust-up with Cedar Falls thugs. Story at eleven."

"I thought he did very well, Polly."

"Yup. He did. Regular boy scout. Pure as the driven snow."

George's face went through a series of wrinkly gymnastics as he tried to figure it out. It can't have been very difficult.

"It didn't work out?"

"Bingo."

"Too bad, Polly."

"Thanks, George."

"I won't say that I told you so." People in love can be so annoying. He was glowing.

"Have you and Susan set a date, yet?" I said.

"A date? For what?"

"Don't tell me your intentions toward her aren't honourable."

"You mean marry her? Polly, we are having a wonderful time. You want us to ruin it by getting married?"

"Just a thought, George. Forget I mentioned it. Can I

borrow the truck? I've got to go into town." I didn't have any reason to go anywhere, but I had to go somewhere.

"Certainly. Yes. Do you want to talk about it?"

"About what?"

"About your policeman."

"He's not my anything." I finished pouring the milk into the pasteurizer, banged the buckets into the sink and started washing them out with a full stream of noisy, you-can't-talk-above-it water.

"Ah," said George and left me to my misery.

Back up at the cabin, I changed out of my overalls and into a clean pair of jeans. I'd go to the mall and shop. Not that I had much extra cash, but sometimes spending twenty bucks at Zellers and the Dollar Store on stupid plastic junk and cheap Chinese candy can cheer me up.

I found myself singing the blues as I freshened up Lug-nut's water bowl. Well, at least I was singing, even if it was all about my baby having left me and my dog having been busted for possession.

I went to the closet where I kept the bag of dog food I'd lifted from Francy's place. I scooped a bunch of the kibble into the bowl and watched with fascination as a fat roll of twenties rolled out of the bag and bounced across the floor. Lug-nut grabbed it before I did.

"DROP IT!" The dog almost dropped his teeth as well. I apologized to him and picked up the money.

There were twenty twenties, rolled up and secured with a rubber band, greasy from dwelling in the bag with the Kibbles and Bits. John's four hundred bucks. No question. A perfect hiding place. If he hadn't been killed, not a soul would have touched the dog food.

After I counted it, I just stared at it. Four hundred bucks may be peanuts to some people, but it sure wasn't to me. And it wouldn't be to Francy. What was I supposed to do with it now?

There was no way the police could get any information from it at this point. I'd handled it. The dog had slobbered on it. It was just currency, covered in kibble crumbs. Francy needed it now, not six months down the road, after the cops got through with it and gave it back, which was not necessarily a sure thing. Not that Becker wouldn't be scrupulous. If he was the kind of guy to contemplate busting his date, then he'd deal with the cash by the book, but there are no guarantees in this world, and this money was real and unmarked.

I pushed the wad of bills into my pocket and went to see Francy.

I knew there was something wrong as soon as I pulled up in George's truck, a little after ten. I could hear Beth wailing with the kind of full-lunged desperation of the baby who has been left too long on her own. I opened the cab door and ran, Lug-nut at my heels, barking.

I opened the front door and found Francy in the kitchen, hanging from one of the big beams over the table. There was a chair knocked over and she turned, very slowly. Her face was black and absolutely horrible. The room stank of shit and piss. There were no beer bottles on the table this time. Just a teapot and a cup. I dived for the phone.

Becker and Morrison arrived after twenty-five hellish minutes. I stood on the porch, holding Beth in my arms, rocking her back and forth, back and forth. She was still crying, but the panic in the sound had changed to one of exhausted distress. She was probably hungry, definitely wet, but my experience with babies was nonexistent, I was in no shape to change a diaper and I had no milk in my breasts.

It was Morrison who held me. He came up the porch steps two at a time and took me in his arms, and it was like being swallowed by a big soft pillow. He produced a hanky the size of a young flag, and I buried my face in it. It smelled of lavender.

Becker plunged stone-faced into the house and emerged a moment later, hurrying to the cruiser to radio for help. Soon Beth was quiet and so was I. Morrison's arms were padded and comfortable, and I felt like I could sleep for year and a half.

Becker came back from the cruiser, and Morrison let go of me gently, easing away with his arms kind of spread, as if he were afraid I might fall over.

"You okay?" Becker said.

"No," I said and tried to smile. My face cracked.

"We'll get you out of here soon. Can you tell me what happened?"

"I came to see Francy. I heard Beth screaming, and I knew something was wrong. I ran inside and found her—like that. I called 911. Grabbed Beth. She was in her carrier right where Francy, right where her mother...right there. I took her outside. Oh, God, Becker. I can't take the baby, too. The dog, yes, but not the baby." I know it's ugly. But that's what I said. I remember it.

"You don't have to take the baby, Polly. It's okay." He reached out a hand to touch me, but I pulled away from him.

"We'll call the Children's Aid," he said. "They'll take care of the kid and get in touch with the family." He used the kind of voice you use on a small child. I whimpered.

"Who did this, Becker?" I said. "Who would kill Francy? How could she let someone hang her up? Francy. She was the gentlest, sweetest woman. She put up with so much."

George came, and soon someone from the Children's Aid showed up. I wouldn't let go of the baby until I had looked deep into the eyes of the worker they'd sent. She was young, younger than me, but she looked capable and concerned. She had to pry Beth loose.

George took me home to his place and put me to bed in the spare room. I guess I had come apart, a bit, like Francy had done after Eddie bonked John on the head. Although my memory was fine, I wasn't planning to do any sleuthing for a while. All I wanted to do was sleep.

"You're on overload," Cass Wright said. George had called her after we got home. She was my GP, one of the last of the breed that makes house calls. She was ancient.

"You've seen too much and your brain can't cope with it," Cass said. "Put this under your tongue, Polly. It'll make you sleep." "This" was a pill, yellow and menacingly small. "The police said they'd talk to you when you're ready."

Not long after the little yellow pill dissolved, I began to drift away, aware that George was right there if I needed him. His hand, which had been holding mine, kind of disembodied itself and started to float around the room like a pale, freckled starship. I addressed the hand.

"There's treasure in my pocket," I told it. It patted me gently. "Really," I said. "Four hundred treasures. Doggy food." I was gone.

Hours later, when I returned to the land of the living, I felt better, although my tongue felt like a towel.

I went to the bathroom to get a drink of water and stared blearily at my reflection in the mirror. I had a little trouble focusing. "Polly Deacon, Private Eye," I said aloud. Then I giggled. I guess there was something mildly hypnotic in the yellow pill, unless I was just going mad.

"Polly? That you?" George called from the hall.

"Yup. I'll be out in a sec." I splashed cold water on my face and stuck my head under the tap, trying to erase the Don King bed-head I'd woken up with.

I heard George shuffle up to the door and lean against it. "Becker the policeman is here," he said quietly through the wood. "Are you ready for speaking to him or do you want to go back to bed for a while?"

"No. I'll talk to him." I combed out my soggy locks with my fingers and stopped caring how I looked.

Becker was sitting at the kitchen table, nursing a cup of coffee. He started to get up when I came in, which was gallant but unnecessary. Embarrassed, I flapped my hand to make him sit down again.

"Hey, Polly."

"Mark."

George muttered something about the goats and went outside.

"Are you feeling any better?" Becker said.

"Some. But whatever the doctor gave me seems to have left me a wee bit stoned. It's legal, though. Prescription. Don't worry."

"I can come back later if you'd rather," he said.

"No, it's fine. Really. It's not as if you haven't seen me stoned before."

I offered it as a giggle, as a test, but he didn't smile. Whatever crashed and burned the night before seemed to be permanent. I could really have used a hug from him—or at least some sign that our night together was at least in his thoughts, but there was nothing. I felt cheap and stupid.

"When did you last see Francy Travers?" he said.

"You mean alive?"

"Yes, alive."

"I helped her clean up the—mess in her kitchen yesterday. About noon or half past."

"Did she seem okay?"

"Well, she certainly wasn't swinging from the rafters at that point."

"Hey, now. Easy, eh? I've got to ask these things."

"I know. Sorry. It's stress."

Becker stared hard at me for a moment, perhaps trying to gauge how tranquilized I really was. My pupils were probably huge. I felt like I was wrapped in cotton wool. Next time he spoke, it was as if he were speaking to a rebellious teenager. He sounded patient, reasonable, with just a hint of anger boiling just below the surface.

"So she was fine when you left her...when?"

"About two o'clock, I guess. And she was still fine when I dropped off some groceries for her a couple of hours later."

"She didn't seem depressed?"

"Not at all. She seemed happier than she's been in a while. She was thinking about ways to get her life back together. She was looking forward to it. Hey, wait. You're not seriously thinking suicide, are you?"

"It looks that way, Polly."

"No way. No goddamn way, Becker," I said. I was getting mad, really fast. "Francy would no more commit suicide than you would. Her father hanged himself. Way back when she was a kid. She was the one to find him. There is just no way she would do the same thing. She saw what it looks like." Poe, who was listening, ruffled his feathers and shifted uneasily.

"So, it runs in the family, eh?"

"Jesus, Becker. No!"

"She left a note."

"What?"

"There was note on the table. She confessed to John's murder, said she couldn't stand the guilt and asked for someone to take care of Beth."

"Somebody else wrote it. No way she did. Who was it addressed to?"

"It wasn't addressed to anybody. It was just there. And it was written on the same kind of notepaper you got your warning message on. I'm surprised you didn't see it when you found her. We think she was trying to scare you away from being involved."

I knew I had to stay coherent. I knew I had to remain calm and reasonable, but I was so angry I was shaking. Poe started clicking his beak.

"You—are—so—wrong," I said.

"Try to accept this, Polly."

"Try to accept it? Accept that my best friend would commit suicide when she was finally free? Accept that she would write a suicide note and not address it to me? Accept that the police are so fucking stupid that they can be taken in by a planted suicide note and a nice neat answer to the murder of John Travers? I don't think so."

"Insulting me isn't going to help," Becker said, standing up.

"What is? You want some evidence? You want me to do your job for you? It was Freddy at the dump who did the squirrel thing, Becker. He practically told me so."

"So, Francy Travers got Freddy to do her dirty work. It's no surprise. We were on to him."

"Bullshit. You were on to nobody. You don't know what the hell you're doing in this case and you never have. You've been trying to pin this whole thing on Francy since it started, and now somebody's tied it up in a nice little bundle for you and you're glad, aren't you? You're glad Francy's dead and you've got a note to tell you whodunnit. Check out the handwriting, you moron. It won't be hers."

"Look, I know you're angry. I would be too, if it was my friend dead. But you're still in shock, and you're saying whatever comes into your head."

"I am not in shock. And what's in my head makes a hell of a lot more sense than what's in yours."

"I haven't been killing my brain cells with drugs, Polly."

I flew forward and attacked him, full out. I really wanted to hurt him. He wasn't expecting it, and my adrenaline must have kicked in, because I landed a few vicious blows before he grabbed both my wrists and twisted me very suddenly so that I was lying face down on the floor, his knee in my back. I felt the handcuffs cold against my skin. It was nothing like my sick little fantasies in the hospital corridor had been. It hurt. It was humiliating. I felt like a jerk. Poe went nuts, cawing and flapping his wings.

The front door banged, and George was in the room. All I could see were his shoes. Becker hauled me to my feet by my arm, none too gently, giving me an angry little shake when I pulled away from him.

"Polly! What's going on?" George said. "Detective Becker. What are you doing?"

"Pauline Deacon, you are under arrest for assaulting a police officer," Becker said. Finally, he was smiling.

Twentythree

She plays his love
like a practice violin,
cold precision, some small art in
her continual adjustment of his tension.
—Shepherd's Pie

It took some negotiating to get Becker to remove the handcuffs. George was diplomatic, but it was obvious that he was as pissed with me as Becker was. They both treated me as if I wasn't there. Becker's eyebrow-cut had opened up again. I guess that was my fault. The handcuffs pinched, and I stared at the ceiling, thinking about how wicked they made me feel. I was a criminal. A dangerous offender. A police officer had needed to restrain me. They made me feel ashamed and oddly exultant at the same time. It was very weird.

"...can overlook it because she was reacting to shock," George was saying.

"She knew damn well what she was doing when she hit me," Becker said.

"It was perhaps a reaction to the sedative," George said.

"It's a reaction to the police acting like fucking idiots," I said.

"Polly, be quiet!" George almost never raised his voice. I shut up.

"I can release her into your custody," Becker said, "but you've got to make sure she behaves herself. No more sticking her nose into police business." I was outraged. What was I? A child? George had no jurisdiction over me, and he knew it, but there he was, nodding and looking sorrowful, like I was a kid caught shoplifting. I swallowed my anger and looked at the floor.

"Turn around, please, Polly." I did as I was told, and Becker removed the cuffs. I massaged my wrists, just like they do in the movies. It's not because the handcuffs cut off the circulation, I discovered. You massage your wrists because you can.

"You will be doing an autopsy, yes?" George said, as Becker headed for the door.

Becker turned and glared. "Whether or not we do an autopsy is our business, Mr. Hoito." He paused, and then took a step towards me. Involuntarily, I took a step back.

He spoke very quietly. "I am willing, for now, to overlook this incident, but I won't forget it. If I hear anything, anything at all about you doing any more nosing around this case, I will assume that you are willing to face the consequences of your actions in their entirety. With drug-possession and assault charges, you could face a prison sentence. Remember that, Polly." Then he left, ignoring Lug-nut on the porch, who had missed the excitement and still wanted to be his friend.

George stared at me, his eyes wide. "Drug possession?"

I blushed. "I offered him a toke last night," I said. George burst out laughing.

"Polly, Polly, Polly," he said.

"I thought it was okay," I said. "He freaked out."

"There are times when I must seriously question your sanity," he said.

"Me too."

"So. How are we going to discover who killed John and Francy Travers?" George said. I hugged him, hard. Poe cawed, flapped his wings and landed with a thump on my shoulder. I gasped and felt immediately taller, more important. I held out a finger, and by God, he nibbled it. My eyes teared up. Animals. They can do magic, sometimes.

We sat down at the kitchen table and started making a list. Poe stayed on my shoulder like a new guardian angel, and his sudden acceptance made my heart hurt.

"Here," George said, handing me a pencil and a scrap of paper. "You must write things down as we think of them. I shall make the tea and be Hercule Poirot."

"Who do I get to be?"

George looked me over.

"Miss Marple?"

"Hardly. She was terribly proper."

"Reid Bennett?" (He's the Ted Wood cop-character who owns Sam, the Wonder-dog. George reads whodunits too.)

"George, I didn't shoot Becker or break his jaw. I only hit him a couple of times. Anyway, Lug-nut will never be a Sam."

"Nancy Drew, then. No. Nancy Druid."

"That's better."

"Good," George said. "Now, how is this to start? Number one. Somebody shot John after Eddie and Francy left the Travers' house, some time after eight o'clock."

"Right," I said, writing it down. "And the weapon may or may not have been John's own gun."

"You saw it in John's truck, yes?"

"I saw what I thought might have been a gun barrel. There's no proof, because someone removed it before the cops got there."

"What does that tell us?"

"That whoever took the gun away knew that I had found the truck, I guess."

"Maybe, but that is only speculation. It may have been a coincidence."

"True. Anyway, Eddie saw me coming out of the garage and told everyone at that holy rollers meeting that I was there, so anybody could have known."

"Do you think the holy rollers are involved?"

"I don't think so. They're a weird bunch, for sure. Otis and Donna-Lou especially. And the Travers. But murder? I hardly think so. But people gossip around here, eh? The news about me was out."

George brought tea to the table and pulled up a chair. "We know that the killer took John's body to the dump, because we found it the next morning," he said.

"Well, we don't know that it was the killer who moved the body," I said. "It could have been an accomplice."

"And it might have been someone working with Freddy, because Freddy hit Spit Morton on the head to get him out of the way," George said.

"We don't know that for sure," I said. "Freddy and Spit could just have had an argument that had nothing to do with the murder at all."

"We are not getting very far," George said. "What do we know for certain?"

"Somebody hid John's truck in his garage. We know that for sure. And covered it up so it would be hard to find. And there was blood in the truck, so we sort of know that John's body was in there at some point."

"Good. Put that down."

"And I'm also going to put down what I know for sure.

That Francy didn't kill John, or herself."

George put his hand on my arm. "How can you be sure, child?" he said. "I know you have always had trust in her, but she was unstable, was she not?"

"I know because I know. There are some things you don't question." I sounded more definite than I felt. Especially after hearing about the alleged suicide note. Still. You had to have faith.

"So, somebody hanged-up little Francy and put a false note telling the police that she had killed her husband. Was that to make them stop investigating?"

"I guess. But what I can't understand is how Francy let herself be hanged."

"She was probably drugged first, Polly. They'll find out when they do an autopsy."

"If they do an autopsy. And George, Becker said that the note was written on the same notepaper the squirrel note was on. If that's true, then whoever did the squirrel thing also killed Francy. Freddy. It's Freddy."

"We don't know that for sure."

"What we also don't even have a clue about is why John was killed in the first place. The truth of it is that when he turned up dead, nobody cared very much. It must have something to do with the money. Oh God. The money."

I reached into my pocket and pulled out the kibble-cash.

"Where did that come from?" George said. I explained where I'd found it, and that I would have given it back to Francy if she'd been alive when I got there.

"So that was the treasure you were talking about before. I thought it was *harha-aistimus*—a vision, a hallucination. Did you tell Detective Becker?"

"No. I forgot."

"You were too busy trying to punch off his head, you mean."

"Something like that. Now what do I do with it? I'm not supposed to butt in anymore, right? Or Becker will lock me up and throw away the key."

"You could talk to Morrison."

"But as soon as I call the station, they're going to know that I'm still butting in, aren't they? I'm scared, now, George. Becker was serious about arresting me. If only out of spite. I don't want to give him the excuse."

"You could call and ask about the funeral arrangements. I didn't hear anything about a funeral for John. Did you? But there must be someone who will want to give Francy a good-bye. I would not want to miss it."

"The funeral. Of course. The police will know all about that, won't they?"

"The logical people to ask, I would say."

When I got the receptionist, I asked very specifically for Morrison. We had been working on our sleuth-list for long enough that Becker was probably back at HQ by now, and I didn't want to take any chances.

Morrison came on the line just as John Denver began telling me that life on the farm was kinda laid back. I was grateful for the interruption.

"You have Muzak," I said, accusingly.

"Yes, we do. It's supposed to keep our callers calm. But from what I hear, Muzak won't work on you, eh?"

"Is Becker there?"

"You want to speak to him?"

"NO! No. I want to speak to you, Constable Morrison. I need some information."

"After what you did to my partner, I don't owe you shit,"

he said. "He's mad as all get out, and although I don't know the details, I know damn well you're responsible. You know how hard he is to work with when he's like that?"

"I can imagine. Sorry."

"I'll just bet you are."

"Listen, I know you don't owe me anything. But there's something I really need to know."

"What makes you think I care?"

"You cared enough about Lug-nut to ask me to take him in."

"So?"

"So, don't tell me you don't care. I know I'm supposed to mind my own business from now on, but I'm wondering about the funeral arrangements. I never heard anything about a funeral for John. Have you released the body yet?"

"Yesterday. The day after we questioned Mrs. Travers. She had it sent to North Bay, to his parents."

"Really? Why?" There was a pause, as if he was making up his mind about something. Then his voice got quiet and he spoke rapidly.

"She told us she didn't want to play the grieving widow. Said his folks wouldn't want her at the funeral anyway."

"That's weird."

"Yup. Backs up what was in the note, Becker says. She knew her in-laws wouldn't want John's killer to be present." In the background, I heard a door opening and a murmuring question. Morrison covered the receiver with his hand and said something which sounded like "funeral home". Then he was back on.

"That's crap, Constable. She didn't kill him."

"I know."

"I beg your pardon?"

"We don't have that information yet, ma'am," he said, loudly.

"Are you telling me that you think that note's a fake?"

"Yup."

"Should you be saying that?"

"Nope."

"Is Becker listening?"

"Yup."

"Can you meet me for coffee at the Tim Horton's in Laingford at nine? I have some new information and I can't give it to Becker."

"Yup. Okay, ma'am. I hope that clears things up. We'll let you know about the arrangements for Mrs. Travers."

He hung up, and I was left staring at the phone. I turned to George, who had been listening openly, a grin on his face.

"Morrison is onto it, yes?" he said.

"I think so. I'm going to meet him later. I'll tell him about the money then. And find out about Francy's funeral."

"He was a fine wrestler, was Earlie Morrison."

"Pardon?"

"Morrison. The policeman you were just talking to. He used to wrestle in his high school, won all the local championships. He wrestled as a professional for some time after he graduated, then he decided to become a police officer. Moved back to Laingford when he got a job on the force here. Now he coaches the high-school wrestling team. He is a good man, Earlie."

"I'll bet nobody calls him Earlie to his face," I said.

"Everybody does," George said, fixing me with a look. "Everybody except your Becker."

215

Twentyfour

I'm so happy, so happy said he,
bought me a coffee at a quarter to three,
meanwhile his happiness waited at home,
in an unhappy bed near a silent phone.
—Shepherd's Pie

The Tim Horton's in Laingford is no different from any Tim Horton's you've ever been in. First thing that hits you is the smell of hot fat, followed by a big wall of white-noise—coolers, Coke machines, fluorescent lights—the inexorable buzz of fast food places everywhere. It never used to bother me until I stepped out of the mainstream and crawled off to live in a cabin in the woods. At home, I can hear a mouse chewing its fingernails, and anything electronic is instantly recognizable and horribly annoying.

One thing about Tim's, though, the coffee is always good, and if you like donuts, they've got 'em.

Morrison was sitting at a formica table by the window, a black coffee in front of him, no donuts. He'd probably already had three while he was waiting. He grinned when I came in and threatened to get up, but he was sort of wedged in the plastic modular chair which was part of the table, designed by someone who thought every ass in the world was skinny. He stuck halfway, grinned even wider and settled back, his butt overflowing the seat. I felt sorry for him. Not so much because his size was unappealing—I mean, I didn't think "poor guy, he'd be very attractive if he'd only lose some weight." I just thought that his bulk must be a bit of a pain sometimes, that's all.

"Hey, Morrison."

"Hey, Goat Girl." He must have picked it up from Spit, but he said it in a friendly way, so I didn't mind. Soon I would try out "Earlie" on him and see if he flinched.

"Just let me grab a coffee, and I'll be right there." There was a queue, but the Hortonites were efficient, and soon I was at the front of the line. Someone was just bringing out a fresh tray of sour-cream cinnamon donuts, my favourite. I ordered two, one for me, one for Morrison. I guess it was a sort of bribe, but I didn't think he'd worry about it. I handed it to him when I got back to the table. He looked at it, grinned, and pushed it gently back across the table to me.

"Thanks, but no thanks," he said.

"It's only a donut," I said.

"I can see that," he said. "Can't stand 'em. It's Becker who likes donuts, not me." I shrugged and another stereotype bit the dust.

I dug in. After a moment, Morrison gazed at my chin and silently handed me a napkin.

"I brought some paperwork," I said, swallowing and wiping my mouth.

"Oh, yeah? What kind?" I explained that George and I had written down everything we knew about Francy and John and the murders.

"Should be interesting. Is there anything in there you haven't told us?"

"I'm not sure. There's stuff I told Becker that I didn't tell you, but I'm sure he let you know about it. You're working together, right?"

Morrison didn't answer. He was reading.

"What's this about four hundred dollars in the dog food?"

"Well, you know how I took over the care and maintenance of Lug-nut, right? After you suggested it. Why did you make out that it was Becker's idea, by the way?"

He pursed his lips. "Figured you'd go for it sooner if it came from him, eh? You did, didn't you?"

"It didn't matter whose idea it was. Lug-nut's a great dog. He's out waiting in the truck."

"My Uncle Dwight's dog, Sheila, is his mother," he said. "I heard Travers treated his dog bad. It's good to know he's in good hands now."

"Jeez, everybody's related around here, aren't they? If not by blood, then by dog."

"Yup. So, the four hundred bucks?"

"Well, I went to get Lug-nut on Tuesday, after you told me he was abandoned, and I kind of, you know, slipped past that tape over the door to get the bag of dog food that John kept under the sink in the kitchen."

"Yeah? It's okay. I'm not going to arrest you—yet."

"I wish you guys would stop threatening to arrest me. It's wearing me down."

Morrison frowned. "I was joking," he said.

"Becker wasn't."

"Becker threatened to arrest you? Why?"

"Didn't he tell you?"

"He never tells me anything."

I told him. I left out some important details, like what exactly Becker and I were doing at my place, but I think he knew anyway.

"So that's how he got the bruise over his eye. Yeah, he's got a thing about dope. Most cops do, but some take it more seriously than others. You be careful, kid. Becker said the ding was from that bar brawl in Cedar Falls last night."

"Well, it was. I just kind of nudged it later and it started bleeding again."

He didn't laugh. "Becker is not the kind of guy you'd want to be pissing off," he said. "That was real stupid."

"I know, I know. So. The dog food."

"Yeah. You found the money in the dog food at the Travers' place? Before you found the truck? Why didn't you tell us?"

"No, I found it this morning, when I went to feed Lug-nut. I took the dog food from Francy's to my place. The money rolled right out of the bag this morning. I was going to give it back to her this afternoon when I found—you know."

"Yeah, I know. Pretty awful for you."

I didn't want to get into it, or I might start to cry. "Anyway, here it is." I pulled the roll of bills out of my pocket and put it on the table.

"Put that away," he hissed, startling me. "People will think you're trying to bribe me." I whipped the wad back into my pocket and glanced around. There were a lot of people in the place, but nobody near our table. Still, in a town the size of Laingford, people know you. No doubt there were several people there who had heard about Mark Becker and the pickup boys the night before. There would be tales told if I was seen handing Becker's partner a wad of bills, I guess.

"Sorry," I said.

"So you found Travers's cash. And you were going to give it to her and not tell us?"

"Well, Lug-nut got to it before I did and we had a tug-of-war. I figured that the dog slobber probably erased any prints."

"That's withholding evidence, Goat Girl."

"Add it to my sheet, Earlie."

He grinned. "From you, I'll take it. The name, I mean," he added quickly, as I reached into my pocket. "Not the money. The money goes to Becker."

"Couldn't it go into trust for Beth, or something?"

"Eventually. But now it's evidence. It means something. Don't know what, but it does. What does it say in your Nancy Drew thing here? The four hundred dollars is somehow important? Yeah. I think so too."

"Have you guys been able to find out who he owed money to?"

"Nope. But Becker's talking to some of Travers's poker buddies over at Kelso's tonight. Maybe you should go find him there and give him the money. Explain how you come to have it."

"Me? Go into Kelso's? Becker would kill me."

"You have a point. Besides, the only women who go in there are usually working."

"Working? You mean professionals? Dancers?"

He eyed me. "Not that you couldn't pass. With the right clothes. A bit of makeup."

"Thanks a bunch, Earlie. Just hang on while I run out to the truck and slip into my bunny suit."

He laughed. "I took you for one of those feminists with no sense of humour."

"Oh, I have a sense of humour, don't you worry. We feminists find it comes in useful when we're dealing with bottom-feeders."

"Well, you'll find plenty of them where you're going. Bottom-feeders just about sums it up. In both senses of the word."

"Will you come with me?"

"To protect you from Becker, or the clientele?"

"Both. He'll go ballistic when he finds out I've been holding out on him. On top of everything else."

"He'll go ballistic, as you say, when he finds out I met you behind his back, too. Maybe you should be protecting me."

"I don't think you need much protection. You're bigger than he is." I hadn't meant it to be mean, but he looked hurt.

"I may outweigh him, but he has seniority."

"Oh. There's that."

He busied himself folding up my sleuth sheet and putting it away carefully in his pocket. He was in plainclothes—wearing the biggest tweed jacket I'd ever seen.

"We're doing a post-mortem on Mrs. Travers," he said.

"Good. I bet it shows she was drugged before she was hanged."

"What would that prove? We found her stash. She was a regular dope-smoker and a pretty heavy drinker. If there's evidence of drugs in her system, it'll just indicate that she doped herself up before she did it. Pretty sad."

"Sure, Francy smoked dope, but then so do I," I said. "It was no big deal. Neither of us did coke. Neither of us took pills."

"We only have your word on that. Don't forget the note."

"Are you going to look for the notepaper?"

"Already did. Found a big pile of it in the desk in the living room."

"That's crazy. It must have been planted by the killer. And besides, any handwriting expert will tell you it's not her."

"How can you be so sure?"

"I just am, okay? Are you guys checking it?"

"I don't know. You'll have to ask Becker. You have a sample of her handwriting?"

"Yup. A note she left for me recently." There was the "we'll be fine" thing she left in my stash-box. It felt awful to think what optimism in her had written it, now. "But there's probably stuff she's written in her house. Thing is, I know for sure that there was no lilac paper there yesterday."

"What makes you say that?"

I explained how Francy and I had torn the place apart the day before her death, looking for the money.

"I searched that desk myself. There was no lilac notepaper there then."

"So your theory is that somebody went over there, got her drunk or stoned enough not to put up a struggle, hanged her, left a suicide note, planted the notepaper and left? That it?"

"That's it."

"Huh. You'll have a hard time convincing Becker. He thinks he's got the case all sewn up. He thinks she was nuts. I finally got him to agree with me that any woman who stays shacked up with a guy who beats her has to have a couple of screws loose."

"There's always way more to it than that. It's not a case of just stay or go. Don't you ever read about it? Don't you guys ever do training courses?"

Morrison glared at me. "Of course we do. Sensitivity training and all that. Still doesn't help when you come up against some poor girl who's had her arm broken in three places and still won't make a statement against the guy who did it."

"Sometimes they stay for the sake of the kids," I said. If we were going to hash the whole issue out at Tim Horton's, we'd need another couple of donuts and a whole pot of coffee.

"Listen, Polly Deacon. I got all the training courses I could handle when I was a kid." Morrison stared at me fiery-eyed for a moment and then looked away, out to where the lumber trucks were whizzing past on the highway. I didn't say anything, just waited. Then he started talking quietly, as if he and I were the only people in the room. "The Honourable MPP who ran up against your aunt in that election way back then isn't my real father, eh? He adopted me. My real Dad was a drunk—hit all of us every goddamn night and used my mother for a punching bag. She never left, never made the break, until Dad set fire to the couch one night. We all got out, but he just lay there in front of the goddamned television and burned to death. Mom snapped like a broken twig, and I spent two years bouncing around from one foster family to another. Now, tell me again how staying with a fucked-up wife-beater is good for the kids. Go ahead." He had said it all very quickly, sending his words like darts straight into my gut. Francy's story had been like that. Gut wrenching. Leaving me feeling inadequate, like my own deal wasn't nearly as bad, so who the hell was I to talk? There was so much tension coming at me over the table that the air crackled.

"Oh, man, Earlie. I'm sorry. That's horrible."

"Damn right. Francy Travers just made me mad. I talked to her, and she just said the same things my mother used to say. Her, with her face half burned off. Did Travers do that to her? She didn't tell me—not that I asked, eh."

"No, that wasn't John. It was her father a long time ago, back when she was a teenager living in the States. She didn't talk about it much."

"Did you ask her right out?"

"Nope. When you carry scars like that, everyone who knows you probably has it at the back of their mind all the time, but there's just no opening to ask, you know? Like 'So, Francy, how about telling me who burned your face off?' I don't think so."

Morrison nodded.

"Francy told me just after she got pregnant," I said. "We were up at the cabin, partying a bit, and got to talking about fetal alcohol syndrome and 'smoking can harm your baby'—that sort of stuff. Francy was having a hard time quitting the old vices, but she said that at least her kid wouldn't inherit the scars. She just came out with it and then laughed. I waited and she told me what happened. Her father was like your Dad was, except he didn't torch the couch. He torched his daughter."

"Why?"

"Why? Does there have to be a reason? Like maybe she did something to deserve it? Like maybe you did something to deserve getting beat up by your dad? I don't know, Earlie. She didn't tell me that. All I know is that after the accident, as she called it, he hanged himself. She moved up here to stay with a family as a nanny, and she never went back. She said that after a childhood like hers, she could handle anything. I guess that's part of why she stayed with John. She compared her early experience to the stuff he doled out and figured she was in heaven."

"Poor kid."

"Uh-huh. She had a blind spot where John was concerned. But after he was killed, she certainly wasn't consumed by guilt, as that stupid note apparently says. She was getting on with it. She was happy."

"Becker won't buy it."

"Then how come he's at Kelso's trying to talk to John's friends? He must have some doubts."

"Loose ends, mostly."

"And so if he finds out something that points the other way, he'll ignore it, right?"

"That would be unprofessional."

"Uh-huh."

"Well. It might just get him thinking. He knows I don't think Francy Travers killed her husband, but what I think doesn't count for nothin' with him."

"How come you guys don't get along?"

"He always gets the girl, eh?"

"Quick, Earlie. Very quick. But really. How come you dislike him so much?"

"I was up for promotion, and he swings in from the city and snatches it away from me. How about that? Or, he's a hundred and fifty pounds of muscle and I'm a slob. How about that? Or, he hates my dog. How about that? I got my reasons."

Morrison's face was red, and his tone was vehement enough to turn a head or two.

"Hey, hey. I'm sorry. Rude question. It's none of my business anyway."

Morrison took a swig of cold coffee and grimaced.

"Okay, let's go," he said. "Next stop Kelso's." He looked at what I was wearing. "Couldn't you have worn a mini-skirt or something?" he said.

Twentyfive

Hey, boys, those boobs would do that
even if they all just lined up
jump jump jumping the whole number.
—Shepherd's Pie

Kelso's tavern is the oldest drinking establishment in Laingford—and the sleaziest. It's housed in an old wooden former-hotel on the ridge overlooking the train tracks. Long ago, the ridge was a prestigious address, with its spectacular view of Lake Kimowan and the mist-covered, pine-studded hills on the horizon. Then, during the Depression, the neighbourhood started slipping and it hasn't stopped.

Kelso's still hops, though. It was boarded up like its neighbours for a long time after the hotel trade died, but a guy from North Bay bought it in the seventies, gutted it, painted over the windows and stuck a couple of neon signs at eye level. A big billboard in the parking lot says GIRLS GIRLS GIRLS.

Morrison had left the cruiser back at the station, which was, rather happily for the local constabulary, right next door to the Tim Horton's.

"If a cruiser pulls up at Kelso's," Morrison had said, "the place'll empty faster than a loose bowel. Er, excuse me, ma'am." He snickered. I stared at him, memory flooding back from the night before, at the community hall in Cedar Falls.

"You don't have a relative who's a musician, do you?" I said.

"My brother Dave's the lead for Baggy Chaps," he said. "Why do you ask?"

"Baggy Chaps. Were they playing the Cedar Falls Harvest Dance last night?"

"Where Becker's brawl was? Yup. So?"

"Nothing. Just wondering."

I let Morrison come with me in the pickup, although it meant Lug-nut would have to sit in his lap. The dog really liked him. I guess he has a thing for cops, like I used to. Morrison did rather resemble Luggy's big, brown pillow at home. The dog kneaded Morrison's mammoth thighs like a cat would, then settled down with a sigh and moaned as Morrison played with his ears.

My palms were slick on the steering wheel. I felt like I was taking my Young Driver's test all over again. I hadn't felt that way driving Becker the night before, but then, there had been enough sexual tension to make the rules of the road absolutely secondary to the rules of the dance. No sexual tension with Morrison. I felt him watching my every move. I just prayed that he wouldn't ask me to parallel park.

When we got there, it was ten-thirty, and the lot was half-full. Becker's Jeep Cherokee was parked a couple of rows over, and I chose a spot well away from it. No sign of the pickup boys, thank God. I could feel the bass-rumble from the open door through the soles of my boots.

"Remind me why we're here, again?" I said.

"To give Becker the money," Morrison said. "You're not nervous, are you?"

"Maybe. Look at me. No way I'm dressed for this." I wasn't wearing barn-chore clothes, but it was close. I had changed out of my rubber boots and overalls, but I hadn't dressed to go dancing—either on or off the tables. I was wearing the kind of outfit that sometimes elicits homophobic comments from the kind of guys who go to places like Kelso's. You know what I mean. I had on baggy jeans. Work boots. A flannel shirt and a baseball cap. It was the same thing I had worn in the Lumber-R-Us store the week before, when a guy behind the counter had said "Can I help you, sir?" When I told him I was a ma'am, he was so embarrassed he scuttled away and got someone else to serve me.

Sometimes, I get called a dyke. I think it's because I don't bother with makeup and I have short hair. It doesn't bother me, in fact, it sort of makes me feel proud. I know that this kind of attitude is likely to offend genuine lesbians, but I can't help it. It's called "passing"—as in "you could pass for a lesbian." It's a form of fraud, I suppose. Still, I like to reserve the right to be non-gender-specific.

However, I was about to walk into Kelso's Tavern in Laingford (GIRLS GIRLS GIRLS), and looking even remotely like a stereotypical lesbian could get me into trouble. I ditched the baseball cap, undid a couple of buttons of my flannel shirt and tucked it in. I caught Morrison looking, but he wasn't smiling.

"Well?" I said. "I don't want to get slugged."

"I know," he said. "Too bad about the workboots."

"I left my pumps at home." I tried to fluff out my hair. There isn't much to fluff.

"You got any lipstick?"

I felt like I was about to go undercover. This was getting ridiculous.

"I'll wet my lips at the door and keep my mouth open. Maybe giggle a bit. What do you think?"

"Couldn't hurt," he said and eased himself out of the cab.

"Stay, Luggy," I said to the dog. "If anybody tries to break in, bite their hands off." Not that anybody would. Lug-nut was ugly and looked mean. He licked my face, then settled down. I don't know how I ever managed without a dog before. They make you feel warm and fuzzy all day long.

There was a cover charge, and Morrison paid it. I just stood next to him and simpered, which earned me a peculiar look from the guy at the door, who stamped our hands with a rubber stamp and said "Have a good time" in the kind of tone that meant we probably wouldn't.

As we headed into the murk, Morrison muttered, "You don't have to act like a moron, for Chrissakes. We're not walking into a pit of rattlers."

We walked straight into a pit of rattlers.

Maybe we should have paid more attention to the cluster of big, black motorcycles parked near the door. There were bikers everywhere. Leather-wrapped, either bearded or Nazi-shorn, rings attached to places I've only seen on livestock and oozing a negative aura which would make any New-Ager reach for his or her crystal in self-defence. Some of these guys made Morrison look like Michael Jackson.

I peered into the smoky gloom, trying to catch a glimpse of Becker. The sooner we found him, the sooner we could get out of there. I saw him at the end of a bar, talking to a ferrety man with glasses and a flat cap. I tugged Morrison's arm and pointed.

"He's over there," I whispered, which was dumb, considering that the music was so loud it was altering my heartbeat. Still, Morrison got the picture and we started moving.

"Hey, honey. Wanna dance?" Someone grabbed my arm and I almost screamed. I turned to see who it was. He was shorter than me, with a grey beard which came down to his chest. From his right ear dangled an earring in the shape of a skull, and his grin revealed a set of well-kept teeth, which looked sharp.

"Uh, no, thank you," I said, pitching my voice to sound as much like a bar-bimbo as I could manage. "Me and my brother here are looking for our cousin Marky who's just got outta jail."

I heard a snort from Morrison.

The biker's grin faded. "Oh. Too bad. My name's Grub, eh? Just asking. Hope you find him. Have a nice evening." He grinned again and moved away. I stared after him in astonishment. This was a biker dude? Skull and leather and all? Have a nice evening?

We walked over to Becker.

"What the hell are you doing here?" he said when he saw me. It seemed to be a customary greeting with him. He'd probably still be saying that when we both met again on the banks of the Styx.

"Hi, Becker. Nice to see you, too. How's your eye?" He just glared at me, so I turned away from him and leaned over the bar to get the attention of the bartender, who had so many tattoos on his arms I thought he was wearing a denim shirt, until he got close.

"I just love your arms," I said, quite sincerely. They were fascinating. Snakes and daggers and Japanese Samurai warriors warring with hearts and flowers and the names of a dozen women. He smiled.

"I guess everybody says that, right?" I said.

"Not many women do," he said. "Mostly they look for names that aren't theirs. What can I get you?"

"Two draft, please." I forked over a five and got more

change than I expected, which I left on the bar. I'm nobody's fool. I handed one of the glasses to Morrison, who nodded his thanks, then I turned back to Becker.

"How's it going?" I said, casually. The ferrety man had melted into the crowd and Becker was fuming. Before he could reply, the music suddenly cut out and somebody announced the floor show. The lights on the postage-stamp sized stage flared up and the announcer howled "Heeeere's Candy!"

Candy strutted onstage dressed in black leather and chains, possibly a last-minute change in the program due to the guests of honour, who were currently hooting and breaking glasses in the front row.

"You shouldn't be in here," Becker said to me. He turned to Morrison. "Why the hell did you bring her in here? Are you out of your mind?"

"She has something for you. I didn't think it could wait, seeing why you're here and everything."

Candy was doing some very interesting gymnastics and had appropriated a beer-bottle from one of the bikers. I stopped looking.

"What couldn't wait until tomorrow? I was just getting some information from Jed Sheeney that could have wrapped that money-issue right up."

There were shouts from the front table and I glanced over at the stage just in time to see the beer bottle disappear. I felt like throwing up.

"Isn't that illegal, you guys? I mean, geez," I said and knocked back my draft, which tasted like weasel piss.

Morrison moved over, so that my view of the stage was blocked. I can't say I minded much.

"Yeah, Ms. Deacon, it is illegal. Like some other things,"

Becker said, "but there's no point trying to do anything about it. Know what I mean? Strippers keep these guys off the street, where they could do real harm. What's so urgent? You still can't keep out of it, eh?" He moved in a little and I stood my ground, reached into my pocket and brought out the money, which I held out to him. It occurred to me that, while Morrison had been worried about being seen to accept money in the Tim Horton's, Becker had no such compunction about it in Kelso's. He grabbed it.

"What's this?" he said, taking off the rubber band and counting it.

"It's John's four hundred bucks," I said. "The money-issue you wanted to tie up. I found it in a bag of dog food I took from Travers' kitchen when I picked up Lug-nut. Morrison said you were here trying to find out who John owed money to, and we thought it would help if you actually had it."

He was turning it over and over in his hands, then he stashed it away in his leather jacket. It was a nice jacket. Made him look just like one of the boys.

"When did you say you found it?" he said and caught my eyes and held them. It wasn't a look that had anything to do with his question. I didn't know what he was asking, but I felt a vague fluttering of something that could have been optimism.

"I found it this morning, Mark," I said, "just before I went over to give it to Francy." I had a sudden flash of him naked. Ouch. Then it was juxtaposed with the memory of Fancy, hanged. I flinched. He was staring into me, and I suddenly realized he was wondering if I was high. The questioning glance had nothing to do with sex. It was that other thing. He would always wonder that, I decided. No matter where we met, no matter what the circumstances, he would always wonder.

"You found *it* before you found *her*, you mean," he said. "And you didn't tell us until now."

"I meant to tell you, but I kind of forgot," I said. Okay, so I'm sorry for trying to hit you for being a dink, I didn't say.

"Good timing," he said and turned toward the stage and Candy.

"I was kind of freaked out, Becker," I said.

He didn't look at me.

"I did find it just before I went over and found her hanging from a rafter in the kitchen," I added. He still didn't take his eyes from the stage. Boy, was I ever wasting my time. Nothing makes a woman feel more alone than the sight of a man watching a stripper. "I found it just before I phoned in a bomb threat and held up the convenience store in Cedar Falls." Nothing. The police officer was fantasizing about being a beer-bottle, maybe. Illegal is as illegal does. I turned to Morrison.

"Something tells me this could have waited until tomorrow," I said and found that my throat was a bit tight. He nodded. The ferrety man had reappeared from the washroom area and was making his way towards Becker. Becker glanced back at me for the briefest of moments, then pushed away from the bar and moved towards him.

On our way out, Grub reappeared in front of me.

"Leaving so soon?" he said. "You find your cousin?"

"Yeah, we did," I said, doing my bimbo-impression again. "He's the same asshole he always was. Jail didn't change him none."

"It never does," Grub said. "Hey, if you ever need any accounting done, though, here's my card." He handed me a square of cardboard. "Miles Gruber, Chartered Accountant," it said, and gave an address in Hamilton.

"You're an accountant?"

"Yup. The bike's a hobby, eh? Me and the boys come up here to get away. So, like, if you ever need your taxes done or anything, just give me a call. Take care, now." Grub patted my arm affectionately and walked away, the chains on his boots clanking like Marley's ghost.

Morrison and I grabbed each other and ran, giggling like schoolkids, the whole way out to the parking lot.

Twentysix

*We're all trying to harness faith,
the sun you gotta worship
to be warmed by.*
—Shepherd's Pie

After I dropped Morrison off at the police station, I headed home. The Kelso's experience had left me feeling a bit queasy, partly from the bad draft, partly from Becker's coldness, but mostly from Candy and the beer bottle. On top of the murders, it was just too much. I had read about stuff like that from time to time, but I'd always figured it was the result of some fiction-writer's diseased imagination—something to say "eeew, gross" about and then turn the page. There would be no page-turning for Candy, though, and thinking about her and how she got to where she was, doing what she was doing, made me feel rotten. And helpless. What could I do when even the police said there's no point in trying?

I entertained a fantasy about going to Kelso's the next morning, finding the stripper and having a good heart-to-heart with her, then helping her to a new life feeding goats, eating healthy foods and living in George's house. Fat chance. She'd just tell me to piss off and mind my own business, which would be about what I deserved. The bucolic life I'm so fond of touting as the answer to everything isn't the answer at all for most people. Candy and other people like her, would probably choose beer bottles and bikers over goat poop any day.

When I got back to George's place, his town car, an elderly Toyota, was gone, so I figured he was at Susan's again. Poe was half-asleep on his shelf and croaked rudely at me. I left a note for George on his kitchen table telling him I'd fed the cats, which I proceeded to do. At least, I put food in their bowl, which usually brought them running, but there was no sign of them. Then I went down to the barn to check on the goats before going home.

They were all settled in for the night and I found the cats curled up in a ridiculously photogenic bundle with the new kids, all warm and toasty next to Erma Bombeck.

"From sleaze to saccharine in one fell swoop," I said, but the sight did actually make me feel a bit better. Erma bleated at me and I bleated back, then turned out the light.

I smoked a little dope when I got home, but didn't have the heart to work on the puppet. A friend of mine had died, I'd been stupid about a man (again) and rather than fill me with creative energy, as a toke usually did, it just made me more depressed. What was the point, anyway? The puppet would get sold at the Artists' Consignment Depot, I'd take the money and live on it for a while, and then have to make another one, and so on. What big hairy difference did it make to the world? Goats got born, goats died, but at least they made milk. People got born. Sometimes they got beaten up by people they loved, sometimes they danced on tables and did unspeakable things with beer bottles to entertain other people, but they all died too, sooner or later. There just didn't seem a point to anything.

I thought about praying, but I've never been able to scrape

even a tiny hint of belief together about a supreme being. God has always seemed to me to be a huge, powerful mess of wishful thinking. I knew this because the only time I ever thought about it was when I needed comforting, and the comfort never, ever materialized, no matter how hard I prayed.

My dead parents had been serious Catholics, and my early years were steeped in religion, but even though I was outwardly as devout as I was expected to be, I had secretly been sure that nobody was listening.

They were killed in an automobile accident on their way to visit me at summer camp. It was parents' night and I was the master of ceremonies. When they didn't show up, I still went onstage. I did my bit, fuelled by an incredible anger. There would be excuses later, of course. A religious meeting or something they had forgotten about—too important to miss. It had happened before. It never occurred to me that something might have happened to them. Children assume the worst, and for me, the worst wasn't death, it was indifference.

The news came during the juice and cookies party afterwards. The camp chaplain, a boisterous, overly friendly man called Father Bob, deftly cut me out like a slice of cake from the group of parents I was being praised by. He annoyed me, and I was rude to him, the way a big-headed ten-year-old who's been told she's hot stuff tends to be.

"I need to talk to you, dear," he said.

"What? Can't it wait? I'm busy." The words ring in my head still. It's one of those bad moments in life that grow more horrific with age and will not fade no matter how hard one tries to forget. The adults who had been praising my performance went suddenly silent, shocked at my behaviour.

The sweetness turned in my mouth, as if I'd bitten into a chocolate and found it full of dust. Father Bob drew me away gently and told me my parents were dead. It was like a punishment. If I hadn't been rude, my parents would be okay.

After that, I went to live with my Aunt Susan in Laingford. Susan was, and still is, an agnostic. She was beside me at the funeral mass (which was incredibly long), and later she told me that, although she was perfectly willing to discuss God and religion if I wanted to, she would not be accompanying me to church again. That suited me just fine. After the initial numbness had worn off, I had experimented with prayer, probing my customary lack of faith like a sore tooth, and found that nothing had changed. There was still nobody listening, and nobody left to insist that there was.

But early training stays with you. In times of trouble, I still find myself probing that empty place in my brain where Christians promise divine comfort is.

Sometimes I feel like an Icharus lost in a flock of twentieth century frequent flyers. They all buy their tickets and whizz off to the tropics while I'm still stuck on the ground gluing chicken feathers to my arms.

That search for meaning continues, of course, and up until the day I found Francy hanging in the kitchen, I was content to putter along believing implicitly in the goodness of humankind, the healing power of the earth and my own efforts to leave as small an ecological footprint as possible. That had been enough.

However, after two murders awfully close to home, and after seeing Candy onstage at Kelso's, it struck me that composting, making herbal tea and living the simple life of a craftsperson was absolutely pathetic.

I sat at my worktable and cried. Lug-nut plunked his head

in my lap in that endearing way dogs have of trying to help, and I thought about what to do. Become a social worker? Start counselling battered women? Go to cop college and become a caped avenger with a gun? Start a farming co-op for ex-strippers? Write a self-help book for New-Age artists with step-by-step instructions for changing the world? Hang myself? Or, dammit, find out who killed John and Francy and erase them from the planet?

My parents were killed by a drunk driver. I wanted to kill him back, for the longest time. Then I met him when he got out of jail. I was fourteen, and he got in touch with Susan and said he wanted to see me. She said it was entirely up to me. I said okay, because I'd never seen him and I wanted a face to go with my hatred.

We met in Susan's front room, both sitting on the edges of our chairs, fragile as porcelain. He was thin and pale, like a root vegetable, and he wept when he saw me, the tears seeping out the corners of his eyes and dripping off his unlovely chin. He wanted to give me money. (I didn't take it. Now, I would. Then, I couldn't.) His hands were damp and they trembled. He smelled of fear and sweat. He had little white yuckies in the corners of his mouth. He made me feel sick, but I stopped hating him. He didn't seem to be worth the trouble. Then he asked me to forgive him.

I used to think forgiveness was a big mystery, something you could only understand if you had been touched by God, which I hadn't. The real Christians I know (as opposed to the bogus ones) speak of it with a kind of wonder. Forgiveness is tangled up in reams of theological wool, though. God forgives everyone everything because of his divinity, and those who believe in him look for forgiveness; they need it, beg for it, even. What's more, they seem to get it. Non-Christians (at least this one) sometimes shy away from the concept because of all the trappings. But after meeting the man who schmucked my parents to a bloody pulp because he was driving pie-eyed, I discovered that forgiveness is actually a piece of cake. You just do it. You say "Okay, I forgive you," and then you forget it. That's what I did.

So, finding John's killer, and Francy's (if it was the same person, which was likely) and killing them back, was out. I suppose I used up all the revenge-juice in my body the last time, and there was none left. Finding the killer and forgiving him or her was an idea that stopped my tears and prompted me to light up another joint.

First of all, why should I forgive them? I mean, why me? Francy and John weren't mine. Francy was my friend, that's true, but I didn't own her the way I had, in a sense, owned my parents.

If someone breaks a teacup, which is yours, you can say "Oh, that's okay. it doesn't matter," and it doesn't any more. But that's a teacup, not a person. Forgiving that man for killing my parents was something I gave him because he needed it, and so did I. I owned my anger, he owned his remorse. Together, we gave them up, or gave them away, which was good.

I certainly had anger about John's and Francy's deaths, for different reasons. John didn't deserve to die, although he was a shithead and a wife-beater, and he deserved something, but not murder. My anger about John's death came under that big, amorphous heading "wrong", the kind of thing that saints and superheroes fight against. Francy's murder came under the "wrong" heading too, but I was madder about hers because it was wronger. She deserved no bad thing. She deserved better. The killer had stolen her life from her (wrong), her friendship and company from me (personal wrong) and the killer was getting away with it (extremely wrong.) Why did I want to find the killer, then? To punish them? Nope. To stop them from doing it again? Maybe. To find out if there was any remorse, so I could mix it with my anger and come up with a magical recipe for forgiveness? That was pretty close, although I felt uncomfortable with the missionary zeal of it. "Admit that you have sinned and ask forgiveness." Yuck.

And what, I asked myself, would I do if I found the killer and discovered that they had no remorse whatsoever? What then? I would be left with my anger and nowhere to put it. I think that's where revenge comes in. "Oh yeah? Well, I'll make you sorry."

What if the killer not only lacked remorse, but still had an unhealthy desire to keep on doing the "wrong" thing? To me, maybe. Then my anger would be gone, certainly, as well as my ecological footprint. I would become the best composter a human being can be. I would be dead.

At this point, I had worked it out. I couldn't just go back to making puppets and drinking herbal tea as if nothing had happened. I would have to find the killer, danger or not, before he killed someone else, like me. As for starting a co-op for ex-strippers, well, maybe in my next life.

Twentyseven

This tadpole has gathered
the reins of my body,
altered my courses,
flicked open the dam of my instinct.
—Shepherd's Pie

Francy's mother came up from the States for the
funeral, which was, to my surprise, organized by the Chapel of
the Holy Lamb—the Schreier's church. Apparently, Francy
and John had at one time belonged to the group, although
Francy had never mentioned it to me. When I found out, I
wondered if Carla had nabbed Francy in the A&P and my
friend had been too polite to say no. Anyway, I had known her
for three years, and I was reasonably sure that she hadn't
attended during that time.

Francy's mother was a small, defeated-looking woman with
no eyebrows. She had painted them on, which gave her caved-
in face a look of unutterable surprise, even when she was
crying. Her mourning attire was vintage American trailer-park
and her permed hair was pale lavender. I introduced myself to
her outside the Chapel and she immediately backed away.

"You're her, ain't you?" she said, rather loudly.

"Her? Who her?"

"The witch. The one who led her away from the Lord. Get

away from me." She turned and scuttled past a group of Lamb-ites, disappearing into the interior of the Chapel. Several people turned to stare at me, and I met the eyes of Carla Schreier, who smiled brilliantly, then turned to say something to her stocky husband, Samson. He looked over too, and I couldn't help feeling that I was the subject of her remark. Could it have been Carla that made Mrs. Delaney so hostile towards me? Had she called me a witch? Why would she do that?

George, who had been standing by my side, touched my arm. "Grief affects people in strange ways, Polly. Don't take it personally."

"How could I not take it personally? The mother of my best friend just called me a witch."

"The mother of your best friend just called me the whore of Satan," said a deep voice from behind me. I turned and threw myself into the arms of Ruth Glass, the angel-voiced lead of Shepherd's Pie.

"I thought you were on tour," I said.

"I was, but Rico called me on the road and told me what happened. I cancelled a booking in Timmins to get back here, so I could pay my respects. Francy was a good friend. I'll miss her. Maybe you could help me write a song for her, later." I squeezed her arm and nodded. It would have to be later, though. I wasn't ready to write about Francy yet. Not until I knew what had happened.

Several of the funeral-goers had noticed Ruth and were whispering and moving in. Ruth gets a lot of press, and she's a big woman, easy to recognize. Eddie came over to say hello, and once again I felt Carla's eyes. I looked over and then looked away, quickly. It was a smile, all right, but it wasn't a very nice one. I wondered what I'd done to deserve it. Maybe someone had reported to her the disparaging remarks I'd made about her baking.

"Hey, Eddie. How are you doing?" Ruth said.

"I'm okay, Miss Glass," he said. His black eye had faded a bit, but he still looked haunted. He probably wasn't sleeping well. His face was pale and he looked like he had lost weight. "Thanks for the postcard, eh? I showed it around at school."

Ruth put a hefty arm around his shoulders.

"Boy, you're getting big," she said. "You're taller than your dad, for Pete's sake. When are you going to stop growing?"

His face got even paler and he squirmed away. "Soon, I hope," he said awkwardly and walked back to where his parents were standing.

"Did I say something wrong?" Ruth said to me quietly.

"Well, he's been kind of jumpy lately. He was pretty involved with Francy and John. This thing hasn't been easy for him."

"I guess not. God, everybody's here, eh?"

Everybody was. Rico Amato, immaculately dressed, leaned on his vintage caddy, chatting to Aunt Susan. With them was Spit Morton, wearing an actual suit of questionable lineage which made him look like an undertaker from the fifties. Freddy, also in formal attire, stood behind him with a placid smile on his face. I guessed that Spit had decided not to press charges and they had made up. I saw Morrison and Becker lurking in the background, both in civvies, and several other locals who had turned out for the spectacle, although I would bet that they hadn't known Francy to speak to. People had started to move inside, so I figured that the service was about to begin.

"You'd think that the Holy Lambers would have a thing about suicide," I said to George, who had taken my elbow to steer me through the crowd like I was a shopping cart. "I'm surprised this is such a public do."

Otis Dermott, just in front of us, turned to blow a wave of sweet, rye-breath into my face. "We're all equal in the eyes of the Lord, Polly Deacon," he said. "Francy Travers may have died by her own hand, but she's in the arms of the Lord, now."

"Did you know her well, Otis?"

"Knew John better. When they was coming regular to chapel, we used to socialize a bit. Didn't get a chance to say goodbye to him, though. She sent his body up north, I heard."

"That's where his parents are," I said.

"I know. Thing is, they're in a home, eh? Barely holding on. Don't know why she didn't just bury him here. Would've been easier."

"Maybe it was too painful for her."

"More likely she knew she wouldn't get much sympathy as the grieving widow, eh?" Otis leered and winked. I wanted to hit him, but George squeezed my arm gently.

"Steady," he said in my ear.

"'Course, they married right here, must have been ten years ago. Lot happens in ten years. She was plenty in love with him then."

"Did they meet at the Chapel?"

"Nope. Francy came up here from the States on a fellowship mission when she was a teenager. Was a nanny to the Schreier's kid, Eddie. He's calmed down a lot, now. He was a little demon back then. She met John somewhere in Laingford and when he started courting her, she got him to come to our meetings. Things happened pretty swift after that."

I was flabbergasted. Francy had told me none of this. I mean, she'd once mentioned that she was a nanny up here, but she never told me it was for the Schreiers. Why not? Was she ashamed of it? More likely, I thought, I'd come on so strongly anti-Christian that she'd just left that part of her life closed to me. I felt a wave of shame for being so insensitive. I'd betrayed her. There was so much about her I would never know, now.

I couldn't believe that she'd never told me about the Schreier connection, although I suppose I could have figured it out if I'd thought about it enough. Eddie and Francy were pretty close. I'd chosen to see it as something vaguely sexual, though. Some loyal friend I was. I turned to George.

"Did you know all this?" I said.

He shook his head. "I didn't know her at all until you met her."

"Francy isn't related to the Schreiers, is she, Otis?"

"Heck, no. Church connections, that's all." We had stopped moving to talk, and we were the only ones left on the steps.

"We'd better hurry or we'll miss the testimonials," Otis said. We followed him in.

The Chapel of the Holy Lamb is built in the middle of a grove of pines in the heart of Cedar Falls farm country. Next to the road, there's a big billboard with BELIEVE IN JESUS written on it in huge black letters. It is not a mild reminder, it's a command. The building is squat and boxy, sided in pale, peach-coloured vinyl. Gathered around its perimeter are those squat, pointy-headed cedar trees, which Aunt Susan calls Holy Shrubs. The shrubs were painfully well-groomed, flanked by carefully tended beds of late-blooming chrysanthemums, giving off their usual, disconcertingly unpleasant scent. The chapel has a big parking lot. On Sundays, when I've driven past it, the lot is usually full.

Inside, there was soft organ music playing, but the service

had not yet begun. The place was packed and everybody was whispering. There was the feeling of suppressed excitement and the whispers sounded like wind in a dry meadow just before a thunderstorm.

Aunt Susan had saved us a seat near the back. We slipped into the pew—a rough wooden bench, really, no prayer books or hymnals to be seen. The seat was hard. Being a Holy Lamber, I suspected, was hard too.

On a platform at the front was a casket, closed understandably and covered in lilies. Beyond it was a podium, and behind that a stained glass window of the generic, abstract variety, all surging arcs and crayon colours. Francy would have hated it.

A thin, hot-eyed man with a bushy moustache got up and lifted his hands for silence.

"Brothers and sisters, we are gathered here today to mark the passing of our sister in Christ, Francine Grace Travers, née Delaney. Francy is in the arms of Jesus now, but those she left behind have a duty to mourn her, to share their love for her and to keep Christ alive in her memory."

In the front pew, Francy's mother, Mrs. Delaney, began sobbing loudly. Carla Schreier, next to her, put an arm around her and held on. Eddie, on the other side of Mrs. Delaney, hung his head and edged away.

The man at the podium continued. "I will now call on Samson Schreier, Francine's mentor in the Lord, to say a few words."

"Mentor in the Lord??" I hissed to George. "Golly."

Samson Schreier was a short man, powerfully built, with a face baked red by the sun and a belly which hung over his belt like a sack of Shure-Gain. He looked distressed, as if there were an unpleasant smell lodged in his nostrils. He stood slowly and walked to the podium as if he carried a great weight with him. When he turned and faced the gathering, I could feel the tension mount in the room. Samson Schreier had something important to say. He took a deep breath and let it out slowly in a hiss which sounded like hellfire to me.

"Brothers and sisters, Francine was an innocent child, easily led astray," he said. "When she came to us, she came in trust from the bosom of her mother here, and she was as pure white as the first snow, washed clean in the blood of the lamb."

"Wouldn't that make her pink?" I whispered to George. Funerals always make me silly. The woman in front of us turned around and frowned at me.

Samson continued. "She tended our boy Eddie with a loving heart, worshipped with us, shared bread with us, and we rejoiced in her young, fresh life."

Eddie had sunk so far down in his seat that his head was barely visible.

Samson inhaled through his nose, as if he required extra oxygen for the next bit. "Then she met a man of the world, a man who showed her a path that forked, brothers and sisters, forked away from the true path like the forked tongue of Satan that was his master. Oh, he put on the clothes of the lamb for a short time, he pretended to be one of the chosen. He has done this before, brothers and sisters. He married her right here in God's house. But soon he convinced her that the path of Satan was more interesting, and he spirited her away from us. John Travers was the right hand man of Satan himself. He chose lambs and led them to the slaughter. He led our Francine to her death."

His voice had risen, he was spitting a little, and the people gathered in the chapel shifted in their seats, as if they were watching an exciting movie. I risked a quick look behind me to the door, where Becker and Morrison were leaning, staring at Samson with narrowed eyes.

"See?" I wanted to shout. "See? There's more here than you ever dreamed of. Maybe Samson did it. You probably never even questioned him."

Samson seemed to have talked himself out. His shoulders sagged and he returned to his seat in the front row. The thin man mounted the platform again.

"Thank you, Brother Schreier. Next we will hear from Brother Einarson, who has asked me if he may speak."

Freddy stood. Freddy? Freddy of the dump, Freddy of the late-night hooch-fests and the gutted squirrel? Freddy was a Holy Lamber? Gosh. Their rules must be pretty flexible. The room hushed for a moment. Obviously, Brother Einarson's request was a surprise to more than just me. There was a burst of hissing as neighbour whispered to neighbour.

He made his way to the podium and stood, waiting for quiet. He swayed slightly, and I wondered if he had been hanging around with Otis Dermott and the rye-bottle.

"Brothers and sisters in the Lord," he said. "I have strayed from the true path and I have done many things I'm sorry for. But I'm back now, and I want to make a confession to you, here, while you are gathered in love to send Francine's soul to heaven."

At the word confession, everybody sat up a little straighter in their seats. I could feel Becker and Morrison behind me take a step or two forward. Freddy, I thought. Freddy did it. Not Samson. Freddy.

"Let me tell you a story. Once upon a time there was a little boy who was very unhappy. Nobody knew he was unhappy except me, but I couldn't do anything about it except love him from far away. The people in this little boy's life were hard on him, always wanting him to be something he wasn't. Then, one day, an angel appeared. An angel straight from heaven, Francy Delaney. She took this little boy by the hand and guided him. She protected him from the demons that he was doing battle with. She loved him as I loved him and taught him right from wrong. I will always thank the Lord for Francy Delaney and what she did for my son, Eddie." Freddy, tears running down his cheeks, left the podium and ran out of the room, through a back door which led God knows where. Carla Schreier sat motionless, the stunned eyes of the room on her back.

Samson, to whom this revelation did not seem to come as a surprise, sat still also. Eddie, who had sunk so low in his seat he was almost on the floor, scrambled to his feet and ran for the main exit, where Morrison and Becker grabbed him and hustled him outside. Eddie? Francy's young friend Eddie? What were they grabbing him for? He wouldn't hurt a flea, for Chrissakes. I stood and hurried outside myself. Morrison and Becker were putting Eddie into the back of the cruiser and I ran over.

"What are you doing?" I said. Becker shut the door—the one with no handles on the inside. Eddie sat in the back seat, tears streaming down his face.

"I am taking this kid in for questioning, that's all," Becker said. His face was grim. "What's your problem, Ms. Deacon?"

"Don't you dare call me Ms. Deacon, Mark Becker. What about Freddy? What about Samson Schreier?"

"We think the kid did it, Polly. He probably hated Travers for taking her away from him. Then Mrs. Travers was killed to cover it up. She trusted him. She drank with him. He made it look like suicide."

"I thought you were sure Francy had hung herself."

"That was before the post-mortem. There were enough Seconals in her blood to knock out a horse. And besides, the suicide note was a fake. We checked." Becker was so smug. He had worked it out, and he was bragging, trying to make me realize that he'd had everything in hand, right from the beginning. Too bad he was wrong.

"Eddie got the pills from home," Becker said. "We know Mrs. Schreier had a prescription. We checked. And the marks on your friend's neck indicated that she was hanged long after she went off to la-la land."

"You think Eddie knocked her out with pills, then hanged her? Eddie?"

"Eddie. We found a scrap of that lilac notepaper in his bedroom wastebasket last night, Polly, when we went to question him again about the night of John Travers's murder. Guy at Kelso's tipped us off. Said John and Eddie had a yelling match one night. Eddie said he was going to kill him. It all fits.

"He did your squirrel, or he got his real dad, Freddy Einarson to do it. That guy would do anything for his son, eh? We even found a newspaper with the letters cut out of it. As to the note, we know it's not Mrs. Delaney's writing. We'll get the kid to give us a sample of his. No problem. Eddie may have just knocked Travers out with a wrench to begin with, but later he went back to finish the job. Carla Schreier's statement indicated that she and Mrs. Travers went to bed shortly after Eddie and Francy arrived. He just went out again later. We found his fingerprints all over the Travers' house."

"This isn't right, Becker. There are too many holes. You can't prove any of it."

"We won't have to," he said, smiling. "The kid has already confessed."

"What??"

"Just before we put him in the car, he said 'Tell Mom I'm sorry for everything.' We all know what that means. We'll get a statement from him soon enough, Polly. It's over."

"You're making a big mistake, Mark."

"No, you are."

They pulled away, and I went back inside.

Things had calmed down some, back in the old Chapel of the Holy Lamb. The Schreiers had not moved from their seats and Mrs. Delaney was still sobbing. Nobody seemed to have noticed, or nobody seemed to care that Eddie Schreier had just been taken away in a police cruiser. The thin man was wrapping up the meeting, but I didn't pay any attention.

"They just took Eddie away," I whispered to George as I slipped back into place.

"Can they do that?" he whispered back.

"I don't know, but they did. I'll have to tell Carla, I guess. She'll probably start praying all over me."

After the final words were spoken, the crowd stood and began milling around. I pushed my way through the throng to get to Carla, who was supporting what was left of Mrs. Delaney. For a woman whose infidelity had just been made public, Carla seemed to be bearing up reasonably well. I touched her arm, gently.

"Carla?"

"Pauline. What is it?" Her eyes were clear and very bright. Her voice was even more child-like and breathy than usual, as if she were walking and talking in her sleep. She looked enormously relieved, almost euphoric, and very pretty.

"The police just took Eddie away for questioning, Carla. You should go to the station."

"Don't be silly. I can't go anywhere," Carla said and giggled. I wondered if she had taken one of those Seconals Becker said she had a prescription for. "I've got lots of people coming back to our place for a reception, " she said. "Eddie'll be fine. They'll let him go. Jesus will look after him."

"Carla, they think he murdered John and Francy. He's in big trouble."

"No, he's not. Don't you think that Jesus is watching out for him?" she said, still in that dream-like tone of voice. "Eddie's a good boy, even if his father's a drunk from the dump." She giggled again. Then she touched my arm. "Land sakes, I'll tell you, that's a load off my heart. Now everybody knows. No secrets in the Lord, you know." She smiled radiantly. Then she leaned very close to me and whispered in my ear. "Samson always knew, of course. It was a long time ago, before I found Jesus. But now he's so very happy. He'll be getting a son of his own." She patted her belly with one hand, still keeping a tight grip on the weeping Mrs. Delaney.

"Oh. Well, congratulations, Carla."

"Thank you. And thanks for telling me about Eddie. You're a good person, Pauline. But I'm sure he'll be fine." I headed for the door, my brain so full I could hardly see.

"Polly? You okay?" It was Ruth. "Listen. A bunch of us are going back to Rico's for a wake. You coming?" I looked back for one more eyeful of Carla.

"I'll meet you there," I said. It had just struck me. Nestled between Carla Schreier's breasts was Poe's gold cross—last seen around the neck of a very happy, very alive Francy Travers.

Twentyeight

Who's she? How'd she get to be so old?
What's she done that's good?
—Shepherd's Pie

In all the whodunits I've ever read, the detective always gets a flash of insight right near the end and goes charging off alone to confront the killer. They always end up in grave danger, and the murderer confesses all in a cold-blooded way while sharpening a knife to chop the hero up into little bits.

I've always hated that. Not the knife part—that's exciting, because you know somebody'll be along at the last second to foil the villain—but the going off alone part. I could never figure out how the detective, who was always so clever, so brave and so calm, would actually be so stupid at the same time.

Stupid isn't hard. It's easy. I know.

I told George I wanted to talk to Samson about Eddie, and I'd show up at Rico's later.

"What are you up to?" George said.

"I'm just worried about Eddie," I said. "Carla doesn't seem to realize the danger he's in. I just want to make sure Samson knows what's going on, that's all."

"You want the truck?"

"No, thanks. I'll get Samson to drive to Laingford to check on Eddie, and he can drop me off at Rico's on the way. Either that or I'll take the bush road home and grab my bike. I need the exercise anyway. You go along, George. I'll be there later."

I waited around until everyone had left. The Schreiers and Mrs. Delaney and the preacher were still inside. It was getting chilly and I regretted not bringing my Cedar Falls dinner jacket with me—the plaid flannel coat the locals wear with pride to everything but a funeral. When they came out onto the front steps, the sun went in behind a cloud. I was standing in the middle of the parking lot and it felt like the last showdown at the OK corral.

I moved toward the group slowly, with what I hoped was a friendly expression on my face. The preacher was holding up one side of Mrs. Delaney, who could barely walk, and Carla was on the other, still wearing that weird euphoric expression. Samson looked troubled when he saw me, as if he couldn't quite remember who I was. He came to meet me.

"Can I help you?" he said.

"Mr. Schreier, you don't know me, but—"

"Of course I know you. You're that woman lives with George Hoito, aren't you? Carla's told me all about you."

"Nothing bad, I hope," I said, laughing to show it was a joke. He didn't get it. "Look," I continued, "sorry to be a nuisance, but I don't know if you realize that the police were at the funeral. When Eddie ran out after Freddy Einarson said, uh, what he said, they took the boy away to the station in Laingford."

"Carla has told me that," he said. "What's your point?"

"Well, aren't you the least bit worried?"

"Why should I be? Eddie's done no wrong that I know of, so the police can't do him any harm. They'll bring him back as soon as they figure that out. If he has done wrong, then he'll get what he deserves. I've got no call to be chasing off after him like a nursemaid. He's a big boy."

"He's not that big."

"Bigger than me, anyway. About as big as Freddy Einarson, you might say. Ever since he found out that Einarson was his real father, he hasn't spoken a word to me. If I went down there, he'd just clam up, and the police would get the idea he had something to hide. He hasn't, has he?" He fixed me with an eye and waited.

"How should I know?" I said.

"Seems you know a lot about this business, Miss Deacon. More than you should, maybe."

"I don't know what you mean."

"What's your interest in Eddie, anyway?"

"He's a friend of mine," I said. "I'm worried about him."

"You stay away from him. He's had enough trouble with older women. Look where Francine got him, once she got hooked by Satan. You're the same. If Eddie hadn't got himself involved with people like you, none of this would have happened." I guessed then that it was Samson who told Mrs. Delaney I was a witch. Nice guy.

"What do you mean 'none of this'? None of what? You mean Francy wouldn't be dead? John would still be alive?"

"Don't go putting words into my mouth. Eddie wouldn't be dealing with the police if he'd stayed away from those two to begin with, that's all."

"How could he stay away from her?" I said. "She was his nanny, wasn't she? He didn't have any choice. Anyway, you said in there, she was the best thing to happen to him."

"I didn't say that," Samson hissed. By this time, Carla and the preacher had settled Mrs. Delaney into the Schreier's car and were looking over at us. "It was Freddy Einarson said it. She was good for Eddie, only until she met Travers. She turned her face away from the Lord after that and poured poison into Eddie's ears. Nothing but poison after that."

Carla started to walk over to us.

"I have to get these ladies home," he said. "We have guests waiting." He clearly had no intention of inviting me to join the party.

"And Eddie?" I said.

Samson suddenly went all paternal on me. He put a heavy hand on my shoulder and smiled in what he probably thought was a caring way.

"He'll be brought back when the time is right. Don't you worry about him. You just go back to your goats and your friends and keep out of our business. It'll be the best for all of us if you do as I say." I felt my insides go cold. Stick to your goats. Gosh.

Carla had arrived at his side and took his arm possessively, smiling at me as if in apology.

"Samson, I'm so tired, dear. I need to rest, to lie down. The baby, you know. Can we go?" Samson's face softened as he looked at her. A kind of wonder filled his eyes at the word "baby" and he put one of his large hands over her small one.

"Carla," I said, in a last-ditch attempt to get through. She looked up with a surprised expression on her face, as if she had forgotten I was there.

"Carla, where did you get that crucifix?"

"Excuse me?" she said. She was wearing a coat, but I knew it was there, underneath, hanging significantly around her neck.

"The crucifix. The one you have around your neck. I noticed it earlier. It's lovely. Where did you get it?"

"You're mistaken," she said. "I would never wear an image of our suffering Lord as an ornament." She opened her coat to show me her unadorned neck, then she smiled, very sweetly.

"Carla was brought up Catholic," Samson explained, indulgently, "but she's put all that idolatry behind her, haven't you, little one?"

Carla snuggled into him like a kitten. "Please can we go?" she said. Her little-girl voice was starting to get to me. It made me feel big and dumb. I also wondered if I had been hallucinating, earlier. I was sure I'd seen Poe's cross around her neck. All this death was making me crazy. Carla gave me a little, waggle-fingered wave, then they turned their backs on me and walked to their car, got in and drove away. I stood for a moment, thinking, then walked briskly over to where the preacher was mounting the steps to go back into the Chapel.

"Mr. Er—pardon me. Sir?" He turned as if surprised to find me there, which was odd, seeing as I was the only other human being around, and I'd been there as long as he had.

"Ma'am?" If he had been wearing a hat, I swear he would have raised it.

"Do you think I could talk to you for a minute?"

"Of course, sister. I always have time for talk. Come on in." He opened the door for me and lead the way purposefully past the chapel, where Francy's body in its closed casket lay in state below the ugly window. I followed him into a small office, presumably his, which was no different from any church office in the world. Not to say that I've been in many, but they are all, it seems to me, furnished by the same company, who make blonde wood desks and chairs padded in burnt orange nubby stuff. There were pictures of Christ in various gentle poses hung on the walls and the bookshelves were full of theological texts and stacks of pamphlets. The carpet was beige. The air smelled melancholy—a mixture of furniture polish and dusty bibles. He waved me to a chair, opened the window a crack, then opened a drawer from which he extracted a cigar and an ash-tray.

"Do you mind?" he said. "I always like to smoke after a testimonial. It clears the air, so to speak." I drew my cigarettes from my pocket and held them up, grinning. We understood each other and lit up, no words being necessary.

"What can I do for you?" he asked, blowing a scented smoke-ring.

"Well, it's kind of complicated. I'm not really sure." I wasn't. I was feeling very odd—mostly because I hadn't set foot in a religious establishment for a long time and it brought back uncomfortable feelings I had thought were long-buried. I liked this man, although I didn't know him. I'd heard him speak at the funeral, using all the God-words I had come to distrust, but the way he said them somehow made them all right, as if it were a language he was comfortable using, but wouldn't force it on anybody who didn't speak it. Strange that some of his congregation (Carla, at least) felt it necessary to seek recruits, but he didn't seem to. Maybe, as the leader, he was exempt from that obligation.

I didn't know why I was there. It had something to do with the fact that I had seen a crucifix around Carla Schreier's neck one minute and she had denied its existence in the next. It had something to do with my own grief, as well, which was building up like a migraine behind my eyes. But why I was sitting in the office of the guy in charge of the Chapel of the Holy Lamb, watching him puff on a cigar as he waited patiently for me to say something—that in itself was a mystery. The silence grew until he cleared his throat.

"By the way, I'm Pastor Garnet Larkin," he said. "I don't

think we've been formally introduced."

"I'm sorry. I should have told you my name right at the beginning." This was not good. I was feeling inadequate already. The churchy atmosphere made me feel guilty. As if I were to blame for something. I was regressing rapidly, back to when I was ten.

"I'm Pauline Deacon," I said and reached a hand across the desk. He shook it firmly.

"Pleased to meet you, Ms. Deacon. You knew Mrs. Travers personally, didn't you?"

"Yes. She was a close friend of mine. I found her, you know. In her kitchen. I was—kind of involved in the murder investigation up until then, but after that..." A large, fist-sized knot was working its way up into my throat. My head felt hot, and my eyes started burning. He shoved a box of kleenex across the desk at me.

"Cry," he said. "It helps." I did. In fact, I cried totally and horribly in a very messy, non-communicative way for quite a long time. Pastor Larkin just sat there, smoking his cigar and gazing off into space. None of that "there, there" stuff for Larkin. I liked that. He just waited until I was finished.

I blew my nose and tossed the soggy mess into his wastebasket.

"Thanks," I said.

"Don't mention it. Tears clarify things pretty good, I find." He leaned forward. "Now. Did you want to talk to me about something?"

"Well, actually, I just wanted to ask you if I could see Francy. The body, I mean. I know the coffin is closed and all that, but you see, the last time I saw her, she was hanging in her kitchen and I guess the image is haunting me a bit. I was going to ask her mother if I could, but she doesn't like me much." I was making it up as I went along, but it felt right. It fit the way I was feeling. I did want to see her, although the thought hadn't occurred to me until the request popped out of my mouth.

"I can't see why Mrs. Delaney wouldn't like you," the Pastor said. "Seeing as you were a close friend and all."

"Well, I suppose someone might have told her some things," I said. I didn't want to accuse Samson of slander, although I was pretty sure it had been him. "I'm not much of a church-goer. Mrs. Delaney called me a witch."

"And are you?"

"Not that I know of. Unless living alone in the woods counts."

"It might. Are you Godless, Ms. Deacon?" Oh, boy. Here it comes, I thought. The pitch.

"Not really. I keep my mind open, that's all," I said.

"That's the first place He'll come knocking, then," the Pastor said and smiled gently.

"So I hear." We sat and smoked in silence for a minute. Having decided to pay my last respects to Francy, alone in the Chapel of the Holy Lamb, I felt calm and strangely peaceful. I hadn't felt like that for a long time.

"Well," the Pastor said, "I don't see why I can't let you take a look at her. She hasn't been prettied-up much, seeing as it was a closed coffin and all, but I saw her just a short while ago and she certainly doesn't look as bad as how she probably looks in your mind. She'll be buried tomorrow. We usually do it right away, but her mother wanted her to stay in the Chapel for one night. Mrs. Delaney will be back to sit with her, she said."

"She didn't seem to be in any shape to sit up all night," I said, following him down the corridor.

"Well, if she doesn't come, I guess the job will be mine. She wanted someone to pray over her, you see. A few prayers. Some thinking. No harm in that."

He opened the chapel door and we walked together up the aisle to the casket. I tugged at the ring on my finger—an opal that my mother had given me for my eighth birthday, which, as I had grown, I had had re-set several times to fit. I had worn it always, but in that short walk to Francy's casket, I decided, in a catch-all, ritualistic sort of way, to give it to Francy. The Pastor opened the lid for me and then discreetly stepped aside.

Somebody had fixed her up a bit—maybe the police, or whoever had done the post-mortem. The Pastor was right, she certainly did look better than she had swinging from the rafter in her kitchen. Because the funeral hadn't included a public viewing, she wasn't slathered in horrible pancake makeup the way bodies sometimes are, but neither was she green and wormy, the way I was expecting. She was very dead, though, and her face was still too dark.

No blood pumped through those veins, nor ever would again. No muscle would jump again to open those eyes, which by now were probably dull and opaque. Francy's face, alive, had sparkled with mischief. No mischief now. I resisted the temptation to lift the eyelids and peer in. A kind of corpse-oriented vertigo took hold of me. I wanted to sweep her up in my arms and dance with her. I reached out to touch her hand. It was cold and stiff. Rigid, in fact. Putting my ring on her finger was going to be tricky.

I felt the Pastor behind me.

"She looks peaceful, any road," he said.

"She does," I said. I showed him the ring. "I wanted to give her this. Can I put it on her finger?"

He sighed gently and smiled a bit. "Seems to be a trend,"

he said, and, reaching out, opened the stiff fingers of her right hand. "Samson Schreier had the same idea. Took it off his wife's neck and said a little prayer over it."

From those dead fingers fell a gold crucifix, on a chain, which slithered quickly out of sight into the satin folds of the coffin.

Twentynine

I shall stew you and chew you
and wear your bones
in a clattering jangle at my neck,
your teeth strung
on a ring hung
in the ruin of my face.
  –Shepherd's Pie

I'd like to report that I kept my cool. After all, Pastor Garnet Larkin had been kind to me. But cool wasn't happening.

Before slipping beneath the folds of satin, that crucifix had glinted, and I knew it wasn't a mirage. It had glinted at the neck of Carla Schreier during the funeral. It had glinted when Poe had carried it in his beak the day after John's murder. It had glinted when it hung around Francy's neck the day I gave it to her. The cross was the key to the whole damn thing and if Samson Schreier had removed it from his wife's bosom and hidden it in the hand of a woman who was about to be buried in the ground, then I figured it was more than a scrap of gold he was trying to bury. Where had he been the night of John's murder? At a farming conference? I don't think so.

I swore loudly, and the Pastor flinched.

"No call for that, ma'am," he said. "None of us has a monopoly on gifts to the dead."

I reached my hands into the coffin, scrabbling around underneath Francy's cold body like a grave-robber until I caught hold of the chain. Pastor Larkin gasped and put a hand on my arm. I wrenched away from him and ran out of the Chapel of the Holy Lamb just as fast as I could go.

I didn't have much time. I had to get to a phone and get in touch with Becker and Morrison, and I had to do it before they charged Eddie with murder. In spite of what Samson and Carla had said, I didn't think that Jesus was going to make everything okay.

The Chapel was just down the road from the Schreier's place and my quickest route to a phone was to take the nearby bush-road to George's place that Francy and I had taken the week before. Actually, my quickest route to a phone was to drop in on Samson Schreier, the fanatical holy roller who had announced publicly that he had hated John Travers and had tried to bury some evidence with the body of his second victim, Francy. But I wasn't ready to confront Samson yet. Not without some big cop standing right behind me.

I hadn't figured it all out yet. I mean, just because Samson had put the crucifix in Francy's coffin, it didn't prove that he was the murderer. I just had a very strong feeling about it. The slim gold chain and pendant was vital evidence. That much I knew. I ran along the path for a while until a pain in my chest told me I'd better slow down or I'd collapse. I was wheezing and my heart was thumping loudly in my ears. I didn't even think about bears. I wasn't afraid of them any more, anyway.

As I hurried along, my brain kicked into overdrive to keep up with my lungs. Why had John been murdered? Revenge? Anger? Had Samson been so enraged at John's having taken

Francy away from the Schreiers that he had harboured a grudge for ten years before doing anything about it?

Was it something to do with the four hundred bucks? What was that money for, anyway? Maybe it had nothing to do with the case at all. Maybe it was just some sort of "just in case" stash. Or maybe John had owed it to Samson and the farmer had become tired of waiting. Still, four hundred dollars is a puny sum to kill for.

According to Eddie, the two men had hated each other, and Samson had made his feelings pretty clear at the funeral. I wondered if Becker had even bothered to check out Samson's alibi. Probably not. He had been convinced from day one that Francy had done it.

But if Samson had murdered John, why had Freddy Einarson become involved? I was sure it was Freddy who had nailed the warning and the dead squirrel to my front door, but Freddy had no reason to defend Samson, had he? If anything, the two men should be sworn enemies, not buddies, seeing as Freddy had dallied with Samson's wife sixteen years ago, if not more recently.

I wondered why Samson had been so relaxed during Freddy's confession in the Chapel. Perhaps he had learned to live with it. But that suggested a self-control which did not match with the idea of Samson killing John in a murderous rage.

Where had Poe picked up the crucifix and how had it come to be around Carla's neck?

Why was Eddie hanging around the Travers place after the murder? Was he looking for Lady Chatterley, or something more dangerous? Did he really get the shiner by walking into a door?

Why did someone kill Francy and leave a fake suicide note?

Why did Freddy bonk Spit over the head unless he was involved in John's murder?

The questions came thick and fast, crowding into my brain until they became a chant. Where? Why? Who? How? The words echoed with every step I took, and my heart was still pumping loudly in my ears so I didn't even hear the all-terrain vehicle until it was nearly on top of me.

It was Carla Schreier, and she did not have any pamphlets with her, she had a shotgun. Maybe she was scared of bears, too. She killed the engine and hopped off the ATV.

"Hi, Carla," I said. "What's up?" I stepped towards her. Had Samson flipped out and tried to attack her? Did she need help?

"This is loaded," she said. Her baby-doll voice had an edge to it, like a toy made of razor-blades. Up close, her smile, which had seemed friendly, pulled into focus. This was the grin of someone about to do murder. Mad. Totally, frothing mad. I almost wet myself. The dull gray of the gun barrel indicated that it could easily have been the one I saw in John's truck, but I didn't think it would be smart to ask.

"Loaded? I see," I said, careful not to startle her.

"You know, Pauline, walking around in the bush this time of year can be very dangerous. Especially if you're not wearing protective orange. There are a lot of crazy hunters around."

"Gosh, you're right. Maybe I'll just slip home and grab my jacket."

"No need for that. No need." She seemed to be enjoying herself. Then she raised the gun and pointed it at my chest.

"Carla, I don't know what your problem is, here. If you need to talk to me about something, that's fine. But I'm in a bit of a hurry. George is expecting me at any moment."

"No, he's not," she said. "He phoned us from that faggot

antique dealer's a little while ago, asking where you were. I said you told us that you were tired and had decided to go straight home. You see, just before that, we received a very interesting little call from the Pastor."

"Oh," I said. Her language shocked me. I wouldn't have thought that "faggot" was in her vocabulary.

"I believe you have something of mine, Pauline. I want it back."

"I don't know what you're talking about."

"Yes, you do. My cross. I want it back."

"But an hour ago you denied ever having worn one."

She grinned, looking quite lovely for a moment. "I lied," she said. "Now, you can either give it to me now, which will give you a few minutes more, or I can blast a hole in you first and search you afterwards."

"Nice choice," I said, starting to cry. Don't get me wrong— I wasn't begging her yet. But I was awfully scared, she was obviously intending to kill me, and I wasn't ready to die. She started to take careful aim.

"Wait! For Chrissakes, wait a second, will you? You don't want to get blood on your dress, do you? That would complicate things, don't you think?" She was still wearing her funeral dress. Pale pink with little spriggy flowers on it. Very becoming, if you were twenty.

She lowered the gun. "Well, yes. Getting bloody would be a shame," she said. "How thoughtful. But you know, when I shot John, I didn't get a spot on me. Not a spot."

"Good for you," I said. "Why?"

"I wore an apron, you see. I burned it. Wasn't that smart?" she said.

"I mean, why did you shoot him?" I figured that if I was going to die, I might as well take the truth with me. Maybe I could explain it to John, when I got there. Except that I was reasonably certain that there was no "there", which was why I was crying.

"Oh. Well, there was a good reason. You know that God tells someone to execute abortionists so they won't keep on killing babies? It was like that. I was just defending my baby."

"Who? Eddie?"

"No, silly. This." She pointed to her belly, which was swollen with the new life inside her. "He told me I had to get rid of it. If I didn't, he'd tell Samson and then where would I be?" She giggled. "Silly boy. He should have known God wouldn't allow it. Anyway, this baby is a miracle and John Travers had nothing to do with it at all."

"He was the father, though, right?"

"He was the messenger, Pauline. Samson's impotent, but he has a lot of faith. In the Lord. In me. I couldn't have that destroyed now, could I?"

"I see," I said. So that was what the four hundred bucks was for. A nice little Toronto abortion. Even John Travers would know that a government-funded, Laingford Memorial procedure was out of the question. That would also explain why he'd stashed it in Lug-nut's food bag. He'd got the money together, but the person for whom it was intended wouldn't take it.

"Tell me, Carla. Did Samson think Eddie was a miracle baby too?"

She didn't like my tone. "Samson knew all about Eddie right from the beginning," she said. "Don't mock me. He married me knowing that I was carrying Freddy Einarson's child. It was after that I found the Lord. I haven't looked back since." There was a fundamental flaw in her logic, but I wasn't about to point it out to her.

"So you and John Travers were having an affair, I take it," I said.

"It wasn't an affair. It was the Lord's work. We prayed before and after." The image was nauseating.

"Did Francy know about it?"

"That little scatterbrain? You must be joking. Too busy picking weeds with her witch-friend and fooling around with my Eddie, who is turning out to be just as sinful as his father, Freddy Einarson. I wouldn't be surprised if that Beth wasn't my granddaughter. That's a sick little thought, isn't it? No. John married Francine because she was pure, and when she dirtied up, he turned to me. She was too wrapped up in her baby to notice."

My head hurt, but I had stopped crying. Now, I was just ragingly angry.

"Carla, what's all the fuss about the crucifix? After all, nobody knows about it but me. You Holy Lambers don't even like crucifixes. Nobody thinks it's important at all." Dumb thing to say. But I was thinking out loud.

"Exactly," she said, glad that I had pointed out why she had to kill me.

"But the cops—I mean, I could show it to the cops, say that I found it and gave it to Francy, tell them that Samson put it in the coffin, but what would that prove? You could easily say you lost it somewhere, or you could deny ever knowing anything about it."

"I could, but then they'd start wondering about me, wouldn't they? I don't want that. Can you give it to me now, please?" She said it quite sweetly, holding out her hand.

"Before I do, could you tell me why you killed my best friend? I just need to know."

She told me. It made a weird kind of sense, if your brain

worked the way Carla's obviously did. It was ugly, though, and stupid. A stupid reason. Just like the stupid reason she had for killing me.

"Now, I think it's time to stage a little accident. Just toss me the cross, would you?" I did. I was numb with fright, and I had a hideous vision of her cold hands rooting around in my clothing after I was dead. She caught it deftly.

"This won't take long, Pauline," she said kindly. "You won't feel a thing. Just don't move around."

I lost it. I fell to my knees and gibbered. I used all sorts of God-words which hadn't passed my lips since my parents died. I even started saying the Lord's prayer. I closed my eyes, heard a heavy rustling in the bush off the trail and knew all at once that my power-animal the bear had come to take me to the other side. I yelled, there was an enormous noise and my heart exploded.

Thirty

Here is the cycle of living and dying
solemnly sung by the waves
in the throat of the bay.
—Shepherd's Pie

The bear was upon me, licking my face and whining.
I threw my arms around it and wondered if it would be safe to
open my eyes. I was ready for anything. My chest hurt, but
that was because the bear was so heavy. Well, not that heavy,
actually, but I supposed that things were different in the
afterworld.

I heard something big moving towards me, but I figured
my bear would protect me, and anyway, I was dead, so what
did it matter? I opened my eyes and found myself looking into
the bear's mouth, which was big and red and smelled like dog
kibble.

"You okay, Polly?" If that was the voice of God, I was
definitely in trouble. It was Morrison. I sat up carefully, my
arms still around the bear, which looked suspiciously like
Lug-nut.

"Oh God. I'm not dead. Oh God." At the same time
somebody else was saying "Oh God Oh God" too, over
and over.

I looked over at Carla Schreier. She was crumpled in a

small heap, shivering and moaning in fright.

"Make it go away, Jesus," Carla whimpered. "Make it leave me alone."

Things happened pretty smartly after that. Some other cops I didn't know showed up and everybody asked a lot of questions. Lug-nut stayed glued to my side, which I liked a lot.

Carla insisted that she'd been attacked by a bear and had shot at it in self-defence. But there was no sign of any bear.

"I didn't see a bear," Morrison said to a superior who wasn't Becker. Where was he, anyway? "I saw Carla Schreier pointing a gun at Polly, and I drew my own weapon, but I didn't have time to use it. Schreier screamed, the gun went off, and then they both fell to the ground. I thought she'd got you, Polly."

"If there had been a bear, Lug-nut would be chasing it right now," I said.

"There was a bear, I tell you," Carla insisted. She was flanked by two police officers, and the shotgun had been whisked away. "It came out of the bush straight for me, roaring. That's why I fired. Look, it scratched me." She offered her sleeve for inspection. The sleeve was perfectly okay, the skin unharmed. She stared at it in astonishment and then went apeshit.

I made sure the cops had the crucifix in hand, although it didn't really matter. Carla was incriminating herself all over the place and praying for me to be struck by lightning. She called me a witch a dozen times, and they took her away, shrieking and struggling.

Morrison drove me to the Laingford cop-shop to make a statement. Becker was there waiting for me in a drab little interview room, tapping a pencil and looking like he hadn't slept in a week. We sat opposite one another, a battered wooden table between us. Someone had carved their initials into the surface—"D.W. was here"—and I wondered fleetingly what D.W. had used to make the marks. They'd searched me for weapons. Hadn't they searched D.W.?

"I have to go fill out a report," Morrison said. "You want a coffee or anything, Polly?" I shook my head and he left us.

Becker's face was tight and he was all business. He banged out question after question concerning the past hour or so, and I answered as truthfully as I could, trying not to feel aggrieved. I didn't think I was going to get an apology from him. After all, he had just been doing his job. The only thing he did wrong was to get involved with a suspect—me.

When we got to the part about Carla and the gun, I got a tad emotional. I wanted to tell him how frightened I had been, to explain that looking into the face of Death had been monstrous and horrible, but I couldn't shake the feeling that anything I said would be chalked up to my own drug-dependent flakiness.

"Now, you said that Carla told you why she killed Mrs. Travers? Tell me about it," he said, pencil at the ready.

"Won't that be hearsay, Detective?"

"She'll tell us something, I expect, but from what Morrison has said, she's gone off the deep end, so your testimony will be important."

"Will it be admissible?"

"What do you mean?"

"I mean, I'm a pot-head whose friend was murdered. How can you be sure I'm telling the truth?"

His face softened a little and he reached across the awful table and touched my hand. I grabbed it and held on.

"Polly, you blush like a mad thing whenever you lie. Top to toe. You know that," he said.

"So you do remember. I wondered if you'd just wiped it out of your mind."

"I won't ever be able to do that," he said and extricated his hand, massaging it as I had done when he took he cuffs off me ages ago. "I'm still kicking myself for it. It was a mistake. We shouldn't have done it."

"'Shoulds' really piss me off," I said. "Somebody says 'should' and I immediately avoid doing whatever it is. Somebody says 'don't' and it makes me want to do it more. Tell me, Mark Becker. You had a good time, didn't you? Before, you know, I made my oh-so-tragic mistake?"

"Yeah. I did. But please don't want more, Polly Deacon. We're incompatible. I'll see you around and I don't want to think every time I do, that I made a dumb move and I 'should' re-think it. I'm too damn busy. You need some sensitive artist-hippie-guy who doesn't care what you do to yourself, and who has the time to double-check every move he makes. That's not me. Now can you tell me what Mrs. Schreier said, please?"

I got my face under control, whipped my mind back to Carla and the forest and told him.

"Could you tell me why you killed my best friend?" I'd said to her. Carla had taken a moment to gaze up at the tree I was standing under. There was a slight breeze blowing, making that whooshing sound pine trees make when they're dancing with the wind. I had thought it was one of that last sounds I'd hear, ever.

"Well, that was just a little mistake of mine, actually," Carla said. "I didn't realize it until you told me just now that you'd given my cross to her. Where did you find it?"

I had told her briefly about Poe.

"What a pity, " Carla said. "Maybe she didn't have to die at all. You see, after John's death, I felt badly for her and went over to see if there was anything I could do and to tell her about my baby—you know, share some womanly conversation. When I got there she was acting strange and she was wearing my cross. The last time I'd seen it was the night John died. I was wearing it when Eddie and Francine came home, telling me that Eddie had hit John. I reached for it and held it and prayed, oh, I prayed that John was dead. Then, after I'd put them to bed with a nice hot drink, I went over to see for myself.

"I still had it on when I called Freddy to come help, because he smiled at it—he gave it to me, you know. It must have fallen off when we were moving the body. That's why Samson put it in Francine's coffin. He told me that part of our lives was behind us now."

"So you killed Francy because she was wearing your crucifix?"

"Of course. She had found it, don't you see? She knew it was mine. I'd worn it for years, when she lived with us. It was a part of me. Oh, I know it went against Pastor Garnet's ideas, but I found it comforting. I figured she'd found it in her house and I've only been there once, when I went to execute John. I've worn it for sixteen years. She wore it to mock me."

"She didn't, Carla. She just said it looked familiar, that's all."

"Well, how was I to know that? She looked at me. She knew. So I made her a nice hot drink there in her kitchen to help her sleep."

"Then you wrote the note and strung her up like a bag of potatoes?"

"Oh, she was much heavier than a bag of potatoes. But we farm-women are strong, you know?"

"I know."

That was when Carla had told me to relax and not move around, then she'd lifted John Travers's shotgun to her eye and taken careful aim. That was when I had been saved by a bear that didn't really exist. I tried to explain that part to Becker, but he didn't seem too convinced.

"I'm glad you're okay, Polly," he said, putting away his notebook. "You'll probably have to testify."

"Will it come out that we slept together?" I said.

"I doubt it. It was incidental."

"Great. Incidental. Great."

He came out from behind the table. "Dr. McCoy," he said, really close to my face. "That goat-poison? There's an antidote. It's called work. Law. Stuff like that." I kissed him, right on the mouth, despite the likelihood of cameras in the interview room and guys checking us out behind the mirror next door. Becker did not struggle, much anyway. Then he touched my face with a sad hand and led me out of the room.

Morrison took me back to George's place. George made coffee and plopped his bottle of Glen-sneeze on the table beside our mugs. Morrison sighed deeply and reached for it before I could, but he poured a hefty slug into mine first.

"Thanks," I said.

"You're welcome," Morrison said. "It was a close call, Polly Deacon. We could have lost you if it hadn't been for that bear."

"But there was no damned bear."

"Well, there might have been. A second before we got there."

"And Lug-nut didn't notice? You got there before she fired at me, right? But she said it attacked her."

"The bear must have been in her mind," George said. "I 've

got a friend at the Rama reserve who would say that was powerful medicine." I had a flash of the Vision-Quest workshop and Dream-Catcher. Good medicine, good medicine. Maybe my hamster had grown up, finally. I would never know for sure.

"Anyway, you did get there in time, Earlie. That was a good thing," George said.

"Yup." Morrison explained that it was Eddie who put the pieces together. "Poor kid was keeping a lot of secrets," he said. "He knew his mother was carrying on with Travers. Knew it right from the beginning because he walked in on them in the Schreier's barn. Knew she was pregnant, too. Heard her throwing up in the morning, he said. He's had a hard time."

"He didn't have anything to do with John or Francy's deaths, though, did he?" I asked.

"Not really, aside from covering up. He says you caught him in the Travers' house after the police tape was up. How come you never told us?"

"I thought he was looking for a book Francy had lent him, one his mother had made him return. He confirmed it himself, later. I didn't really think he was up to anything bad in there."

"His mother sent him over to look for the crucifix," Morrison said. "She told him that Francy had stolen it. He didn't believe her, but I guess he realized it was important, somehow."

"Was he carrying on with Francy, like Carla said? I hoped not, but I did wonder."

"Not according to him, no. He just liked her, that's all. He said that Samson had forbidden him to go over there, but he did anyway. His mother didn't seem to mind. Probably gave her a chance to see Travers."

"Was it Samson who gave him the black eye?"

"Nope. That was Freddy. Seems Eddie always suspected that Samson wasn't his real father. When Carla let slip that the crucifix had sentimental value on account of the fact that his father had given it to her, he figured it out. Samson Schreier didn't hold with that sort of thing, he knew that. So the kid sniffed around for a likely father and came up with Freddy."

"Why would Freddy hit him?"

"The kid went over to the dump for the big father/son confrontation. Didn't go too good, it seems."

"Ah."

Eddie had told the cops about the squirrel note, which his mother had pasted together one night when she thought that he was asleep. The police had grilled him for a while, and then decided that they needed to talk to the Schreiers senior.

"Just before we left we got a call from the Pastor at the Chapel," Morrison said. "He told us that you had grabbed the crucifix and made a run for it. He said he'd called the Schreiers, figuring you'd gone over there, asking for you, and he let the story out. Carla Schreier's reaction was a bit wild, he said, and he got worried."

"Nice of him," I said, faintly.

"That was when I high-tailed it over to your cabin. When Lug-nut saw me, he barked once, then ran off along the bush road. Kept looking back to make sure I was following."

Lug-nut the wonder dog. I was bursting with pride. I patted Luggy's head and he slobbered all over my hand.

"I called Carla Schreier, too," George said.

"I know. She told me," I said.

"After the telephone call I realized that you would never miss one of Rico's parties, particularly if Ruth was there with her guitar. So I set out to bring you back and encountered a large number of screaming police cars headed for the Schreier's farm. I knew that if there was trouble, you would be there."

"Thanks, George."

It was nine o'clock. I suddenly thought of Ruth Glass singing *My Life, My Death* in that haunting, healing voice of hers.

"Do you think they're still at it?" I said. Then the phone rang. It was Rico, wondering where the hell we were. We looked at each other after George hung up.

"Earlie," he said, "you off duty yet?"

He was.

EPILOGUE

Carla Schreier ended up in a criminal psychiatric facility. It wasn't a pretty trial, especially after the media got interested in it. We all had our pictures in the paper a few times, but eventually the fuss died down and people stopped talking about it. She lost the baby, and I feel bad about that. It wasn't its fault and Carla would have loved it fiercely. Still, that's another very, very big issue.

Freddy disappeared and people say the authorities are still looking for him. George thinks he's probably managing some dump up in Temiskaming or somewhere. Nobody seems to care much.

None of us knows where Samson Schreier is either, although there's a rumour going around that he and Mrs. Delancy opened up a bed and breakfast in Minnesota. Could be true. As far as I'm concerned, they deserve each other. Bet there's a Gideon Bible at every bedside.

Eddie moved in with Aunt Susan after his mother was arrested, because he said he couldn't handle living with Samson any more. He doesn't like high school much and he and Susan fight a lot, but he's still there, tossing bags of grain around the feed store. He wants to be an Olympic wrestler. Earlie Morrison's coaching him.

I'm still living in George's cabin with Lug-nut. A large family of squirrels has moved into the attic and they drive both of us crazy.

Every so often we take a hike down to the Chapel of the Holy Lamb to visit Pastor Garnet and put flowers on Francy's grave, which is covered in snow, now. I still miss her a lot.

I finished the Becker puppet and then was at a loss as to

what to do with it. I thought about giving it to him (minus the extra piece, which I pulverized), but I decided it would embarrass him, so I gave it to Earlie. He says he put it in his bathroom, which is fine with me. Becker and I haven't kept in touch, and I try not to think about him. I'm still smoking dope, anyway.

Last week I signed a contract to build a bunch of black-light puppets for the Steamboat Theatre Company in Sikwan, a town south of here. I guess it's back to contact cement fumes and theatre people, but we all have to eat.

Oh, and I stopped dreaming about bears.

photo by Laura Bombier

H. Mel Malton was born in Oxford, England, but was raised in Bracebridge, Ontario. After studying at the Ontario College of Art, Ryerson Polytechnic and Acadia University, she toured North America for ten years in the professional theatre business as both actor and stage manager. She currently works as a reporter/photographer for a community newspaper in Huntsville, in the Muskoka region of Ontario. Her work in a small town community gives her unlimited material for her creative writing, which has appeared in numerous literary journals.

Mel can be reached at mel@muskoka.com.